DEPTHS OF DEPRAVATION

Trying to push him away, she finally succumbed and placed her hand behind his head and returned his kiss. Their mouths pressed together, their tongues entwined, Belinda let out a rush of breath as Tony slipped his hand up her skirt and sank his fingertips into the warm swell of her panties. It had been so long since anyone had paid her so much attention, she reflected. But she was married, this was her next-door neighbour, another man . . .

DEPTHS OF DEPRAVATION

Ray Gordon

This book is a work of fiction.
In real life, make sure you practise safe, sane and
consensual sex.

First published in 2005 by
Nexus

10 9 8 7 6 5

Typeset by TW Typesetting, Plymouth, Devon

ISBN 9780352339959

Penguin Random House is committed to a sustainable future for
our business, our readers and our planet. This book is made from
Forest Stewardship Council® certified paper.

Printed and bound in Great Britain by Clays Ltd, Elcograf S.p.A.

You'll notice that we have introduced a set of symbols onto our book jackets, so that you can tell at a glance what fetishes each of our brand new novels contains. Here's the key – enjoy!

cp (traditional)

cp (modern)

spanking

restraint/bondage

rope bondage/hojojutsu

latex/rubber/leather/enclosure

fem dom

willing captivity

medical

period setting

uniforms

sex rituals

One

Belinda peered round her daughter's bedroom door and smiled. The sixteen-year-old was sitting at her desk, sifting through her mock exam papers and tapping on her computer keyboard. With long black hair framing her fresh face and cascading over her shoulders, Desiree was extremely attractive. Her dark eyes, full pouting lips and olive complexion gave her the appearance of a Mediterranean beauty. She was also academic. From her early school days, she'd loved studying and had been top of her class in just about every subject. With her stunning looks and intelligence, Belinda was certain that her daughter had a good future ahead of her.

Unnoticed by the studious girl, Belinda thanked God that Desiree hadn't yet taken an interest in boys. She knew only too well that falling in love at sixteen wasn't conducive to studying and passing exams. Fortunately, Desiree was young for her age. She was extremely naive and had giggled when she'd told her mother that a boy had asked her out. Belinda knew that the girl's hormones would fire up at some stage. But, hopefully, not until she'd finished at university and got her degree.

Recalling her own teenage years, Belinda bit her lip. She'd discovered boys, and sex, at an early age. She'd then met a boy and thought that she'd fallen in love – and failed her exams. Rather than study, she'd enjoyed partying, dancing, drinking ... Never giving a thought to the future, she'd lived for the moment and enjoyed nights of sex. She'd only realised her fatal mistake when her friends had gone to university and she'd ended up in a menial office job. It would be a devastating waste to watch her daughter follow that path.

'How long have you been standing there?' Desiree asked, looking up at her mother.

'Not long,' Belinda replied. 'How's it going?'

'I'd like to get this finished this evening, but I think I'll take a break.'

'Good idea,' her mother agreed. 'You don't want to burn yourself out. By the way, the new people have moved in next door.'

'Oh? What are they like?'

'I've only seen the son. Well, I assume he's the son. Perhaps we should go round and introduce ourselves?'

'Yes, why not?' Desiree trilled, switching her computer off. 'I'll finish my work later.'

Eyeing her daughter's jeans and baggy top, Belinda was thankful that she'd not turned out like some of the other girls at the college. Kathy, in particular, was tantamount to a slut. Desiree had been rather too friendly with Kathy at one stage, and Belinda had banned the girl from calling at the house. Kathy wore very short skirts and flaunted her young body. Flashing her tight panties, wearing revealing tops, she went with one boy after another and talked about sex constantly. Desiree not only understood her mother's concern, but agreed that Kathy was an undesirable character.

Belinda's real problem with Kathy was that she saw herself in the girl. During her teenage years, Belinda had worn short skirts, flaunted her curvaceous body, thought about nothing other than sex, chased after boys ... Thankfully, Desiree was turning out to be a delightful girl. She helped her mother around the house and even did her share of the cooking. A friend as well as a daughter, Belinda couldn't have wished for more from the girl. To have a boy ruin everything now . . .

'I hate it when Dad's away on business,' Desiree said with a sigh, following her mother along the path to their neighbour's house. 'Tokyo is a million miles away. And six weeks will seem more like six years.'

'I know,' Belinda said, ringing the doorbell. 'When he gets back, he's got a month off. A whole month without having to go to work.'

'Oh, hi,' a young man said, opening the door.

'We thought we'd introduce ourselves,' Belinda said. 'We live next door.'

'Come in, come in,' he invited them. 'The place is a bit of a mess, I'm afraid. The removal people just dumped everything and left. I'm Tony, by the way.'

'I'm Belinda and this is my daughter, Desiree.'

'Desiree?' he echoed, smiling at the girl as she followed her mother into the hall. 'What a lovely name.'

'Are your parents home?' Belinda asked him.

'Er . . . No, no. They live up north. This is my house.'

'Your house? Oh, I . . . I'm sorry.'

'Look, I can't offer you tea or anything. I haven't even got –'

'No, no, we don't want tea,' Desiree broke in. 'We only came round to say hello.'

'That's very nice of you. I'm pleased to meet you both.'

'We'll leave you to it,' Belinda said, casting her eyes over several cardboard boxes blocking the lounge doorway. 'You've obviously got a lot to do. Once you've settled in, you'll have to come round.'

'Yes, yes, I will. Talking of tea, is there anywhere round here where I can buy some milk?'

'There's a corner shop. If you walk to the end of the street –'

'We have plenty of milk,' Desiree broke in, her dark eyes frowning at her mother.

'Yes, of course,' Belinda said. 'I'm sorry, I didn't think.'

'I'll bring some round,' Desiree offered.

'Thanks, I could do with a cup of coffee.' Tony caught Desiree's gaze and smiled. 'It's good to know that I have nice neighbours.'

'It is,' Belinda agreed. 'The woman who used to live here was ... I shouldn't gossip. Right, we'll leave you in peace.'

'I'll be back in a minute,' Desiree said, following her mother out of the house.

Taking a bottle of milk from the fridge, Belinda thought how pleasant Tony was. He was a nice man, she mused as she passed the milk to her daughter. Wearing jeans and a T-shirt with his dark hair cut short, he was also very good looking. But she thought that he seemed rather young to have bought a fairly expensive house. Reckoning that he'd either been left some money or had an extremely good job, she told Desiree to explain that her father was away on business.

'I don't want Tony to think that I'm a single mother,' Belinda said chuckling.

'Of course he won't,' Desiree returned with a giggle.

'Tony has a lot to do, so don't be long. The last thing he'll want is you under his feet.'

'I'll only be a minute,' Desiree said as she walked through the hall. 'Besides, I have my work to finish.'

Desiree wandered through her neighbour's open front door and found him unpacking in the kitchen. It must be awful to live alone, she thought, coming home to an empty house, having to cook dinner and do the washing up and housework ... But he seemed happy enough, she decided as he locked his dark eyes to hers. She placed the milk on the table and he offered her a cup of coffee.

4

'I'm really pleased that you're my neighbour,' he said. 'Hopefully, we'll become good friends.'

'I'm sure we will,' she agreed readily. 'Don't you mind living alone?'

'It can be pretty boring at times,' he said, filling the kettle. 'There again, with you living next door ... It would be nice if you called round sometimes. Sorry, I'm jumping the gun.'

'No, not at all. I'd love to come round. Oh, Mum said to tell you that my dad's working away. She doesn't want you to think that she's a single mother.'

'Where's he working?'

'Tokyo. He's going to be there for six weeks.'

'Lucky devil. I love Tokyo.'

'You've been there?'

'Several times. I'm an IT consultant. The work takes me all over the world.'

'Wow.' Desiree gasped. '*You*'re the lucky one. Have you been to America?'

'Yes, I have. I know I shouldn't ask but ... Do you have a boyfriend?'

'No,' Desiree murmured, nervously twisting her long black hair around her slender fingers. 'What about you? A girlfriend, I mean.'

'No, no. I've been out with one or two girls, but I've never met anyone I've really liked.'

Desiree felt her stomach somersault as she pondered on the prospect of becoming Tony's girlfriend. But she'd only just met him, she reminded herself, as she watched him pour the coffee. And he'd said nothing about taking her out. Did he like her? she wondered, suddenly becoming conscious of her dowdy clothes. She reckoned him to be in his late twenties, but decided that he wasn't too old for her. Her heart fluttering, her dark eyes sparkling, she wished that she'd brushed her hair and worn something more feminine. She had a short skirt but had never bothered to wear it. Spending most of her

5

time studying in her room, there'd been no reason to dress up.

Feeling quite at ease with her new neighbour, Desiree brushed her long black hair away from her fresh face and wondered whether she should explain why she was wearing dowdy clothes. Although she was relaxed, she felt self-conscious about her baggy jeans and didn't want him to think her a tramp. Again wishing that she'd worn something more alluring, she said that she'd been helping her mother in the garden. Tony looked her up and down and smiled.

'You'd look beautiful in anything,' he complimented her.

'Thanks,' she said, her stomach fluttering.

'What do you normally wear? What sort of clothes do you like? Are you into goth stuff or –'

'A skirt,' she broke in, wondering whether to go home and change. 'A short skirt.'

'I like girls to look feminine. You'll have to show me the next time you come round.'

'I could change now,' she proffered eagerly. 'It'll only take a few minutes.'

'All right. I'll carry on unpacking while you're gone.'

Desiree rushed home, bounded up the stairs to her room and yanked the wardrobe door open. She grabbed her short red skirt as she recalled Tony's words, kicked her shoes off and tugged down her jeans. *I like girls to look feminine*. She'd never looked feminine, she reflected. Spending her money on reference books, she'd never given a thought to clothes. She changed into a T-shirt, donned the skirt and eyed her reflection in the full-length mirror. She had a pretty good figure, she decided, turning this way and that, and hoped she'd meet with Tony's approval. She looked OK, but she was going to have to buy some decent clothes.

Desiree heard her mother chatting on the phone in the lounge as she went downstairs. Slipping out of the house unnoticed, she took a deep breath before showing herself to Tony. Her stomach was somersaulting and her hands were trembling slightly; she'd never felt like this before. And she'd certainly never dressed up for anyone. Unfamiliar sensations were rippling through her young womb and she didn't know what was happening to her as she pushed her neighbour's front door open and called out.

'In here,' Tony said, emerging from the lounge. 'God, you look . . . You're amazing, Desiree.'

'Thanks,' she said shakily, feeling self-conscious as he looked down at her long legs.

'You're so like your mother. Long black hair, a lovely olive complexion, big dark eyes . . . Is there a drop of Mediterranean blood in your family?'

'My grandmother is Greek. On my mother's side, of course.'

'Ah, that explains it. I've taken your coffee in here,' he said, leading her into the lounge.

'Wow.' She gasped. 'A wide-screen television. And hundreds of DVDs. You must be rich.'

'Hardly.' He chuckled. 'Here, sit down,' he invited, clearing the sofa of cardboard boxes. 'So, tell me about yourself.'

'I don't know where to begin,' Desiree said. 'I'm at college, hoping to go on to university . . . I'm pretty boring, really.'

'Not at all,' he said, eyeing her naked thighs as she sat on the sofa. 'You're a very attractive girl, Desiree. We'll have to go out for a drink one evening.'

'Oh, er . . . I'm not old enough to drink,' she confessed sheepishly.

'How old are you? If you don't mind my asking?'

'Well . . . Almost seventeen.'

'I know that we've only just met,' he began, again eyeing her naked thighs. 'But . . .'

'Yes?' she trilled expectantly.

7

'Well, I was wondering whether . . . No, it's too soon.'

'Please . . . What were you going to say?'

'It doesn't matter. You probably think I'm too old for you, anyway.'

'No, no, I don't.'

'Desiree, I've never met anyone like you before,' he said softly, joining her on the sofa. 'I know this is going to sound ridiculous, but I have to say it. I think I've fallen for you.'

'Oh, right,' she murmured, unsure what to say. 'I . . . I've fallen for you, too.'

As he placed his hand on her knee and pressed his lips to hers, Desiree closed her eyes and enjoyed her first kiss. Unable to believe that he felt this way about her, she thought that she'd found love. This was heaven, she mused dreamily, lost in the passionate kiss. Love at first sight? With Tony living next door, she'd be able to see him every day and . . . As he ran his fingertips up her naked thigh, she moved back and frowned at him.

'I'm sorry,' she said, lowering her head. 'I . . . I think . . .'

'What is it?' he asked. 'I thought you felt the same as me?'

'I do. It's just that . . .'

'You don't want me? Is that it?'

'No, it's not that I don't want you. It's just that I'm not ready for –'

'I can't believe how wrong I was,' he interrupted her, shaking his head.

'Wrong? No, no, you weren't wrong.'

'Wasn't I? You pushed me away, Desiree.'

'No, I didn't.'

'It's all right, you don't have to explain. I'd better get on with unpacking.'

'Tony, I . . .'

'I've got a lot to do, Desiree. I'll see you around some time.'

'I'll see you tomorrow?' she asked as he stood up.

'Maybe.'

'Don't you want me to come round?'

'What for? I mean, what's the point?'

'Because I thought . . . You said that you'd like me to call round. You said that we'd become good friends and –'

'Yes, I did,' he cut in. 'But, obviously, you don't want to become good friends.'

'Tony, I'm not ready for that sort of thing.'

'You're too young for me,' he said despondently. 'I should have realised that.'

'No, I'm not too young. I've never had a boyfriend before. Please, give me a chance.'

'All right, come round tomorrow evening. But don't mess me about, OK?'

'OK. I'll see you tomorrow.'

Leaving his house with a tear rolling down her cheek, Desiree was sure that Tony didn't want her. She'd ruined everything, she thought, as she avoided her mother and headed for her bedroom. She'd let Tony down, let herself down, and ruined any chance of a relationship. But things had moved so quickly. She'd only been with Tony for a few minutes and he'd kissed her and tried to slip his hand up her skirt. She'd not felt ready for sex. To have allowed him to go further . . . Wondering whether she should have consented to his slipping his hand up her skirt, she knew that she was going to have to go further with him at some stage.

'Are you all right?' her mother asked, peering round the door. 'Oh, you've changed into your skirt.'

'Yes, I . . . I thought . . .'

'Are you going out?'

'No, I've been to see Tony.'

Belinda frowned. 'You came back to change?'

'Yes, I wanted to show him my skirt.'

'Oh, right. So, er . . . What do you think of Tony? Do you like him?'

'Yes, I do,' Desiree said, sighing.

'He must be about thirty years old,' Belinda said, realising that her daughter was feeling emotional. 'I expect he's got a girlfriend.'

'No, he hasn't,' Desiree returned defensively. 'He said that he's never met anyone he's really liked.'

Belinda felt her stomach churn as she feared the worst. 'Are you going to finish your work?' she asked.

'No, I'm not in the mood. I'll do it tomorrow.'

'Are you coming downstairs? There's a film on in about ten minutes.'

'I might come down later.'

'All right.'

Closing the door and making her way to the kitchen, Belinda hoped that she was wrong about her daughter's feelings. But she could see the signs and instinctively knew that the girl had a crush on Tony. This had to be stopped before it got out of hand, she thought, gazing out of the kitchen window. Tony was almost twice Desiree's age. And he was only a few years younger than Belinda. Old enough to be the girl's father? Deciding that this wasn't going to become a nightmare situation, she wondered whether to talk to Tony.

Again recalling her own teenage years, she knew that she'd have gone mad if her mother had intervened. In later years, she'd wished that her mother *had* said something. If she'd tried to tell her where she was going wrong and what the future would hold if she didn't bother with her studies . . . Belinda knew that she wouldn't have listened to her mother. If anything, she'd have rebelled. To now find herself in the position of the worried mother was ironic. She knew how teenage girls thought, how her daughter felt. She'd been there. But what could she do to save Desiree from her inevitable fate?

Belinda noticed Tony dumping some boxes in his back garden. She stepped out onto the patio and wandered across the lawn. The sun was sinking behind the trees; it was a beautiful summer evening. Normally, she'd be pottering in the garden with Desiree or enjoying a walk in the local park. If her husband was home, they'd probably be having a barbecue. He would be in Tokyo just when she needed him, she thought dolefully, as Tony leaned on the fence and remarked on the weather. Desiree would probably listen to her father, take his advice and forget about the boy next door. Boy? He was a grown man.

'Is Desiree around?' Tony asked, glancing at the open back door.

'No, she's . . . she's studying,' Belinda replied, doing her best not to come out with something she might regret. 'She has exams coming up so the more time she spends studying the better.'

'She's a lovely girl. You must be very proud of her?'

'Yes, yes, I am. Tony, I . . . It would be best if Desiree wasn't distracted.'

'Distracted?' he echoed. 'What do you mean?'

'I don't quite know how to say this. She's only sixteen and she's not yet taken an interest in boys. The longer it stays that way, the better off she'll be. She plans to go to university and . . .'

'If you're saying what I think you're saying, then you have nothing to worry about,' he reassured her. 'She's a lovely girl and I like her very much. But that's as far as it goes. I agree with you, she should be concentrating on her studies.'

'Thanks for being so understanding,' Belinda said with some relief. 'She's bound to call on you again. When she does . . .'

'She said that she'd come round tomorrow. I won't upset her, but I will make it clear that we're friends and nothing more. Besides, she's far too young for me.'

'Thanks, I really appreciate your understanding.'

'No problem. Obviously, I'll not mention our little talk to Desiree.'

Belinda chatted with her neighbour for several minutes before returning to the house. She felt at ease after hearing his reassuring words. He was right, Desiree was far too young for him. How the girl would react when she realised that Tony was to be nothing more than a friend, she didn't know. But, hopefully, this would be nipped in the bud and Desiree would again concentrate on her studies.

Desiree moved away from her bedroom window and sat at her desk. Wondering what her mother had said to Tony, she gazed at the papers strewn over her computer keyboard. She wasn't in the mood for studying. Her thoughts centring on Tony, his hand slipping beneath her short skirt, she left her chair and stood before the full-length mirror. She'd made a fool of herself, she reflected, as she lowered her skirt and kicked it aside along with her shoes. Pulling her T-shirt over her head and gazing at her slender body, she hoped that her prudish attitude hadn't ruined everything.

Eyeing her young body, she noticed that her boyish figure had transformed into the curves of womanhood. Releasing her bra and gazing at her firm breasts, the ripe teats of her nipples, she knew what Tony wanted. But could she give it to him? Slipping her panties off and focusing on the dark curls veiling her tightly closed sex crack, she realised that she'd never scrutinised her naked body before. Her breasts had developed without her really noticing. Her veil of pubic curls had sprouted without her registering that she'd become a woman.

Parting the fleshy lips of her pussy, she again eyed her reflection in the mirror. As the moist petals of her inner lips unfurled, swelled, she realised that her arousal was heightening. A droplet of milky fluid clung to her inner folds and she pulled her outer labia further apart and focused on the solid bulb of her ripe clitoris. Dragging her milky sex fluid up her open crack, she caressed her clitoris with the pussy-wet tip of her finger. The sensations permeated her contracting womb and she let out a rush of breath as her young body trembled uncontrollably. Instinctively she slipped her finger into the virgin sheath of her vagina and massaged her hot inner flesh.

This is wrong, she thought, as she fingered her tight vagina. Nice girls didn't touch themselves. Only sluts played with their pussies and masturbated. But her longing to bring herself sexual pleasure was overwhelming. It was as if she'd woken some latent desire, she mused, as she drove a second finger into her hot sex. Massaging the solid tip of her clitoris, she repeatedly withdrew her fingers from her vagina and drove them into her hot duct. Trembling, breathing heavily, she felt her breasts harden, her nipples ripen.

She withdrew her wet fingers from her vagina and locked the door. Then she crawled beneath her quilt and lay on her back. She knew the time had come to explore her mounds and crevices, as she recalled Tony's passionate kiss. Her hand between her parted thighs, she ran her fingertip up and down her waking sex valley. Her feminine desires were stirring, her hormones rousing, her juices of lust flowing in torrents. Her clitoris calling as she caressed the sensitive tip, her breathing fast and shallow, she closed her eyes and again recalled her lips locked to Tony's.

Moving down her drenched valley of desire, she again slipped her finger into her tight vaginal entrance and explored her sex sheath. Hot, creamy-wet, yearning . . . Massaging her erect clitoris with her free hand, she stifled her gasps of pleasure as her young womb rhythmically contracted. This was the first time she'd attempted to masturbate, and she couldn't think why she'd neglected her young body. Had meeting Tony roused her latent desires, fired her hormones? Her thighs twitching, she parted her legs to the extreme and arched her back as her pleasure heightened. Her self-induced orgasm approaching fast, she knew that this wouldn't be the last time she masturbated.

Desiree was a late starter. It was at least two years ago when Kathy had first talked about the delights of clitty frigging and pussy fingering. And it had been some time since the girl had told Desiree about losing her virginity. The thought that she was still a virgin playing on her mind, Desiree knew that Tony would be the one to tear down her curtain of innocence. Imagining his solid penis entering her tight vagina, his shaft sliding in and out of her well-lubricated sex sheath, she threw her head back and let out a cry as her pioneering orgasm shook her young body to the very core.

'Yes,' she cried rather too loudly. Hoping that her mother wouldn't hear her, she did her best to stifle her gasps of self-induced pleasure. Her womb contracting, her vaginal muscles tightening, gripping her thrusting finger, she massaged her clitoris faster as her orgasm peaked. Never had she dreamed that she could derive such immense pleasure from her naked body. She'd neglected her femininity for years, she reflected. The ripe teats of her breasts, her tight vagina, her yearning clitoris ... She should never have ignored her teenage body.

Quivering uncontrollably, she thrust a second finger into her cream-drenched vagina and lost herself further in her sexual delirium. Again and again, waves of pure bliss crashed through her young body as she writhed and squirmed beneath her quilt. Her clitoris pulsating, transmitting waves of pleasure deep into her pelvis, she writhed on her bed like a snake in agony. Massaging her sex-button faster, she forced a third finger into the restricted duct of her pussy. Whimpering in the grip of her orgasm, panting and gasping for breath, she brought her knees up to her chest to allow her fingers deeper penetration of her spasming vaginal sheath.

'Are you all right?' her mother called, tapping on the door.

'Yes, yes,' Desiree managed to answer, slipping her wet fingers out of the burning sheath of her vagina and lowering her legs.

'May I come in for a moment?' her mother persisted.

'Hang on, I'm not dressed.' Desiree leaped out of bed and grabbed her dressing gown. She brushed her long black hair away from her flushed sex-face and finally opened the door. 'Sorry,' she said. 'I was . . . I was almost asleep.'

'It's very early, Desiree,' her mother said. 'Your face is flushed. Are you feeling all right?'

'No, I . . . I think I have a fever,' she lied. 'I feel hot one minute, and shivery the next.'

'You'd better get back into bed. I'll bring you up a drink of something.'

'No, no, it's all right.'

'Well, if you're sure?'

'Yes, I'm sure. I'll try to get some sleep.'

'It might be best if you stay in bed tomorrow. Give college a miss.'

'I'll see how I feel.'

Closing the door as her mother went downstairs, Desiree breathed a sigh of relief. She slipped beneath her quilt and again allowed her fingers to delve into her creamy-wet sex crack. If her mother discovered that she'd been masturbating, the embarrassment and shame would be too much to bear. Massaging her swelling clitoris, her thoughts turned to Tony. Good looking, plenty of money, passionate . . . But he'd been unfair, she reflected. He should have understood that she wasn't ready for sex. To thrust his hand up her skirt when they'd only just met . . . All he'd done was run his fingers up her thigh, she mused dolefully. Was that so bad?

Wondering whether she was the one who'd been unfair, as her clitoris transmitted ripples of sex deep into

15

her young womb, she thought about Tony's age. Nearing thirty, he was a mature man with adult thoughts. Of course he'd want sex, she reflected, slipping a finger into the wet heat of her tightening vagina. He was a grown man who wanted sex and ... She wasn't even old enough to have accepted his offer of taking her out for a drink. She'd lose him before a relationship had even begun, she was sure. Unable to enjoy a drink with him, unwilling to have sex ...

She slipped her finger out of her hot vagina, curled up into a ball and closed her eyes. She'd at least allow him to fondle her, she decided. The next time he made a move ... But, would he make another move? Sure that she'd ruined everything, she drifted in and out of sleep and dreamed of having sex with Tony.

Two

'How did you get on at college?' Belinda asked as Desiree closed the front door and dumped her bag on the floor. 'Did you feel all right?'

'I felt fine,' the girl replied. 'I'll get changed and then go and see Tony.'

'Desiree, you've only just got home.' Belinda sighed. 'Surely, you're not going straight round to Tony's?'

'I just want to see whether he's settled in.'

'What about your work?'

'I'll do it later.'

'All right, but don't be too long.'

Changing into her short skirt, Desiree caught sight of her reflection in the mirror. Eyeing her naked thighs, her shapely legs, she recalled Tony's words. *Don't mess me about, OK?* The last thing she wanted to do was mess him about. If he made a move, if he kissed her and ran his fingers up her thigh ... She was bound to make a fool of herself, she knew as she pulled her T-shirt over her head. Her inexperience would show and Tony would probably decide that she was too young for him. All she could do was play it by ear.

'I won't be long,' she called, bounding down the stairs.

'Are you wearing a bra?' her mother asked her, emerging from the kitchen and gazing at her daughter's nipples clearly defined by her tight T-shirt.

17

'Of course I am,' Desiree replied indignantly. 'For God's sake, Mum.'

'I'm sorry, I just thought . . .'

'Just thought what?'

'Nothing. I'll see you in a while.'

Watching the girl leave the house, Belinda wrung her hands and bit her lip. Although Tony had reassured her, said that Desiree was far too young for him, Belinda was uncertain. Desiree was an extremely attractive girl, and Tony was a red-blooded male. All she could do was hope that he'd been honest when he'd said that they were friends and nothing more. Flopping onto the lounge sofa, she glanced at her watch. Five o'clock. Perhaps Desiree would only be ten minutes or so.

'I'm almost finished,' Tony said, dumping the vacuum cleaner in the under-stairs cupboard. 'It's taken me all day, but I'm almost there.'

'The place looks lovely,' Desiree said, following him into the lounge. 'Where did they come from?' she asked him, gazing at a huge bunch of flowers on the window sill. 'Did a girl send them?'

'A woman,' he replied.

'Oh, I see. Have you known her long?'

'All my life,' he said with a chuckle. 'Desiree, my mother sent them.'

'Oh, right.' Feeling stupid, Desiree sat on the sofa and crossed her long legs. 'What did my mum say when you were in the garden last night? Did she talk about me?'

'She talked about the weather, the house, the garden . . . Nothing of importance. I'm going to have a glass of wine. Are you going to join me?'

'Er . . . Yes, yes, I will.'

'Had a good day at college?' he called, as he grabbed a bottle of wine from the fridge.

'Not bad,' she replied, wondering whether alcohol was a good idea as he placed two glasses on the coffee table. 'Pretty boring, really. When will you go back to work?'

'I'm back tomorrow. I'm off to Ireland for a couple of days.'

'You're going away?' She sighed dolefully.

'Belfast. There's a computer network problem ... I won't bore you with that.'

'How often do you have to go away?'

'During the last six months, I've been out of the country most of the time. Things are hectic at the moment.'

'So I ... I won't be seeing much of you?'

'Probably not. We'll have to make the most of our time together.'

Feeling despondent as she sipped her wine, Desiree was sure that a romantic relationship with Tony would never develop. How could it? she pondered. He'd be working away most of the time and ... and she'd rebuffed him when he'd made an advance. As he sat next to her on the sofa and placed his hand on her knee, she knew that she'd have to allow him to fondle her. If she wanted a chance of a relationship, she'd at least have to allow him to touch her.

'I'm sorry about last night,' Tony said. 'You must have thought me pretty unreasonable?'

'No, no.'

'It's just that you're such a beautiful girl. I couldn't help myself.'

'You don't have to apologise,' she replied, smiling at him. 'It was my fault. I've never had a boyfriend. I've never had sex and I felt that things were moving too fast.'

'I promise to behave from now on,' he said as his hand left her knee.

'I'm going to miss you while you're away,' she said softly. 'Will you phone me?'

'Yes, of course. When I get back, I'll only have twenty-four hours and then I'm off to Thailand.'

'Thailand?' Desiree said, her dark eyes widening. 'How long will you be there?'

'A week, most probably. The reason I always volunteer for the work abroad is because there's no one to come home to. The other lads are married so they'd rather not be away too much. As far as I'm concerned, I might as well be in Thailand as here in the UK. And the money's a lot better.'

'Oh, I see,' Desiree murmured.

'If I find someone and settle down, then I'll not go for the jobs abroad. In the meantime, I might as well earn all the money I can.'

'I don't suppose we'll ever get to know each other properly. With you away most of the time . . .'

'I don't have to do the Belfast job. Ian, my colleague, has relatives in Ireland. He wanted the job but I got in first. As I said, I have no one to come home to.'

'I'm here,' Desiree said hopefully.

'I know, but . . . You said yourself that you're not ready for a relationship.'

'I didn't say that. I do want a relationship. It's just that . . .'

'You only want half a relationship? I'm not trying to push you, Desiree. But there's more to a relationship than chatting and sipping wine. I know that you don't want to rush things, but I'm away for two days and then I'll be in Thailand for a week and . . . Unless we make the most of our time together, we'll never get anywhere. It could be months before we really get to know each other. There's a job coming up in California. It's a three-month contract and I'm trying to get it.'

'Three months?' she echoed, her heart sinking.

'If I had someone here, I wouldn't go for the job.'

'You have me, Tony. I'm here.'

'Yes, but . . .'

'I do want a proper relationship. But I don't want things to move too fast.'

As he leaned over and kissed her full lips, Desiree felt his hand squeeze the firm mound of her breast. She daren't back away as he stroked her sensitive nipple through the thin material of her T-shirt. This was probably her only chance to begin a proper relationship with Tony. If she messed this up, if she backed off or pushed him away . . . As he slipped his hand beneath her T-shirt and lifted her bra clear of her young breasts, she closed her eyes. He stroked her nipples and squeezed her milk teats, sending waves of pleasure through her trembling body as he kissed her passionately.

Desiree did her best to relax as he pulled her T-shirt up and exposed her naked breasts. Until now, no one had seen her mammary spheres, the ripe teats of her brown nipples. Embarrassment flooded her as he scrutinised her teenage breasts and she wondered whether they were big enough. Some of the girls at college were huge with deep cleavages. Hoping that Tony was happy with her petite mounds, she felt a quiver run through her young body as he encircled each nipple in turn with his fingertip.

'They're beautiful,' he whispered, squeezing the hardness of her mammary spheres. 'You have perfect tits, Desiree. Hard and pointed . . . They've developed into perfect tits.'

'Yes,' she said, not sure what to say.

'They're so hard. And your nipples are so long and suckable.'

Sucking her ripe nipple into his hot mouth, tonguing the sensitive protrusion, he slipped his hand beneath her skirt and massaged the soft swell of her tight panties. She could feel her clitoris stiffening, her juices of arousal seeping between her fleshy vaginal lips as he sucked hard on her erect nipple. How far did he intend to go? she wondered. Would he want full-blown sexual intercourse? She wasn't ready for that. This was getting out of hand, going too fast for her. Fondling and massaging was one thing, but to have sex with him . . .

'It's all right,' he whispered as her wet nipple slipped out of his mouth. 'Just relax. I promise I won't go too far.'

His words comforting her, she again closed her eyes as he sucked on her elongated milk teat and squeezed the firm mounds of her young breasts. As his fingers pulled her panties aside and massaged the fleshy swell of her moist outer labia, she let out a gasp. The feel of his intimate caress sent her into a dreamlike state and she parted her thighs further. This was heaven, she mused in her sexual delirium. This was what he'd wanted to do. This was love.

His finger slid deep into her hot vagina; this was the first time she'd been touched, the first time she'd found heaven. Her vaginal muscles tightened, hugging his finger, and she recalled masturbating the previous evening. The sensations had gripped her naked body, taken her to hitherto unknown heights of sexual ecstasy. Would Tony now take her to orgasm? she wondered. Opening her legs, allowing him access to the most intimate part of her teenage body, she hoped she'd experience another mind-blowing orgasm.

Writhing on the sofa, breathing heavily as he massaged the creamy walls of her tightening vagina, she wondered whether his penis was erect. Should she reach out and touch him there? she mused, as he slipped his finger out of her vagina and again caressed her solid clitoris. Should she run her hand up and down the hard shaft of his penis and bring out his sperm? She was learning, she mused. Learning, experiencing . . .

'God,' she whispered, trembling uncontrollably as he massaged her solid clitoris faster. Tremors of ecstasy rolled though her young body. She threw her head back and parted her thighs to the extreme as he continued to suck on her sensitive nipple and masturbate her. His teeth bit gently into her nipple, adding to her immense sexual pleasure. Suddenly she jumped as the doorbell rang out. Tony sat up, his fingers leaving her yearning clitoris as he gazed at Desiree.

'Who the hell's that?' he whispered.

'It's probably my mum,' she said, leaping up from the sofa and adjusting her clothing.

'That's bloody bad timing.' He sighed, walking into the hall.

It *was* bad timing, Desiree reflected. Her panties wetting with her flowing pussy-milk, her clitoris yearning for attention, she again pondered on the future. A relationship with Tony was impossible, she decided. What with her mother lurking and Tony working away … She'd hoped that, living next door to each other, they'd have been able to spend a lot of time together. Perhaps it wasn't meant to be, she thought dolefully. Brushing her long hair away from her flushed face, Desiree smiled as Tony led her mother into the room.

'I … I was just about to come home,' she stammered guiltily.

'Your father's on the phone,' Belinda said, frowning at Desiree. 'He wants to talk to you.'

'Yes, right. I'll see you later, Tony.'

Belinda waited until the front door had closed before saying anything to Tony. 'Have I interrupted something?' she finally asked him.

'No, not at all,' he replied with a chuckle. 'We were just chatting. As Desiree said, she was about to leave.'

'Is that wine?' Belinda said, eyeing the two glasses on the table.

'Yes, would you like some?'

'I don't want Desiree drinking. She's sixteen, Tony. I don't want her –'

'She's not a kid,' he interrupted her. 'Surely, a glass of wine won't hurt?'

'Did you make it clear to her that you're only friends?'

'Belinda, you're going to have to give Desiree some space. And you're going to have to trust her.'

'I do trust her. It's just that ... I remember when I was her age. My hormones running wild, I thought of nothing other than boys and sex. I don't want Desiree to make the same mistakes I did.'

'We're friends, that's all. Perhaps I shouldn't have given her the wine, but it was only one glass. You worry too much.'

'Not without good reason.'

'What do you mean by that?'

'Desiree came home from college, changed, and then came straight round here. She hasn't finished yesterday's work, let alone ... I'm sorry, I shouldn't be having a go at you.'

'It's all right, I understand. Look at it this way. She's far safer here with me than out somewhere meeting boys. She's only next door so you can call her home any time you like.'

'Yes, you're right. I'm sorry.'

'You don't have to apologise. Why don't you have some wine?'

'No, thanks. I'd better get back.'

'All right. And don't worry.'

'I won't. Thanks, Tony.'

Making her way home, Belinda felt that she'd made a fool of herself. Going on like an old mother hen, she wondered what Tony must have thought. He'd told her several times that he wasn't interested in Desiree, so what was the problem? At least he was understanding, she mused, closing her front door. But she'd rather Desiree didn't call round to see him every day. Realising that her intervention had to be subtle and not seen to be unreasonable or demanding, she decided to have a chat with her daughter. Tony understood, she reflected. But would Desiree? Finding the girl sitting in the lounge, Belinda sat opposite her in the armchair and asked what her father had talked about.

'The line was dead,' Desiree said accusingly. 'Was it a ploy to come and get me?'

'Of course it wasn't a ploy,' Belinda said. 'How could you think such a thing?'

'I'm sorry.'

'If you don't believe me, then ask your father the next time he calls.'

'I said I'm sorry.'

'Desiree, I think we need to talk.'

'We are talking.'

'You know what I mean. You've changed since Tony moved in next door. We used to get on so well, spend time together and . . .'

'I was only round there for a few minutes.'

'Twenty minutes.'

'Oh, you've been timing me?'

'No, no. Talk to me, Desiree. Tell me what the trouble is.'

'What trouble? There's nothing wrong.'

'Talk to me about Tony. How do you feel about him?'

'He . . . I . . . I like him a lot.'

'Desiree . . . I hate to have to tell you this, but he's not interested in anything other than friendship.'

'Did he say that?'

'In so many words, yes.'

'You're lying.'

'Desiree, please . . .'

'If he only wants to be friends, then why did he kiss me?'

'He kissed you?'

'Yesterday, and today.'

'What else has he done?'

'He kissed me properly, on my lips. He said that he wants to be more than friends, so why are you lying?'

'Desiree . . .'

'I'm going to my room.'

Pacing the floor as Desiree bounded up the stairs and slammed her bedroom door shut, Belinda held her hand to her head. Tony had lied, she reflected. She instinctively knew that this was only the beginning of a nightmare. Her worst fears were emerging from the darkness and coming to life. Desiree thought that she was in love and . . . Belinda left the house and rang Tony's doorbell. She had to put a stop to this before it went any further.

'Oh, hi,' Tony said, smiling as he opened the door. 'Changed your mind about a glass of wine?'

'I need to talk to you,' Belinda snapped, walking past him into the hall.

'Talk away,' he invited her, following her into the lounge. 'What's the problem?'

'You kissed Desiree.'

'I don't believe *this*,' he said, shaking his head and laughing. 'Yes, I did kiss her. It was a friendly kiss, Belinda.'

'A friendly kiss? On her lips?'

'Look, you're going to have to allow Desiree to grow up. Chasing after her like this . . .'

'I don't want you to see her again, Tony. Do you understand?'

'I can't stop her from coming round. If she wants to see me, then I'll invite her in. You're going way over the top with all this.'

'Am I?'

'Yes, you are. You come storming round here . . .'

'Has anything happened? Have you done anything with her?'

'What if I have? What if I've taken her to my bed and made love with her?'

'If you dare to . . .'

'She's a very beautiful girl, Belinda,' he taunted her. 'She has a lovely body and –'

'Stop it. I don't want you talking about my daughter like that.'

'All right, all right, calm down. Nothing's happened between us, and it's not going to. I told you yesterday

26

that she's far too young for me. If I was looking for a relationship, then I'd go for someone of your age. We're about the same age, aren't we?'

'I'm older than you,' Belinda said with a sigh. 'I'm sorry, Tony. I know that I'm overreacting.'

'Yes, you are. OK, so I kissed Desiree. As far as I was concerned, it was a friendly kiss.'

'That's not what she thinks. She's fallen for you. She's fallen for you in a big way.'

'Sit down and have a glass of wine.'

'Thanks, I think I will.'

Sitting on the sofa as Tony went to the kitchen, Belinda wondered what Desiree was doing. The girl had never been like this. Moody, argumentative, slamming her bedroom door ... To accuse her mother of lying, making out that her father had phoned as a ploy to get her home ... Taking a glass of wine from Tony, Belinda wondered why he'd said that he'd invite Desiree in if she called to see him. He wasn't helping the situation, she ruminated. Then again, why should he send Desiree home if she called to see him? Feeling confused, she sipped her wine. She knew that she'd gone over the top.

'I don't want to fall out with you or Desiree,' Tony said, sitting next to Belinda. 'If she comes to see me and I tell her to go away, she'll think I'm being rude.'

'I know.' Belinda sighed. 'And I can't stop her from seeing you. She said that you want to be more than just friends.'

'She's got the wrong end of the stick. Either that, or it's wishful thinking on her part. And the kiss was nothing more than a friendly gesture.'

'It's rather stupid to say that you only want to be friends and then kiss her.'

'Where I come from, the way I've been brought up, friendly kissing is perfectly normal. Look, why don't you come round now and then?' he suggested. 'If Desiree knows that you're here, she'll keep away.'

'That's an idea. But I can't come round every evening.'

'You won't have to. Just call in now and then for a chat and a drink.'

'All right, I'll do that.'

'It's nice having Desiree come round, but I'd much prefer to see you. As I said, if I was looking for a relationship, then I'd go for someone of your age. I like you very much, Belinda. You're a very attractive woman.'

'I'm also a married woman, Tony.'

'No, I didn't mean . . . Actually, that's an idea.'

'What is?'

'You and me. If you want me to keep Desiree away from me, then . . .'

'Tony, for God's sake.'

'I was only joking.'

'Don't you say anything like that to Desiree. If she tells her father that I've been . . .'

'Having an affair with me?'

'Yes, no . . . Look, I'd better get back and make sure that she's all right.'

Belinda finished her wine and followed Tony to the front door. She wished that she could turn the clock back as he smiled at her. If she'd not called and introduced herself, if she'd kept Desiree away . . . Locking his eyes to hers, Tony promised her that Desiree would be safe. He wouldn't lay a finger on the girl, she was far too young for him, he'd rather be with someone of Belinda's age . . . As he moved forwards and kissed Belinda's full lips, she couldn't believe what was happening. Finally pushing him away, she gazed wide-eyed at him as he again smiled at her.

'I couldn't resist,' he whispered. 'I'm sorry.'

'That wasn't a friendly kiss,' Belinda said, locking her dark eyes to his. 'Tony, please . . . I'm married.'

'That doesn't make you unattractive.'

28

'And I thought you were after my daughter.'

'No, Belinda. It's you I'm after.'

'There's no future for us, Tony. I can't believe this. I'm happily married.'

'Yes, I know. Why don't you come back later? Check up on Desiree and then come round for a while.'

'No, I don't think so.'

'She'll be studying, you'll be sitting alone, I'll be sitting alone . . . Come and have a couple of drinks with me.'

'No, Tony. I . . . I don't want to.'

'It's a sure way to stop Desiree coming round.'

'No.'

'She did say that she might come back later this evening. If you're here, then she won't bother.'

'Well, I . . . I might. I'll see what she's up to and then . . . I might come back.'

Leaving Tony's house, Belinda couldn't believe that he'd kissed her. Thinking how wrong she'd been about him wanting Desiree, she felt a lot easier. Desiree had obviously fallen for Tony but, ironically, he'd fallen for her mother. Flattered, and feeling rather guilty, Belinda prepared a ham salad but Desiree said that she wasn't hungry and wouldn't come out of her room. Eating alone at the kitchen table, Belinda knew that Desiree would get over Tony at some stage. As long as this didn't affect her studies, everything would turn out fine.

Sitting at her dressing table, Belinda applied a little make-up and ran a hairbrush through her long black hair. Butterflies fluttering in her stomach, she felt like she did when she was in her teens. Sexy, horny, excited . . . Tony had flattered her, but she was old enough not to play silly games. The idea of going to see him was to keep Desiree away, she reminded herself. Once Desiree realised that her mother was also friendly with Tony and called round to see him now and then, she'd forget all thoughts of love.

'I'm going out for a while,' Belinda called, tapping on Desiree's bedroom door.

'Where to?'

'Tony's place. He invited me round.'

'Why are you going to see him?' Desiree asked, opening her door.

'You're stuck in your room and I'm feeling bored. He asked me round to ... to talk about curtains. He's not sure what type of curtains to get.'

'Oh, right.'

'I won't be long.'

Sighing as Desiree closed the door, Belinda made her way down the stairs and decided not to worry about the girl. She'd get over it, she was sure, as she left the house. Knowing that Tony wasn't interested in Desiree was a great relief. The fact that he was interested in her wasn't a relief, but it made Belinda feel good. A teenager again? She wasn't unattractive, she thought happily. Her figure was good, her hair was nice ... And a younger man fancied her. Smiling as Tony opened the door and invited her in, she didn't want to appear too keen so she told him that she couldn't stay for long.

'That's all right,' he said, leading her into the lounge. 'I'm just pleased that you came. Er ... I've got wine or vodka.'

'Oh, vodka would be nice. Do you have any orange juice?'

'Vodka and orange coming up. I'll have to stock up on drinks. And food, for that matter. So, how's Desiree?'

'She's all right,' Belinda replied as he passed her drink. 'She's sulking, but she'll be all right.'

'Now you can see why I don't want silly teenage girls. I don't mean that Desiree is silly.'

'I know what you mean.'

'Giggling one minute, sulking the next, and then tears and tantrums ... That's not for me.'

'We haven't got off to a very good start, have we?' Belinda said. 'As neighbours, we should have –'

'We're fine,' he broke in, sitting next to her on the sofa. 'There's no problem.'

'My daughter's fallen for you, I went off at the deep end, you kissed me . . .'

'It's all sorted out now. Desiree knows that I want nothing more than friendship. I can't say that when it comes to you, though.'

'Tony, don't start that again. All *I* want is friendship, OK?'

'If you say so.'

'I do say so. The only reason I'm here is to keep Desiree away.'

'Really?'

'Well, and because . . . because I'd like to get to know you. As a friend, I mean.'

'Does your husband often work away?'

'Yes, he does. Desiree misses him terribly.'

'Do you?'

'Do I miss him? Yes, of course I do. I feel lonely and bored at times but . . .'

'That's where I come in. When he's away, you can spend some time with me.'

'That's nice of you but . . . Let's get one thing straight. We're only friends, OK?'

'OK. I'll make sure that the fact that I fancy you to bits won't come into it.'

'Tony, don't.'

'Don't what?'

'Keep on like that.'

'Are you weakening?'

'No. Look, I'll go home if you're going to keep on.'

'If you go home, then Desiree will probably come round to see me.'

'Yes, I think she will. Tony, you will make it clear that you just want to be her friend?'

'I've already done that, but I'll tell her again.'

'Why not say that you have a girlfriend?'

'Because I've already said that I haven't. The last thing I want is to start lying to Desiree. I'm a hopeless liar. When I was a kid, my mother used to say that my face went red whenever I lied. And she was right. You're worrying too much again. Just relax and enjoy your drink.'

'Yes, yes I will.'

Sipping her vodka and orange as Tony put some music on, Belinda pondered on her husband. They got on all right, but Brian worked away so much that it wasn't easy to have a proper relationship. She was alone in her bed more often than not and, when he was home, he was busy with the garden or decorating the house. He seemed to spend more time with Desiree than he did with her. They rarely went out these days, she mused. There was always so much to do before he went abroad again.

'Another one?' Tony asked as she knocked back her drink.

'Well, I . . .'

'Go on,' he coaxed her with a chuckle. 'It'll help you to relax.'

'I am relaxed,' she said as he refilled her glass.

'You're tense, Belinda. You're all wound up, and you know it.'

'Yes, you're right. It's all this business with Desiree. I knew that she'd take an interest in boys at some stage. But to fall for a man old enough to be her father . . .'

'Hang on,' he said with a chortle. 'You make me out to be ancient. I'm only twenty-seven.'

'Sorry. You see, she's doing so well with her college work. If she's distracted now, if she neglects her work at this crucial point in her education –'

'I know what you're saying,' he interrupted her. 'If she falls in love, then you can say goodbye to her education.'

'Yes, that's right. God, this vodka is going to my head.'

'In that case, have some more.'

'Tony, I don't want to go home drunk.'

'And I don't want you to go home at all.'

Again sitting by her side, Tony placed his hand on her naked knee and kissed her cheek. Belinda felt her stomach somersault as he locked his lips to hers in a passionate kiss. She tried to push him away, but finally succumbed and placed her hand behind his head and returned his kiss. Their mouths pressed together, their tongues entwined. Belinda let out a rush of breath as Tony slipped his hand up her skirt and sank his fingertips into the warm swell of her panties. It had been so long since anyone had paid her so much attention, she reflected. But she was married, this was her next-door neighbour, another man . . .

'Tony, don't,' she whispered as her outer labia swelled and her vaginal muscles tightened. Ignoring her protest, he kneaded the swell of her vulval flesh through her tight panties. Her body quivering, her heart racing, she knew that this was so very wrong but . . . Her husband was away, no one would know what she'd done, she was safe enough. Again reminding herself that she was a married woman, she pushed his hand away and closed her thighs.

'I'm sorry,' she said. 'I'm sorry, I shouldn't have . . . I don't know what came over me.'

'Why fight it?' he asked her. 'Why fight your feminine desires?'

'Because I don't have feminine desires. Not like that, anyway.'

'You might fool yourself, but you don't fool me. You want me as much as I want you, Belinda.'

'Tony, no.' She gasped as he eased her naked thighs apart and again pressed his fingers into the warm mound of her panties. 'Tony, I don't want this.'

33

'Of course you do.'

'Stop it, Tony,' she said firmly, again pushing him away.

'Perhaps I should have invited Desiree round?'

'What do you mean by that?'

'I was joking, Belinda.'

'Were you?'

'Yes, of course.'

'I'd better get home.' She sighed and rose to her feet. 'It was a mistake to come here.'

'Belinda, I don't want to have to be rude to Desiree. If you go, then she'll come round and . . .'

'And what? This is a ridiculous situation. I have to stay here to keep my daughter away from you? If she comes round, I want you to tell her to go home. Say that you're busy or you're expecting a visitor.'

'No, Belinda. I like Desiree very much. If she wants to come and see me, then I'm not going to send her away. I'm not going to lie to her.'

'Don't you understand that she thinks she's fallen in love with you?'

'Yes, I do understand that. And the best way to deal with it is to stay friends with her and she'll eventually realise that –'

'I'll have to ground her unless you do as I ask.'

'Ground her? Get real, Belinda. She's sixteen years old, for God's sake.'

'Yes, well . . .'

'Stay for a while longer. Have another drink.'

'All right,' Belinda agreed, retaking her seat as he filled her glass. 'I want us to be good neighbours, Tony. The last thing I want is for us to end up not speaking to each other. Desiree is at a difficult age and –'

'I still say that you're making too much of all this,' he broke in, passing her drink.

'Tony, you've kissed my daughter, you've kissed me and put your hand up my skirt . . . I hope you didn't do that to Desiree?'

'Of course I didn't. Can't you get it into your head that I'm not interested in Desiree?'

'You're a normal man, a red-blooded man. You've already proved that by ...'

'I really fancy you, Belinda. But that doesn't mean to say that I want sex with your daughter. You're confused, getting yourself all mixed up.'

'Yes, I am confused. When you kissed me ...'

'You enjoyed it?'

Pondering on his question as she sipped her drink, Belinda couldn't deny that she'd enjoyed his kiss. She'd never been in this situation before. Happily married to Brian, bringing up Desiree in a lovely home ... Never had she dreamed about another man, let alone savoured a kiss or fingers pressing against the swell of her tight panties. Six weeks without her husband was a long time, she thought unhappily. Alone in her bed every night ... Taking a deep breath, she pushed all thoughts of having an affair with Tony out of her mind.

'You haven't answered my question,' Tony persisted, breaking her reverie. 'Did you enjoy the kiss?'

'The answer is no,' she said firmly. 'I didn't enjoy kissing another man. I'm happily married, Tony. And I intend to stay that way. I don't think it is a good idea to come here again.'

'I wasn't suggesting that you ruin your marriage,' he said with a chuckle. 'And why not call round now and then? I'd love to see you.'

'No, it's not a good idea. I'd better be going.'

'Not to worry. No doubt Desiree will come and keep me company now and then.'

'Tony, please ... I have to go.'

Leaving the house, Belinda didn't know what to think. Tony was threatening her, he'd sent her arousal soaring to frightening heights ... Desiree had to be kept away from him, she decided. The girl was young and naive. She wasn't in love, Belinda reflected. Infatuated, but certainly not in love. The trouble was that she might lose her virginity to Tony. If Tony played one against the other, mother against daughter ... he wouldn't do that, she was sure. Or would he?

Three

Gazing at Desiree's short skirt and tight T-shirt, Belinda knew that things were going from bad to worse. The girl had announced that she wasn't going to college, she was taking the day off to spend some time with Tony before he went to Ireland. She pouted her lips as her mother asked about her work and said that she'd catch up while Tony was away.

'You've never taken a day off college,' Belinda said. 'And you've always been well ahead with your work.'

'Perhaps it's time I did have a day off, then,' Desiree said.

'Tony didn't tell me that he was going to Ireland.'

'Why should he when you went to see him about curtains?'

'Well, I thought he might have mentioned it.'

'He's only there for a couple of days, and then he's off to Thailand for a week.'

'Oh, right,' Belinda said, trying not to sound pleased. 'So, you won't be seeing much of him?'

'No, I won't. But he did say that we should make the most of our time together. That's why I'm going to see him now.'

'Well, I have to go into town. I'll see you later.'

Leaving the house, Desiree hoped that Tony hadn't left yet. She'd spent too long in the shower and getting ready, she reflected, as she rang the doorbell. But she'd wanted to look nice for him. Brushing her long black hair away from her face, she rang the bell again. Her stomach sinking, she reckoned that she must have missed him. This wasn't going to work, she mused dolefully. Her mother going on at her, Tony going away ... Hanging her head, she was about to go home when the door opened.

'Oh, hi,' Tony said, smiling at her. 'You're bright and early.'

'I wanted to see you before you left,' Desiree said, walking into the hall. 'I hope it's not too early?'

'No, no, I'm not leaving until ten. You look lovely, as always.'

'Thanks. I should be at college, but ... As you're going away, I thought I'd come and see you. What did my mum say when she was here last night?'

'We chatted about this and that. Nothing much, really.'

'She said that you only want to be friends with me. Is that right?'

'You know how I feel about you, Desiree.'

'But you told my mum that you only wanted to be friends.'

'Yes, I did. I said that because she worries about you. She thinks that I'm too old for you.'

'Do you think that?'

'No, I don't. But I must admit that I'm finding it difficult to start up a relationship with you.'

'Why?'

'Because ... To be honest, I want to enjoy a full relationship with you. By full, I mean ...'

'I know what you mean.' She sighed.

'With your mum watching you like a hawk, it's not easy. Take last night, for example. We were just getting to know each other, and she turned up. Where is she now?'

'At home. She's going into town later, though.'

'So, she'll probably come round in a minute to check up on you?'

'No, well . . . She might.'

'You're going to have to lie to her, Desiree.'

'Lie? How? What do you mean?'

'Don't say that you're coming here. Tell her that you're going somewhere else.'

'And then sneak round here?'

'Yes.'

'I've never lied to my mum.'

'If you want a relationship with me, then it looks as if you'll have to. Can't you see that?'

'Yes, I suppose so.'

'It would be best to tell her that there's nothing between us. Just say that we're friends.'

'Yes, I will. But . . . We are more than friends, aren't we?'

'Of course we are, Desiree. As I said, you know how I feel about you.'

'I wish you didn't have to go to Ireland.'

'I could ring Ian and tell him . . .'

'Really?'

'As I said, he wants to go because he has relatives there. The thing is . . . If I stay here . . . We will have a proper relationship, won't we?'

'Yes, yes we will. Look, I'll go and tell Mum that I'm going to college. You ring your friend and I'll sneak back.'

'OK, it's a deal.'

Leaving the house, Desiree didn't like the idea of lying to her mother. But, as Tony had said, there was no other way if she wanted a proper relationship. She found her mother in the kitchen and announced that she was leaving for college. Belinda smiled, her expression depicting her relief as she grabbed her handbag and said that she was going into town. Desiree waited until she'd left the house and sneaked back to Tony's and slipped in through the front door. Although swamped with guilt, she was pleased to have some time to spend with Tony.

'OK?' he asked as she wandered into the lounge.

'Yes, she's gone into town. Did you phone your friend?'

'Yes, and I'm not going to Ireland.'

'That's great,' Desiree trilled excitedly, her fresh face beaming. 'So, we have all day together.'

'Indeed, we do. Perhaps we should really get to know each other?'

'Er . . . Yes.'

'You don't sound very keen.'

'No, no . . . I suppose I'm a little nervous.'

'We'll play a little game to relax you.'

'A game? What sort of game?'

'Bend over the armchair, and I'll spank you. We'll pretend that you've been a naughty little girl and –'

'No, Tony. I . . . I don't want to.'

'It's only a game,' he said with a chuckle. 'It'll relax you, loosen you up. It won't be a real spanking.'

'It's not right, though. I mean, spanking isn't normal.'

'I really don't see us getting anywhere.' Tony sighed. 'I suppose you're too young to play adult games.'

'I'm not too young,' she returned. 'It's just that . . . What has spanking got to do with love?'

'It's all part of a physical relationship. Come on, Desiree. It's only a little fun.'

'Well, I . . . I suppose so.'

Leaning over the back of the armchair, Desiree bit her lip as Tony stood behind her and lifted her short skirt up over her back. Running his fingertips over the cotton-covered orbs of her firm bottom, he squeezed and kneaded her rounded buttocks. Her long black hair veiled her flushed face as he ran his fingers up and down her bottom-crease. She grimaced as his finger pushed into the groove of her bottom. Although she did her best to relax and enjoy the so-called adult game, this wasn't what she'd expected. She'd thought that they'd go up to Tony's bed and make love and ...

'I don't go much on panties,' Tony enlightened her, pushing the tight cotton material into the groove of her bottom. 'I prefer thongs.'

'I ... I don't have a thong,' she said.

'I'll get you one. You have a beautiful bottom, Desiree. Have you ever been spanked?'

'No, no, I haven't.'

'Not at school by a male teacher or by your dad?'

'No one's ever spanked me.'

Tony rudely pulled her panties down, exposing the firm cheeks of her teenage bottom, and knelt down and kissed each warm buttock in turn. Desiree gasped, her young body trembling as she felt his wet tongue running over the tensed flesh of her bottom. This wasn't normal, she was sure, as he parted her rounded buttocks with his thumbs. This had nothing to do with love, with making love. As his tongue ran up and down the gully of her bottom, repeatedly sweeping over her secret brown hole, she stood upright.

'I don't want you to do that,' she protested, turning and looking down at him.

'For God's sake, Desiree,' he said agitatedly. 'Lean over the chair, or I really will spank you.'

'Tony, I ...'

'This is a complete waste of time,' he snapped. 'If we can't even enjoy a little game together, then ... Perhaps I should forget about you and get to know your mother a little better.'

'What do you mean?'

'Nothing, I was joking. Are you going to bend over or not?'

Again leaning over the back of the chair, Desiree pondered on his words ... *get to know your mother a little better*. What did he mean by that? she wondered, as he again parted her firm buttocks and exposed her anal inlet. His tongue explored her there, wetting the delicate brown tissue surrounding her tight hole and she instinctively knew that this was not normal. But, if that's what Tony wanted, then she had no choice if she was to embark on a full relationship with him.

The tip of his tongue entered her tight hole, slipping into the dank heat of her rectal duct, and he stretched her firm buttocks wider apart. Unable to imagine her father committing such a debased act with her mother, she couldn't understand Tony. He'd kissed her passionately, sucked on her milk teats, massaged deep inside her vagina ... That was normal, she reflected. Warm and loving. But to push his tongue into her bottom hole? Shuddering as she tightened her muscles, she knew that she couldn't relax. If she was supposed to be enjoying his crude attention, if she was supposed to be deriving some sort of pleasure from his anal licking ...

'You taste beautiful,' he whispered. His wet tongue lapped at her anal ring.

'Tony,' she began shakily. 'Tony, I ...'

'You want more?'

'No, I ...'

His wet tongue again entered the tight sheath of her rectum. He pulled her panties down to her knees and cupped her full pussy lips in the palm of his hand. His finger entered her tight vagina, massaging the creamy walls of her sex sheath, and he managed to push his tongue further into her rectum. Desiree trembled, her breathing unsteady as she again thought how wrong and debased his act was. His tongue seemingly driving into the very core of her trembling body, his finger exploring deep into her virgin pussy, he seemed to lose himself in his debauched act. Desiree could hear his mouth slurping, his finger squelching her vaginal juices. Was this normal? she wondered for the umpteenth time.

'Bloody hell,' Tony cursed as the doorbell rang. 'If that's your bloody mother ...'

'She's gone to town,' Desire said, standing and hurriedly pulling her panties up. 'It can't be her.'

'It *is* her,' Tony said, gazing through the net curtains. 'Go out the back way. I'll get rid of her and see you later.'

'I'll come back when she's gone,' Desiree whispered. She dashed into the kitchen and made her escape into the garden.

Tony opened the front door, smiled at Belinda and invited her in. Stepping into the hall, Belinda immediately began quizzing Tony. Had Desiree been there? Where was she? She'd said that she was going to college but she wasn't there. Closing the front door and leading her into the lounge, Tony eyed the woman's full breasts straining the tight material of her white blouse.

'You're very attractive,' he said, lowering his gaze to her short skirt, her naked legs. 'And very sexy. Especially when you're angry.'

'Where is my daughter?' Belinda persisted.

'I have no idea.'

'She has been here, hasn't she?'

'Yes, she called in earlier. She stayed for a few minutes and then went off to college.'

'She's not at the college, I rang them.'

'She probably hasn't got there yet. Perhaps she's at home?'

'I've just come from home.'

'Belinda, I'm not Desiree's keeper. You're her mother. If you don't know where she is then . . .'

'She's upstairs, isn't she?'

'For God's sake. Go and look, if you want to.'

'I thought you were going to Ireland?'

'It was cancelled at the last minute. You really must calm down, Belinda. You're making mountains out of molehills, getting everything out of all proportion, jumping to conclusions and . . .'

'I'm sorry, Tony. I shouldn't be having a go at you.'

'No, you shouldn't. I don't suppose Desiree's got to college yet. How long does it take her to walk there?'

'I don't know,' Belinda said. 'About fifteen minutes, I suppose.'

'There you are, then. When Desiree called round earlier, I again made it clear that we're only friends.'

'And she accepted that?'

'Yes, yes, she did. In fact, she took it very well. If you're going to accuse me of abducting her every time she goes out somewhere . . .'

'I'm not accusing you of abducting her.'

'It seems that way. She goes out, you don't know where she is, so you come storming round here and have a go at me. I've been here alone, washing up the dishes and minding my own business.'

'I said I'm sorry,' Belinda said, flopping onto the sofa. 'It's just that we always got on so well together. Since you arrived, she's changed.'

'I've only just moved in.'

'I know, but . . . You say that she accepted that you're only friends?'

'Yes, she did. She was fine when she left here. No tears or upsets or anything. You worry too much.'

'Perhaps she called into a friend's house on the way to college. Perhaps she's at the college by now.'

'I'm sure she is. Would you like a cup of coffee?'

'No, thanks. I think I'd better go home. I'll ring the college again.'

'Leave it, Belinda. You can't chase around after Desiree like this. Say she's skipped college. So what?'

'Oh, I don't know. I suppose you're right. I wish my husband was here.'

'Why, are you feeling horny?'

'Of course not.'

'Don't you ever feel horny?'

'Yes, no . . . I don't want to talk about it, Tony.'

'When you're in your bed alone at night, do you –'

'I said, I don't want to talk about it. I have enough on my plate without you going on at me.'

'All right, all right. I only wondered what you did for sexual relief.'

'I don't do anything. Look, I'd better be going.'

'You really are an attractive woman.'

'Tony . . .'

'It's not a chat-up line, so you needn't worry.'

'What is it, then?'

'The truth. I can honestly say that I've never met anyone as attractive, and sexy, as you. I hope your husband appreciates you.'

Sighing, Belinda knew that her Brian appreciated her. It was just that he worked away so often and they had very little time together. They'd only made love once in the last two months, she reflected. No sooner had he returned from Germany, and he'd gone off to Asia. What with Desiree around and so much to do in the house and garden, there was never time for loving. To her horror, she found herself thinking that sex with her husband had never been particularly exciting or satisfying.

'He looks after your feminine needs, then?' Tony persisted, joining her on the sofa.

'What? Sorry, I was daydreaming.'

'About sex?'

'No, Tony, not about sex. Look, I really have to go now.'

'Why?'

'Because . . . because I have things to do.'

Belinda closed her eyes as Tony locked his lips to hers and squeezed the full mound of her breast. This was wrong, she knew, as his tongue delved into her mouth. But she needed love and passion like any other woman. With Tony? she pondered, as he tweaked the ripe teat of her breast through the flimsy material of her blouse. Becoming weak in her arousal, she wished that her husband made love to her rather than had sex with her on the odd occasion. She rarely achieved orgasm and was usually left wanting as he snored beside her in the marital bed.

'No,' she said, pulling away as Tony slipped his hand up her skirt. 'Tony, please . . .'

'It's all right,' he whispered, stroking the tight material of her panties. 'Just relax.'

'Tony, I'm married.'

'And you're very lonely. And wanting.'

He parted her thighs and pulled her panties aside. Again she felt his tongue snake into her mouth as his lips met hers. His finger entered her wet vagina, his free hand again squeezed her mammary globe, and she knew that she'd lost her battle. He was right, she reflected. She was very lonely, and wanting. Wanting what? Sex with another man? Sex with a man she'd only just met? Adultery? Was that what she wanted?

While driving a second finger deep into the hugging sheath of her yearning pussy, he managed to unbutton her blouse and lift her bra clear of her full breasts. Lost in her sexual delirium, she felt a quiver run through her womb as he sucked her erect nipple into his hot mouth. This was wrong, she repeatedly thought. But no one would know what she'd done, she decided. After all, it wasn't as if she was having full-blown sex with Tony. This wasn't true adultery, was it?

Her hand reached out involuntarily and she squeezed the bulging crotch of Tony's trousers. She tried to stop herself as she felt the hardness and sheer size of his penis. Groping, fumbling, she finally managed to tug his zip down and slip her hand into his trousers. He was as hard as rock, she mused, gripping the fleshy shaft of his warm cock as he drove his tongue further into her mouth. Her juices of lust flowing over his thrusting fingers, she quivered uncontrollably as she finally pulled his solid cock out of his trousers.

'God, no.' She gasped as he slipped his fingers out of her spasming vagina and dragged her sex-milk up her valley to lubricate the solid nub of her clitoris. Massaging her lubricious cream into the sensitive tip of her expectant clitoris, his mouth left hers and he let out a gasp of pleasure as she rolled his foreskin back and forth over the swollen bulb of his glans. Again he sucked her erect nipple into his wet mouth and he repeatedly swept his tongue over the sensitive protrusion as he expertly massaged her solid clitoris.

In a sexual frenzy, Belinda whimpered and squirmed as Tony masturbated her and she wanked his cock. This was wrong, she told herself for the umpteenth time. Lies, deceit, betrayal, adultery ... So very wrong. Massaging his silky-smooth knob with her thumb, she tried not to think about her husband. This was a one-off, she decided. This was nothing more than two people bringing each other pleasure. Mutual masturbation, no strings, no ties. Never again would she do this, she thought, as she ran her fingertip around the rim of Tony's bulbous glans.

Shaking violently as her clitoris exploded in orgasm, she could feel Tony's sperm flowing in rivers over her hand. Her fingers flooding with another man's sperm, her mind flooded with thoughts of adultery. How could she do this? A one-off? How could she allow another man to finger her vagina and massage her clitoris to orgasm while her husband was working abroad? How could she wank another man's cock and bring out his spunk while her husband was away earning money for his family?

Running her hand up and down his cock, she shuddered as he sustained her orgasm with his vibrating fingertips. This would never happen again, she asserted mentally. The creamy sperm squelching, lubricating her hand as she continued to wank his massive penis, she recalled her schooldays. Meeting boys in the woods, moving her hand up and down their solid cocks, watching the spunk shoot from their swollen knobs . . . But she'd been free and single then. Now, she was a married woman. An adulteress.

'You're a horny little bitch,' Tony finally said as his sperm-flow stemmed.

'Please, no . . .' Belinda said as her orgasm receded. 'I . . . I don't want this.'

'Too late.' He chortled. 'Besides, you were desperate to come.'

'I'm married,' she whimpered, as if reminding herself. 'God, I'm a married woman and I've . . .'

'Allowed another man to bring you off? Wanked another man's hard cock and flooded your hand with spunk?'

'Please, stop it. I . . . I have to go home.' She gazed at the male cream covering her hand and then looked up in horror at Tony's grinning face. 'God, what the hell have I done?' she said.

'Given me the best wank ever,' he quipped.

'You . . . you bastard.'

'That's nice, I must say.'

'You made me, you forced me . . .'

'It was either you . . . or Desiree.'

'What? Don't you dare to say things like that.'

'I was joking, Belinda. Mind you, if I get really horny and you're not around . . .'

'For fuck's sake, Tony.'

'Uptight again? Why the hell you can't relax, I really don't know.'

'Because . . . Get me a tissue or something,' she ordered him, gazing at the sperm glistening on her hand.

'Why don't you lap it up?'

'God, you're vile. Get me a bloody tissue.'

As Tony zipped his trousers and went to the kitchen, Belinda inadvertently allowed his sperm to drip onto her skirt as she stared into space. Lies, deceit, betrayal, adultery – the harsh words battered her tormented mind.

She couldn't believe what she'd done. Even if her husband never discovered her wicked ways, even if Desiree remained ignorant as to her mother's adultery, the illicit act would be forever etched in Belinda's mind. Why? she wondered. Why had she done it? What had possessed her to wank another man's cock and bring out his sperm?

'There you are,' Tony said, returning and tossing a towel onto the sofa. 'God, I needed that. The way you wanked me off and –'

'For fuck's sake, shut up,' she hissed, wiping her hand on the towel. 'Just shut up, Tony.'

'OK, anything you say. You're absolutely beautiful. You know that, don't you?'

'Shut the fuck up.'

'You can be quite a fiery little bitch when it takes your fancy. I like fiery women.'

'I'm going home,' she announced, tossing the towel to the floor as she stood up.

'And I'm going to sit here and have a drink and think about how firm your tits are and how tight and very wet your sweet pussy is and –'

'You won't be seeing me again, Tony. I . . . I made a terrible mistake. This has all been a terrible mistake. Oh, and you won't be seeing Desiree again.'

'Won't I?'

'No, you won't. I want you to forget everything that's happened.'

'Forget how tight and wet . . .'

'I'll talk to Desiree when she gets home. I'll tell her that . . .'

'I'm good with women?'

'Look, I know that you . . . Try to understand that I'm a married woman and Desiree is only sixteen. Please, leave us alone.'

'You certainly didn't leave me alone, Belinda. You unzipped my trousers, pulled my cock out, wanked me off and –'

'Please, Tony. It was wrong of me, OK? I made a mistake, and I want to forget about it. And I want you to do the same. There's no future for us. Surely, you must understand that? And there's certainly no future for you and my daughter. Hopefully, we'll be able to remain friends and good neighbours. Apart from that, there's nothing between us.'

'If you say so.'

'I do say so.'

'What are you going to say to Desiree?'

'I'll tell her that . . . I don't know, yet. I'll think of something.'

'You do that, Belinda. And, in the meantime, I'll invite her in and offer her wine and give her friendly kisses.'

'You really are a bastard, aren't you?'

'You come round here, pull my cock out and give me a wank . . . And then you call me a bastard? What are you, Belinda? What name would you call a married woman who pulls another man's cock out and wanks him off? What name would you give to a married woman who opens her legs and allows another man to bring her off? A happily married, loyal and devoted, faithful and loving wife?'

Belinda stormed out of Tony's house, knowing that there was only one answer to his question. A wanton, adulterous whore. Blaming her husband, blaming her daughter, she took a deep breath and tried to compose herself as she reached home and closed the front door behind her. Adultery. There was no other word for it. But she'd only been trying to protect Desiree, she tried to convince herself. Had the stupid girl not thought that she'd found love, had she got on with her studies instead of . . . There was only one person at fault, Belinda knew as she filled the kettle.

Belinda noticed Desiree lurking in the back garden and watched her for a while. She was obviously waiting

50

for something as she hovered behind a bush. Finally opening the door and calling out to her, Belinda feared the worst. The girl looked nervous, guilty, as she stepped into the kitchen. Scowling at her, Belinda was sure that she'd been about to sneak round to Tony's house.

'What were you doing out there?' Belinda asked her daughter.

'Er . . . nothing,' Desiree replied shakily. 'I was just . . . just enjoying the sunshine.'

'I thought you were going to college?'

'Yes, no, I . . .'

'You were about to sneak round to Tony's house, weren't you?'

'No, I wasn't.'

'You're not to see him again, Desiree. Do you understand?'

'No, I don't understand. Why can't I see him again?'

'Because . . . because he's not a very nice person. He's only after one thing.'

'That's not true,' Desiree hissed. 'He's one of the nicest people I know. And he's not only after one thing. You're jealous, aren't you?'

'Jealous? Don't be ridiculous, Desiree.'

'You've been round there, haven't you?'

'Yes, I was looking for you. You're young, Desiree. You know nothing about men, especially older men. Take it from me, Tony is only after one thing. And whether he gets it from you or someone else makes no difference to him. He's after women, with one thing in mind.'

'Has he been after you, then?'

'Well . . . No, of course he hasn't.'

'That blows your idea out of the window, doesn't it? If he was after a woman, any woman, then he'd go after you.'

'He . . . he has been rather suggestive.'

51

'How?'

'Well, talking about things.'

'What's that on your skirt?'

'I . . . I must have spilled something. Look, Desiree, Tony's no good. And I want you to keep away from him.'

Belinda shook her head as her daughter stormed out of the room and bound up the stairs, and cringed as she heard the bedroom door slam shut. She'd made matters worse, she was sure, as she wiped a tear from her eye. Desiree would rebel, she knew. The girl would now be more determined than ever to see Tony. Recalling her orgasm, the sperm flowing over her hand, she pondered on the idea of giving Tony what he wanted to keep him away from Desiree.

'God, what am I thinking?' Sighing, she wiped the sperm off her skirt and poured a cup of coffee. To have sex with Tony, to satisfy his lust in order to keep him away from her daughter was crazy. She took her coffee into the lounge, sat on the sofa and pondered on the notion. It would probably work, she mused. Bring Tony's sperm out once every day, and his libido would never rise to the point where he demanded sex from Desiree. Again thinking that the idea was crazy, she knew that there was no way she could stop her daughter from seeing Tony. The girl would sneak round to his house, or they'd meet in the park or on the common.

Hearing the front door close, Belinda leaped to her feet and gazed out of the lounge window. Desiree was heading for Tony's house. Wearing her short red skirt, she looked so attractive, so young and beautiful. How could any man resist her? she mused, biting her lip as she imagined Tony's sperm flowing over Desiree's hand. Sixteen years old with long black hair and a beautiful body . . . There was no way Tony could resist her.

'We need to talk,' Desiree said as Tony opened his front door.

'Yes, we do,' he agreed as she stepped into the hall. 'Your mother is becoming a pain.'

'Tony, do you fancy her?' Desiree asked him.

'What? Fancy your mum? Hardly. Whatever gave you that idea?'

Desiree followed him into the lounge and flopped onto the sofa. 'Things she said,' she finally said.

'What things?'

'She said that you're only after one thing. From any woman, it doesn't matter who.'

'She's mad,' he said, forcing a laugh. 'If I wanted a woman, any woman, then I'd go to a pub and pick one up. If I only wanted sex, there are plenty of women who'd oblige. This is ridiculous. I've cancelled my trip to Ireland and your mother comes here going on at me, and now you're asking me whether I fancy her ... I don't know why I'm bothering with all this nonsense.'

'I'm sorry.' Desiree sighed. 'It's just that –'

'It's just that the situation is impossible,' he cut in. 'You, your mother ... Nothing but bloody trouble. I think we'd better call it a day, Desiree.'

'No, please ...'

'Have you got a better idea?'

'I don't know.'

'How can we possibly go on like this? It wouldn't surprise me if your mother arrives in a minute to check up on you. I should have gone to Ireland.'

Tears filling the dark pools of her eyes, Desiree knew that there was no future with Tony. He was right, her mother would probably turn up at any minute. The woman was possessive, she reflected. Possessive, overly protective, unreasonable and ... and jealous? She'd always be there: lurking, hovering, spying, checking up. The situation *was* ridiculous, she decided, recalling Tony's words. Ridiculous and impossible.

'I'd have earned some pretty good money had I gone to Ireland.' Tony sighed.

'I'm glad you didn't,' Desiree said.

'Are you?'

'Yes, of course. I want to be with you, Tony.'

'Prove it,' he said. 'Prove that you want to be with me.'

'How?'

'Shave for me.'

'What?'

'Your pussy, Desiree. Prove that you want to be with me by shaving your pussy for me.'

'Tony, no . . .'

'OK, let's forget the whole thing.'

'But . . . Why do you want me to shave?'

'Because I like it that way. It pleases me. If you're not willing to please me, then . . .'

'But it's not normal to shave.'

'It's what I want, Desiree. If you're not willing to please me, if you won't do the smallest thing for me . . .'

'All right,' she finally agreed. 'All right, I'll do it.'

'Go home now and do it. Then, come back and show me. Come back and prove that you want to be with me.'

'Yes, yes, I will.'

Desiree left his house, made her way home and closed the front door quietly. Thanking God that her mother was out, she climbed the stairs to the bathroom and slipped her skirt and panties off. She didn't want to shave off her pubic hair: it wasn't right, it wasn't normal. She didn't understand why Tony wanted her to shave down there but, if that's what it took to keep him, then she'd do it. She'd do anything, she decided, grabbing her father's shaving foam and razor from the shelf. No matter what, she'd do anything to keep him.

Sitting on the side of the bath, she massaged the foam into the fleshy swell of her outer lips, the gentle rise of her mons. Dragging the razor over her most private place, the blade leaving smooth skin in its wake, she again wondered why Tony wanted her to do this. A thong, she reflected, recalling his words. He'd licked her bottom hole, asked her to wear a thong and now wanted her to shave off her pubic hair.

Her mother was right, Desiree mused, dragging the razor over the swell of her vaginal lips. She knew nothing about men. Perhaps this *was* normal? Perhaps Tony's adult spanking and bottom-licking game was perfectly normal? But, to shave off her pubic hair? She finished the job of depilation, wiping away the foam and black curls with a flannel, and gazed at her reflection in the full-length mirror.

'God,' she said, eyeing the smooth, hairless flesh of her outer lips, her unveiled sex crack. She dried herself with a towel, pulled her panties on and slipped into her short skirt. The feel of her panties against her hairless skin wasn't unpleasant, she thought, as she cleared away the evidence of her illicit shaving. But she didn't feel right. How could it be normal to shave? Had her mother shaved to please her father? She doubted that very much.

'Desiree?' her mother called from downstairs. 'Desiree, are you up there?'

'Yes,' she replied, leaving the bathroom and descending the stairs. 'I was just . . . I was just washing.'

'You're not going out again, are you?'

'No, no,' she murmured, trying to avoid another confrontation with her mother. 'I'm going to get on with my work.'

'Oh, right. Well, I'm pleased to hear it. I've just seen Tony leaving his house.'

'He's gone out?'

'Yes, he has. Your uncle's coming over later. You will be here to see him, won't you?'

'How much later?'

'He didn't say exactly. Why don't you get on with your work for a couple of hours? I'll let you know when he arrives.'

'Yes, all right,' Desiree said softly.

Desiree climbed the stairs to her room and sat at her desk, staring at the blank computer screen. Why had Tony gone out? she wondered. Where had he gone? And why did her uncle have to arrange to call round today of all days? She decided to catch up with her work and switched the computer on. After her uncle had been, she'd make up some excuse or other to her mother and then sneak round to Tony's house. She'd prove that she wanted to please him. She'd show him her shaved pussy, and prove that she wanted him.

Four

'Does your mother know that you're here?' Tony asked, leading Desiree into the lounge.

'I said that I had a headache and was going out for a walk to the park,' she replied. 'She's talking to my uncle. He's been there for over two hours.'

'Did you shave?'

'Yes, yes, I did. Where did you go earlier?'

'I haven't been anywhere.'

'My mum said . . .'

'Said what?'

'Nothing.'

Tony seemed annoyed, angry. He was quick and sharp with her, but Desiree didn't know why. Although she'd never had a boyfriend, she knew that a relationship shouldn't be like this. Something was wrong, but what? Her mother hadn't helped things, she reflected. But, neither had Tony. Asking her to shave to prove that she wanted him didn't seem right. Talking about thongs and licking her bottom hole. Something was wrong. Wondering whether she was imagining things as he smiled at her, she did her best to relax.

'What did your mother say?' he asked her again.

'She didn't say anything. It's just that I thought I saw you go out earlier.'

'I've been in all afternoon, Desiree. All afternoon waiting for you to turn up.'

'I'm sorry, but I couldn't get away. I had to see my uncle. Anyway, I'm here now.'

'Right. Well, you'd better show me what you've done. Show me before your mother comes looking for you.'

'I'm rather embarrassed,' she murmured, brushing a tendril of hair away from her flushing face.

'You'll get over it,' he said unsympathetically. 'Come on, pull your panties down and show me what you've done.'

Lifting her short skirt and lowering the front of her white cotton panties, Desiree revealed the swollen cushions of her hairless vaginal lips, her tightly closed sex slit. Tony gasped, his eyes widening as he knelt before her and gazed longingly at the most intimate part of her teenage body. Praising her, he kissed her naked mons before moving down and pressing his lips against her vulval valley. Desiree quivered and breathed heavily as she felt his tongue running up and down her sex crack. The sensations were heavenly, but she began to wonder whether he was interested in her as a person, or only for what she had between her shapely legs.

Recalling her mother's words as Tony ran his tongue up and down her sex slit, she imagined Tony running after women purely for sex. Any woman, all women. He'd asked her to wear a thong, to play his adult games and shave her pubic hair, he'd talked about spanking. Was he interested in her as a person? she again wondered. He'd taken no real interest in her college work, he hadn't asked her anything about herself. All he seemed to want was her young body.

'So, you like me shaved?' she finally asked.

'God, yes,' he replied. 'You look so young and fresh and . . . and you taste delicious. You have a beautiful body, Desiree.'

'Yes, but do you like me as a person?'

'Of course I do,' he said, rising to his feet. 'What are you getting at?'

'Nothing. I was just thinking that it would be nice to go out somewhere or . . .'

'I'd love to go out for a drink with you, but you're too young to go to the pub.'

'I could have a soft drink.'

'You could but, apart from your age, we have to keep our relationship under wraps. What with your mother watching you like a hawk, we have to be careful.'

'I suppose so.'

'Can you imagine your mother's reaction if she heard that you'd been to a pub with me? She'd go crazy. Anyway, let's not talk about your mother. I have an idea. How about a few photographs?'

'Photographs?'

'Of your beautiful young body,' he said eagerly, taking a camera from the mantlepiece.

'But . . . What for?'

'What for? Because you look absolutely gorgeous with your shaved pussy. Slip your blouse and bra off and I'll –'

'No, Tony,' she stated firmly.

'No?' he echoed, frowning at her. 'Why ever not?'

'I might be naive and inexperienced, but I'm not stupid.'

'I know you're not stupid. What are you talking about?'

'I thought you wanted a proper relationship with me. Taking photographs of my shaved . . . It's not normal.'

'Not normal to want photographs of the girl I love? Desiree, you talk about a proper relationship, and yet you've made no attempt to come anywhere near me.'

'What do you mean?'

'You've not touched me. You've not made one move towards me, have you?'

'Well . . . No, not yet. You want photos because you love me?'

'Why else would I want photos? I don't think you realise just how much I love you. I think about you

59

constantly. I'm always looking out of the window for you. I think of nothing other than you. To have a few photographs of you naked would be great. I could look at them when you're not around. I'll put one in a frame and stand it on my bedside table. No one will see it, other than me.'

'Well, in that case ...'

'I don't want to force you. And I certainly don't think you're stupid. If you'd rather I didn't have photos of you, then ...'

'No, no, it's all right. I want you to have photos.'

Desiree unbuttoned her blouse, tossed it onto the sofa and unhooked her bra. Although she'd agreed to the photos, his words hadn't reassured her, hadn't made her feel any better about the situation. What were his thoughts? she mused, her small breasts exposed to his wide eyes. She dropped her bra onto the sofa, and slipped her skirt and panties off. Standing naked before Tony didn't feel right. His eyes focused on the ripe teats of her teenage breasts and he licked his lips. This didn't feel like love, whatever love felt like.

Watching as he knelt before her and took several shots of her hairless pussy, she didn't feel embarrassed or self-conscious. But she did feel very unsure about Tony's motives when he asked her whether she still had her school uniform. He said how nice she'd look in a gymslip and blouse and white knee-length socks. He asked her whether she'd mind putting her hair into pigtails as he took more photographs of her naked body and suggested that she pose with one foot on the sofa and her legs wide apart.

'Part your pussy lips for me,' he instructed as she stood with one foot on the sofa.

'I thought you wanted normal photographs,' she said. 'Photographs of me, not of my ...'

'That's right. Photographs of every little bit of your beautiful young body. Do you have a gymslip?'

'No, I don't. Mum got rid of it when I left school and started college.'

'Shame. I suppose we could always get you one. And a white blouse and navy-blue knickers. OK, part your little pussy lips as wide as you can.'

Following his instructions, Desiree parted the fleshy lips of her vulva as he knelt on the floor and focused the camera. Although she again felt that this was very wrong, she didn't want to ruin any chance of enjoying a loving relationship with Tony. Sure that once he'd taken his photographs he'd show his love for her, she did as he asked and stretched open the wet entrance to her young vagina.

'I'm feeling cold,' she said finally, hoping that he'd allow her to dress. 'It's quite chilly in here.'

'Gazing at your pretty little tits makes me feel hot,' he quipped. 'So, are you going to touch me or is our relationship going to be one sided?'

Desiree stared open mouthed as he kicked his shoes aside and tugged his trousers down. He was massive, she observed, his penis catapulting to attention as he slipped his boxer shorts off. Were all penises this big? she wondered. Never having seen a naked man, she had no idea about sizes. Focusing on the opening of his foreskin, she could just see the purple surface of his glans. Would he order her to pull his foreskin back and expose his knob? His penis waved from side to side above his heaving balls and she knew that she was going to have to touch it as he ordered her to sit on the sofa. Standing before her as she complied, his manhood only inches from her flushed face, he told her to have a good look at her first cock.

'Touch it and get to know it,' Tony said. 'This is your first cock, Desiree. What do you think of it?'

'It's big,' she answered, reaching out and running her fingertip up and down the veined shaft. 'You haven't kissed me today.' She sighed. 'You've not held me in your arms or . . .'

'There's plenty of time for that. Hold my cock and move your hand up and down. Hold it close to the top and wank me.'

Wrapping her fingers around his fleshy rod, Desiree pondered on his crude word. *Wank*. She didn't like words like that. They were the words her friend, Kathy, had used when talking about boys. Desiree saw no connection between crude words and love. Moving her hand up and down his warm shaft, rolling his foreskin back and forth over the solid bulb of his glans, she wondered how long it would take before his sperm shot out. She'd heard about wanking cocks from Kathy. She knew about wanking and bringing out sperm. But this didn't feel like love.

'That's good,' Tony said, watching her small hand wanking his rock-hard cock. 'Do it faster, Desiree. Do it faster and I'll spunk all over your beautiful little tits.'

Saying nothing, Desiree moved her hand faster up and down the length of his hard penis. His purple globe repeatedly appeared and disappeared. She didn't like the idea of his sperm splattering her young breasts. *Wank, spunk, tits* ... What did Tony want from her? she wondered. When they'd first met, he'd said that it would be nice if she called round sometimes. Called round for what? Sex? Unable to push her mother's words out of her mind as she watched Tony's heavy balls bouncing, she imagined him chasing after women purely for sex. How many girls had done this to him? she wondered. How many girls had allowed him to lick their bottom holes? How many girls had shaved for him? Had he dozens of photographs of naked girls?

'Suck it,' he said, his body trembling uncontrollably. 'I'm coming. Suck ... suck it ...'

Watching his sperm pumping from his knob, running over her hand, splattering her young breasts, Desiree couldn't imagine taking him into her mouth and tasting his male cream. The very notion revolted her. Had other girls sucked his penis and swallowed his sperm? she pondered, as he gasped and again ordered her to take his knob into her mouth. He'd want to drive his penis deep into her tight vagina before long, she knew, as his sperm flow began to stem. Feeling very uneasy about the relationship, she finally released his penis and gazed at the white liquid hanging in long threads from her slender fingers.

'Why didn't you suck it?' he asked her.

'I ... I didn't want to,' she replied, watching his sticky penis deflate.

'You'll soon learn. So, what did you think of your first cock-wanking?'

'I don't know. It was all right, I suppose.'

'All right? What with your dad away, I'll bet your mum would love to get her hands on a hard cock.'

'Tony, please. Don't talk like that about my mum.'

'I was only joking. Are you all right, Desiree? You seem ... Oh, I don't know. You don't seem to be in a very good mood.'

'I'm cold. I think I'll get dressed.'

'Get dressed? But we haven't finished our games, yet. I thought a little spanking might warm you up?'

Desiree felt sickened by Tony's so-called joke. Her parents were a loyal, loving couple. There was no way her mother would want to get her hands on a hard cock. Initially, Tony had seemed so warm and friendly. Was this some darker side of his character emerging? she wondered, as she cupped her sperm-splattered breasts in her small bra. In her confusion, she was pleased that she'd held a man's penis, brought out his sperm. She couldn't have remained totally innocent and inexperienced forever. But she'd never dreamed that the experience would leave her feeling cold and unsure.

Watching Tony pull the armchair into the centre of the room, she didn't want to play his spanking games or endure his bottom licking. *We haven't finished our games, yet*. Games? she ruminated. This was supposed to be love, not a game. She noticed that his penis was stiffening as he turned and grinned at her. He asked her to lean over the back of the chair and again said that a little spanking would warm her up and do her the world of good.

'Only in fun,' he added with a chuckle. 'You have such a beautiful little bum, Desiree. I could really get into spanking games with you.'

'Tony, I . . . I don't want to be spanked,' she said, grabbing her panties and standing.

'What's the matter?' he asked her. 'What's wrong?'

'I don't know.' She sighed, pulling her panties up her long legs. 'I suppose this isn't what I expected.'

'What isn't?'

'The situation, the relationship, us . . . I don't know what I expected, but it wasn't this.'

'I don't know what you mean,' he said. He placed his arms around her and kissed her full lips. 'What you did to me just now was wonderful, Desiree,' he said, the solid shaft of his penis pressing against her naked stomach. 'I'll be honest with you. You're the first girl . . . No one's ever done that to me.'

'Really?' She gasped, her dark eyes locked to his. 'You mean . . .'

'I mean, no one's ever done that. I know you'll find this difficult to believe seeing as I'm twenty-seven, but . . . I'm a virgin.'

'What? You've never . . . You've never had a girlfriend?'

'I've been out with a few girls, but nothing ever came of it. From the moment I set eyes on you, I knew that you were the one for me. I know that I'm going too fast for you, rushing you into things. The reason is that I've had no experience at all and I'm desperate to learn. I feel stupid now I've admitted I'm a virgin.'

'No, you mustn't feel stupid. I'm really pleased.'

'I've seen the odd dirty video and looked at men's magazines so I'm not completely naive. I've read about spanking and ... I just wanted to try things with you, Desiree. Try things and learn about sex, with you.'

'Tony, you've made me so happy,' she trilled. 'I thought ... I don't know what I thought.'

'I suppose I was trying to come across as experienced. Talking about splattering your tits with spunk and ... I didn't want you to think that I knew nothing about sex.'

'I'm so happy,' Desiree again trilled. 'We can learn together, try things and learn about sex together.'

'Don't go telling your mum that I'm a virgin.' He laughed.

'There's no need to worry about my mum because I'm not going to tell her anything. I'm not going to tell her that we're seeing each other. I want her to think that there's nothing between us. That way, she won't cause problems.'

'Good idea. I know that she's overly protective towards you, which is understandable. But the last thing we want is her ruining what we have together. So, shall we try a little spanking?'

'Yes, why not.'

Leaning over the back of the armchair, Desiree closed her eyes as Tony knelt on the floor behind her and kissed each firm buttock in turn. She couldn't believe how lucky she was to have met a man who was also a virgin. As he ran his tongue up and down her anal groove, parted her rounded buttocks and licked the brown ring of her anus, she quivered and gasped. She was able to enjoy his intimate attention now that she knew that he'd never done this before. What she'd thought to be dirty and crude was now immensely satisfying, and she vowed to give herself completely to the man she loved.

As Tony stretched her buttocks wide apart and drove his tongue into her hot rectal duct, Desiree let out a sigh of pleasure. The sensations were amazing, she mused dreamily, her body trembling wildly as his tongue teased the sensitive walls of her anal sheath. This was experimenting with sex, learning together, discovering . . . This was loving. His lips locked to the delicate brown tissue surrounding her anus, he managed to push his wet tongue deeper into her once sacrosanct hole and wake the sleeping nerve endings there.

Her mother had been so very wrong about Tony, she reflected, as her juices of arousal seeped between the hairless lips of her vulva. If only she knew that Tony was a virgin, if only she knew how much he loved her daughter. Desiree had also been wrong about Tony. Doubting him the way she had, she now felt very guilty. He was a kind, loving man, she mused, as he expertly attended her bottom hole with his wet tongue. But there was no point in telling her mother about their love. As Tony had said, they had to keep their relationship under wraps.

'I don't believe it.' Tony sighed. He had slipped his tongue out of Desiree's tight anus as the doorbell rang. 'If that's your mother . . . Grab your clothes and go upstairs. I'll deal with her.'

'I'm sure it won't be her,' Desiree said, taking her clothes from the sofa as Tony pulled his trousers up.

'Who else could it be? I don't know anyone around here. Go upstairs to the front bedroom and I'll call you when the coast is clear.'

Waiting until Desiree had bounded up the stairs, Tony ran his fingers through his hair and took a deep breath as he walked through the hall. It might have been an idea to ignore the bell, but he knew that Belinda would try to look through the lounge window. If she believed that her daughter was there, she'd not go away. Finally opening the door, he donned a welcoming smile and invited her in.

'Is Desiree here?' she asked, stepping into the hall.

'Desiree? No, she's not,' he replied nonchalantly. 'She rang the bell earlier, but I didn't answer the door.'

'Oh, I see. I can't think where she's got to.'

'Out with a friend, perhaps?'

'Maybe,' she murmured, wandering into the lounge. 'Tony, I'm sorry that I called you a bastard.'

Closing the lounge door as Belinda sat on the sofa, Tony hoped that Desiree wouldn't be able to hear their conversation. 'You might think me a bastard, but I've kept Desiree away,' he said.

'So, you knew it was her but didn't answer the door?'

'I thought it best, Belinda. In view of all you've said, and the relationship we now have . . .'

'Tony, we don't have a relationship.'

'Don't we?'

'No, we don't. I only came here looking for Desiree. I like you very much and . . . and I have to admit that I'm attracted to you. But I'm a happily married woman.'

'So you keep telling me. In fact, you've told me so many times that it makes me wonder whether you're trying to convince yourself.'

'That's nonsense. I'm just feeling lost, that's all. I've always looked upon Desiree as a friend as well as a daughter. Whenever my husband's working away, Desiree and I . . . Now that we seem to have drifted apart, I'm feeling a little lonely. Desiree and I did everything together. Walking, shopping, cooking, watching television.'

'Belinda, why don't you come round for a drink now and then? I did suggest it earlier, but you wouldn't entertain the idea.'

'Because I don't want to become involved with another man. I know that I said I feel lonely at times, but ....'

'You don't want me to become involved with your daughter, and yet you don't want to become involved with me. I'm the one who's feeling lonely, Belinda. I'm new to the area and have no friends here. If you're not going to visit me, then I might as well invite Desiree round.'

'Is that a threat?'

'No, of course it's not. All I'm saying is that I live here alone and have no friends in the area. Desiree obviously likes me. To sit here alone when I could enjoy her company seems ludicrous. You've said that you're attracted to me, and I know that you enjoyed what we did earlier. But you won't submit to your inner desires and . . .'

'So, you're saying that it's either me or my daughter?'

'We've been through this before, Belinda. To be honest, I don't see why I should sit here alone when Desiree is eager to spend some time with me. Why won't you spend some time with me? You want me, don't you? It's all very well trying to fool me, but at least be honest with yourself.'

'I'm not trying to fool you, and I am being honest with myself. I don't want a relationship with you. I only came here to see whether Desiree . . .'

'I wish I *had* invited her in now. I've been sitting here alone when I could have been chatting with Desiree. I've been pushing her away because I thought that we might have something together. If we haven't got anything, then I might as well . . .'

'That sounds very much like a threat to me.'

'I don't care what it sounds like. But I'm not prepared to push Desiree away when she obviously wants to be with me and I need company. It just doesn't make sense. You might think me unreasonable, but I need company.'

'If I decide to come round now and then, will you promise to keep Desiree away?'

'Yes, of course I will. I've already done that by not answering the door to her.'

'But, I told you that you wouldn't be seeing me again.'

'I didn't believe you, Belinda. Look, you give me what I want, and I won't give your daughter what she wants. Is it a deal?'

'That sounds like blackmail to me.'

'I'll rephrase it. You give me what I want, and I'll give you what you want.'

Biting her lip, Belinda turned and gazed at Tony as he sat beside her on the sofa. Confused, she didn't know what she wanted. But she did know that she didn't want Desiree to lose her virginity to a man almost old enough to be her father. This was definitely blackmail, she mused, as Tony placed his hand on her naked knee. She couldn't deny that she'd enjoyed his intimate attention when she'd last sat on his sofa, but . . . Again pondering on her virtually nonexistent sex life with her husband, she breathed heavily as Tony slipped his hand up her skirt and pressed his fingertips into the warm swell of her tight panties.

'No,' she murmured. 'Tony, I . . .'

'Let yourself go,' he whispered, pulling her panties to one side. 'You don't have to become involved with me to enjoy sex. Just look at it as two lonely people finding some solace in physical contact.'

'Desiree might be home and . . .'

'Don't worry about Desiree,' he whispered, again hoping that the girl couldn't hear him. 'Just relax and enjoy your time with me.'

Lifting her buttocks clear of the sofa as he tugged her panties down, Belinda knew that she couldn't win the fight against her inner desires. She'd battled against right and wrong for long enough. Adultery, deceit, lies, betrayal . . . Again wallowing in confusion, she didn't know why she'd gone to see Tony. She'd been wondering where her daughter had got to, but she knew deep down that she'd wondered whether Tony would try to seduce her again. And, if he did? She'd tried to fight her inner desires, tried to remain faithful to her husband. She was doing this to save Desiree from Tony, she decided. She didn't want this, but had to endure his crude attention in order to save Desiree from the unscrupulous man.

Closing her eyes and reclining on the sofa as Tony settled on the floor, she allowed him to pull her panties off and part her thighs wide. Pushing her skirt up over her stomach, exposing her neglected vulva, he kissed her naked legs. She could feel his warm breath against the smooth flesh of her inner thighs as his mouth moved dangerously close to the open valley of her vulva. And she moved dangerously close to full-blown adultery.

Digging her fingernails into the sofa cushion as Tony kissed the full lips of her vagina, she realised that it had been years since her husband had kissed her there. He was always working away, Desiree was usually around, there was very little time . . . Gasping as she felt Tony's tongue lapping at the solid nub of her clitoris, she arched her back. Images of her husband looming in her mind, she looked down at Tony. She was offering her body to another man, offering her sex valley to another man's tongue. Her panties lay on the floor, discarded. Her fidelity was in shreds, her marriage vows torn, put asunder. The sensations drove her wild as her neighbour continued to sweep his tongue over the sensitive tip of her clitoris. She didn't want Desiree to experience this. Not yet – and certainly not with Tony.

'You didn't come here looking for Desiree,' Tony whispered, driving two fingers deep into Belinda's sex-drenched vaginal sheath. 'You came here because you were desperate for an orgasm.'

'No, no,' she murmured shakily. 'I had no intention of . . .'

'You were desperate to have your pussy licked and sucked and fingered.'

'No, please, I . . .'

'Relax and allow yourself to come,' he whispered, sucking the bulb of her erect clitoris into his hot mouth.

'I came here looking for Desiree,' she persisted.

'You don't have to lie to me, Belinda. You came here because your sweet little cunt needed me.'

'No, don't talk like that.'

'You came here because your tight little cunt was in dire need of a hard cock.'

'Please, stop it. You ... you don't know what that does to me.'

'You like dirty talk?'

'Yes, no, I mean ...'

'When was your tight cunt last spermed? When did you last get fucked senseless?'

'I ... I don't know. Please, I need to come.'

'You need me to finger your wet cunt hard and suck an orgasm out of your sweet little clitty?'

'God, yes, yes ...'

Guilt swamping her as she listened to the squelching of her pussy-milk, the slurping of Tony's mouth, she quivered uncontrollably and again dug her fingernails into the sofa cushion. Why had she ever introduced herself to Tony? she wondered, moving forwards and positioning her naked buttocks over the edge of the cushion. Why on earth had she bothered to be neighbourly and call on him? Parting her thighs to the extreme, allowing him deeper access to her vaginal sheath, she imagined Desiree discovering her adultery.

The family unit would be in ruins, she reflected. Mum, dad, daughter, nice home ... All in ruins because she'd offered her body to another man. Why was she doing this? she wondered. Recalling her teenage years, she remembered the boys she'd opened her legs to, the cocks she'd taken into her very tight and sex-thirsty pussy. She'd been a slut, a tart. But she was single in those carefree days. Single, free ... Now, she was married, she reminded herself. This was adultery.

71

But she knew that Tony would have pulled Desiree's panties off and licked her vagina if she'd not intervened. Had she not stepped in and saved her daughter . . . She was doing this for Desiree, she tried to convince herself for the umpteenth time. A good mother would do anything for her daughter. Behave like a common slut and commit adultery? She had to shield Desiree from oral sex, pussy-licking, fingering, cock-wanking, spunk-swallowing . . .

Belinda couldn't remember when she'd last enjoyed oral sex. She used to love sucking her husband's cock, drinking his creamy sperm. But things change with the passing of time, she mused, as her clitoris became painfully hard within Tony's hot mouth. As the years pass, the flame of passion burns low, diminishes . . . And eventually goes out? Perhaps she should have rekindled her sex life, she thought. But there was never time for making love, making lust.

'Come for me,' Tony whispered, repeatedly thrusting four fingers deep into the stretched sheath of her vagina. 'Come and pump out your hot girlie cream.'

'I am.' She gasped, her face grimacing as he snaked his tongue around the swollen bulb of her clitoris. 'God, I'm . . . I'm going to come.'

Her curvaceous body rigid, her breathing fast and shallow, Belinda whimpered in her adultery as her orgasm exploded within the pulsating nub of her ballooning clitoris. Wave after wave of sex crashed through her shaking body. Her eyes rolled, her nostrils flared as she rode the crest of her illicit orgasm, her adulterous orgasm. Her husband should be between her thighs, she reflected in her sexual delirium. Brian should be fingering her spasming vagina, licking and sucking on her orgasming clitoris. Not another man. Adultery, lies, betrayal, deceit . . .

Again and again, tremors of sex shook her quivering body as she lay gasping and panting on the sofa. Her climax finally began to recede and she felt drunk on sex. Dizzy, floating, drifting through clouds of lust ... Tony was good, she mused dreamily, as he teased the last ripples of sex from her deflating clitoris. Never had she had her pussy so expertly attended, her feminine needs so fulfilled. Opening her eyes as he slipped his wet fingers out of the burning sheath of her vagina, she focused on his smiling face as he asked her whether she was all right.

'Yes, yes,' she managed to answer shakily.

'I know how to please a woman,' he said, moving forwards and lapping up the cream oozing from her gaping vaginal entrance. 'Do you want to come again?'

'God, no ... Please, no more.'

'I'll suck out your sex-milk, Belinda. I'll drink your hot sex-milk from your beautiful cunt.'

His crude words driving her wild, she listened to his slurping, his sucking and swallowing as he drank from the inflamed sheath of her vagina. He was incredible, she mused, as he cleansed her pussy crack, drained her vaginal duct. He knew exactly what to do. But, although incredibly aroused, guilt began to swamp her again. Finally pushing him away, she knew that she had to stop him. If he carried on, she'd be begging him for another orgasm. Thoughts of Desiree flooded her mind and she realised that things were going too far as Tony unzipped his trousers and pressed the purple globe of his solid cock against the pink flesh surrounding her vaginal entrance.

'No,' she said, moving back on the sofa.

'Come on, Belinda,' he said, grinning at her. 'You know how much you want my cock.'

'No, I can't. Please, I have to go now.'

'Not until you've pleased me,' he said, standing before her. 'Suck it, Belinda. You know you can't resist sucking out my spunk.'

Grabbing his solid shaft and wanking him, she knew that she had to restrain herself. To suck his knob and taste his salt, to bring out his spunk and swallow the product of his orgasm would be heavenly. But the illicit act would be too close to full-blown adultery. To take his cock into her mouth would be as adulterous as allowing him to penetrate her vagina. So far, she'd only enjoyed mutual masturbation. That wasn't adultery, she decided. Mutual masturbation was forgivable. She eased his heavy balls out of his trousers and continued to run her hand up and down his solid shaft as he gasped and swayed on his sagging legs. He was close to his orgasm, she knew, as she quickened her masturbation motion. He was about to pump out his fresh sperm and ...

'Suck it,' he said, clutching her head. 'I'm coming ... Please, suck it.'

As his creamy sperm jetted from his knob-slit and splattered her face, she pulled his foreskin right back and sucked his throbbing knob into her sperm-thirsty mouth. Rolling her tongue over the silky-smooth surface of his glans, she swallowed hard as her cheeks filled with his lubricious cream. She'd not wanted this, she reflected, slurping and suckling on his swollen plum like a babe at the breast. This was wrong, so beautifully wrong.

Kneading his heavy balls, she wanked his solid shaft and slurped on his orgasming knob as he gasped and swayed in the grip of his coming. Her tormented mind was battered with a thousand thoughts, as she repeatedly swallowed her neighbour's spunk, revelling in the adulterous act as she drank from his fountainhead. Her husband was working hard, Desiree was probably at home wondering where her mother was ... Guilt gripped her again.

She slipped his spent cock out of her spermed mouth. 'I have to go now,' she finally said.

'God, you're amazing,' he said, managing to pull his zip up. 'You really know how to suck cock.'

'Tony, I . . .' She grabbed her panties from the floor, stood up and moved to the door. 'I won't be back,' she stated firmly, clutching her panties.

'Whatever you say.' He chortled. 'Just call round when your tight little cunt needs spunking.'

'No, I won't. I've made a fatal mistake and I . . .'

'That's the second fatal mistake you've made. That's the second time you've brought out my spunk.'

'And the last.'

'I wonder whether Desiree would enjoy a mouth-fucking?'

'Stop it, Tony. Please, don't even think things like that about my daughter.'

Belinda left the house, made her way home and closed the front door behind her. Home, the marital home. Her panties in her hand, she climbed the stairs to Desiree's room to find the girl sleeping in her bed. Not realising how fast the time had flown, she wished that she'd not stayed at Tony's for so long. Had Desiree known where she was? she wondered. Thanking God that the girl didn't know what she'd been up to, she went into her own bedroom and closed the door. The day had been a nightmare, she mused dolefully. Never again, she thought. Never again.

Five

'You stayed at Tony's for a long time last night,' Desiree said accusingly as she wandered into the kitchen.

'Yes, I . . . We got talking about curtains and furniture. Would you like some breakfast?'

'No, thanks. Did you get talking about me?'

'No, we didn't. How did you know that I was there?'

'I saw you go in as I got back. Dad rang when you were out.'

'Oh, er . . . How is he?'

'He's fine.'

'Did you tell him where I was?'

'Yes, I did.'

'What did he say?'

'He's going to ring you this morning.'

'So, what are you doing today? It's Saturday, no college.'

'I might go into town,' Desiree said, filling the kettle. 'I want to buy some new clothes.'

'I'll come with you,' Belinda suggested cheerily.

'No, I'd rather go alone.'

'Oh, I see. In that case, I might do some gardening. The geranium cuttings you took will need watering. And I'll carry on with the flower border we were preparing.'

Belinda opened the back door, stepped onto the patio, and looked up at the clear blue sky. The sun was already hot; it was going to be a beautiful day. Not a day of nightmares, she asserted mentally, imagining that she could still taste the salt of Tony's sperm. Determined to get back to normal, into a proper routine, she decided that getting on with the garden would be a good start. When Desiree returned from her shopping trip, she'd suggest having a picnic in the country. It would be like old times, she mused. The times before Tony.

Hearing the front door close, Belinda knew that Desiree was in a strange mood. The girl had never left the house without saying goodbye, she reflected. They were drifting apart, she knew, as she filled the watering can. Desiree had lovingly planted the geranium cuttings, and had now left them to wither in the heat. Was her relationship with Desiree withering? she wondered. They'd always gone shopping together, done the garden together and . . .

'Good morning,' Tony called over the fence.

'Oh, er . . . good morning,' Belinda replied as coldly as she could.

'Sleep well?'

'Very well, thank you.'

'It's hot today. Why don't you put a bikini on and show off your beautiful body?'

'Because I have a lot to do in the garden. Now, if you don't mind?'

'I don't mind at all. I didn't realise that you had green fingers. I know how good you are with your fingers, but I didn't realise . . .'

'Tony, please. I'd like to enjoy gardening without having to listen to you.'

'I thought of you this morning when I was in the shower.'

'I'm not interested in your thoughts.'

'I thought about your pretty mouth, your pink tongue. God, was I stiff.'

'Tony, stop it,' she snapped. 'You're making the situation impossible. If we're to live next door to each other as good neighbours, then . . .'

77

'Very good neighbours,' he quipped. 'Is Desiree around?'

'She's gone into town. And, when she gets back, she's going to get on with her studies and then we're going out together.'

'Oh, I think that's my front doorbell. I wonder who that could be?'

As he wandered into his house and closed the back door, Belinda felt her stomach churn. Had Desiree gone round to see him? she wondered fearfully. She didn't want the constant worry, she mused wearily, watering the geranium cuttings. Things never used to be like this. Then again, she'd not committed adultery before, she reflected, biting her lip as she recalled Tony's throbbing knob bloating her mouth and flooding her tongue with creamy sperm. Finally, placing the watering can on the lawn, she knew that she couldn't enjoy gardening all the time she was worrying about her daughter.

Sitting on a patio chair, Belinda tried not to clutter her head with thoughts of Tony and Desiree. But she couldn't stop pictures looming in her mind of Desiree sucking Tony's cock and drinking his sperm. If Desiree had gone round there, if Tony was feeling horny . . . She got up from her chair and walked across the garden to the fence but couldn't see through Tony's kitchen window. Perhaps they were in the lounge? she pondered. Perhaps Tony was fondling Desiree's young breasts, slipping his hand up her skirt, fingering her virgin pussy and . . .

She walked into the house and made her way upstairs to the front bedroom. She gazed out of the window for an hour. Where was Desiree? What was she doing? If she came out of Tony's house, if she'd lied about going to town and had sneaked off to see him . . . Worry and anxiety driving her mad, she finally returned to the garden. This was a complete mess, she thought wearily. Why couldn't a nice family or an elderly couple have moved in next door? Why bloody Tony? Sighing, she knew that there was nothing she could do to stop Desiree from seeing Tony. Nothing, apart from . . .

Was adultery so bad? she wondered, again hovering by the fence and gazing at Tony's kitchen window. If Belinda's adultery put a stop to Tony seeing Desiree, if her infidelity preserved the girl's virginity, then was it so very bad? Things would be different once Brian was back, she mused. He'd talk to Desiree and she'd listen. And Tony . . . Tony could go to hell. There'd be no need to worry about him once Desiree's father was home. But, in the meantime . . .

'You still at it?' Tony asked her as he emerged from his house.

'Yes, I am,' she replied. 'Who was your visitor?'

'A friend,' he said, grinning at her. 'A very good friend.'

'You said that you didn't have any friends around here.'

'I have now.'

'Tony, if you . . .'

'If I what?'

'Nothing.'

'I might do a little gardening,' he said. 'You have a lovely garden. Perhaps you could give me some advice?'

'No, I don't think so. I don't know much about gardening. Desiree was . . . She is the keen gardener. All I do is help her.'

'She seems to be very good at everything.'

'What do you mean by that?'

'The garden, college . . . She's good at everything.'

'Yes, well . . . Look, I have a lot to do.'

'OK, I'll leave you in peace. I might ask Desiree to come round and help me with the garden. I'm sure she'd be only too willing to give me a hand.'

'Tony, I thought you said . . .'

'You know very well what I said, Belinda. It's either you, or your daughter.'

Her stomach churned again and Belinda knew that she had no choice. *It's either you, or your daughter.* If she didn't give her body to Tony, then he'd use Desiree's young body to satisfy his craving for crude sex. There was no battle to fight now, she mused. Right or wrong, adultery or not . . . If she was to save her daughter from Tony and preserve her virginity, her only option was to give him what he wanted.

'When my husband gets home,' she began, not sure what she was saying. 'When Brian gets home . . .'

'When your husband gets home, you'll still need me,' he cut in. 'You'll still need me to satisfy you, Belinda. Unless he's extremely good in bed, that is?'

'Yes, he is,' she lied. 'I won't need you, Tony. In fact, I don't need you now. I'm only doing this for Desiree's sake.'

'Of course you are. It has nothing to do with the amazing orgasm you experienced with me last night. It has nothing to do with you sucking the spunk out of my cock and loving every minute of it. You only endured a terrific orgasm and a beautiful mouth-fucking for Desiree's sake.'

'Please, don't be so crude.'

'You love dirty talk, Belinda. There's no point in denying it. Right, I think I'll go and put my shorts on. It's getting hotter by the minute, don't you agree?'

'No, I don't.'

'I'll change and then get started on my garden. I won't be long.'

As he returned to his house, Belinda mooched across the lawn to the patio and sat down. There was no point in pondering on adultery, she decided. She'd already committed adultery, so that was no longer an issue. What really worried her was that Tony had been right when he'd said that she loved his dirty talk. *A terrific orgasm and a beautiful mouth-fucking* . . . She'd enjoyed sucking the sperm out of his cock, and she'd loved the way he'd taken her to orgasm with his darting tongue.

Had her husband taken more interest in her feminine needs, had he satisfied her ... But he hadn't and probably never would, she concluded. Trying to push all thought of Tony's hard cock from her mind, she realised that her panties were wetting with her juices of lust. Her clitoris called for attention and her womb contracted, and she knew that she was either going to have to masturbate or ... Go to Tony for the relief she so desperately craved?

Watching Tony walk down his garden with his top bared, she left the patio and grabbed the watering can. He was wearing his shorts, she observed out of the corner of her eye as she watered the geranium cuttings, again. He had a good body, firm, muscular ... And his shorts were bulging. Disappearing into the bushes at the end of his garden, he called out for her. Belinda walked to the end of her garden and peered through the foliage as he again called her. Tony was standing in a small clearing which was well shielded from the house. He was grinning and beckoning her with his finger.

'What do you think of this secluded spot?' he asked as she joined him. 'No fence between us, we can't been seen from the houses: an ideal place for us to meet, don't you think?'

'There was a fence here,' Belinda said, frowning and looking about her. 'Where's it gone?'

'I took the panel away earlier this morning,' he replied, fondling his cock through his shorts. 'There's no need to have a fence here. Besides, it would only get in our way.'

'I have to get on.' Belinda sighed. 'Desiree will be back soon and ...'

'Before you go, why don't you kneel down and suck this?' he whispered, lowering his shorts and exposing his erect penis.

'No, Tony,' she stated firmly, eyeing the solid shaft of his inviting penis. 'Can't you get it into your head that I don't want a relationship with you?'

'I might talk to Desiree, suggest that we meet here.'

'Have you touched her?'

'No, I haven't.'

'Swear to me that you've not laid a finger on her.'

'I swear, I haven't fucked her tight little virgin cunt.'

'Don't talk like that about my daughter.'

'I haven't fucked her – yet. Kneel down, Belinda. As you said, you're only doing this for Desiree's sake.'

'You're a bastard.'

'I do believe I am. You know that you love sucking cock, so why fight it? Do you suck your husband's cock?'

'No, I . . . My sex life with my husband is . . .'

'No good at all? Come on, Belinda. Take what's on offer. Take it before it's offered to someone else.'

'If you dare to touch my daughter . . .'

'You can quite easily keep me away from your daughter. All you have to do is . . . You know what to do, Belinda.'

Kneeling, Belinda wrapped her slender fingers around the hard shaft of his penis and fully retracted his foreskin. Cupping his heavy balls in her free hand, she leaned forwards and kissed his purple knob. Marriage hadn't changed her, she reflected, recalling her teenage years. She'd loved cock-sucking, feeling her mouth flooding with creamy sperm. She'd been a tart, a slut . . . What was she now? she wondered, taking his ripe plum into her wet mouth. A cock-sucking slut?

Thoughts of sex had faded as the years had passed. Even when her husband was away, she'd not thought about sex or craved the relief of orgasm. Sex had become a distant memory, until now. Tony had woken her sleeping desires, roused her libido, juiced her pussy and stiffened her clitoris. She'd once again become aware of her body, her feminine needs. It was like reliving her teenage years, she mused, savouring the salty taste of his swollen knob. After school, she'd gone to the woods and met boys. She'd wanked them, sucked out their sperm and allowed them to take her beneath the trees. The fragrance of the bushes, the decaying leaves scattered over the ground, brought memories of her games in the woods flooding back. Nothing had changed.

'You like a good mouth-fucking, don't you?' Tony asked, clutching her head and rocking his hips. 'You love the feel of my knob gliding over your wet tongue. You're going to drink my spunk, Belinda. I'm going to come in your mouth and you're going to swallow my spunk.'

With her eyes closed as Tony held her head tight and repeatedly drove his swollen knob to the back of her throat, Belinda breathed heavily through her nose. Fondling his rolling balls, she recalled a boy at school who'd referred to cock-sucking as face-fucking. She'd loved face-fucking, she reflected. Remembering the time she'd simultaneously sucked on two knobs, she realised what a tart she'd been in her younger days. The boys had come together, pumping their teenage sperm over her tongue, flooding her gobbling mouth with their orgasmic cream. If Desiree turned out like that, if she went to the woods and sucked cocks and allowed boys to fuck her . . .

Desiree was safe, Belinda thought, as Tony began to gasp and tremble. All the time Tony had her mother's mouth to fuck and spunk, she'd be safe. But nagging thoughts still worried Belinda. Had Desiree gone into town? Or had she been to see Tony? Was Tony keeping his side of the bargain and leaving Desiree alone? He was a bastard, she thought, as he rocked his hips faster. Why should he keep his word? With a beautiful girl of sixteen chasing after him, why should he keep his cock in his trousers?

'Coming,' Tony announced, his cock shaft twitching, his knob swelling. 'God, yes.' He gasped as his sperm bathed Belinda's snaking tongue.

'Mum?' Desiree called from the house. 'Mum, where are you?'

'Drink it all up,' Tony ordered. 'And remember, it's your mouth or Desiree's.'

'Mum, where are you?'

'Suck out every last drop,' Tony ordered Belinda, clutching her head tight as she drank from his throbbing cock-head. 'God, yes. That's . . . that's amazing.'

'I'm here,' Belinda finally called as she managed to pull away and slip Tony's spent cock out of her mouth.

'Where?'

'You'd better go and see your little girl.' Tony chuckled. 'We'll meet later, and I'll shaft your tight cunt until you scream.'

'Mum? I can't see you.'

'I'm here,' Belinda said, emerging from the bushes and wiping her mouth on the back of her hand. 'I was just . . . just doing some gardening.'

'In the bushes?' the girl said, frowning as her flushed-faced mother walked towards her.

'I was clearing the leaves. What did you buy in town?'

'A couple of skirts and a few tops. Your face is all red. What have you been doing?'

'I'm hot, that's all. I think I'll have a cold drink. Come inside and show me your new clothes.'

Belinda led the girl into the house and closed the back door. She downed a glass of water to take away the taste of Tony's sperm. It had been a close thing, she reflected. Had Desiree walked to the end of the garden rather than called out, the sight that would have met her eyes would have shocked her. To discover her mother with Tony's cock in her mouth and sperm running down her chin . . . It didn't bear thinking about. At least the girl had been into town, she mused. At least she'd not been to see Tony and . . . sucked his cock?

Taking an interest in Desiree's new clothes, Belinda thought the skirts rather too short. But she daren't say anything. They were chatting, she mused. Mother and daughter chatting like old times. If only Tony hadn't moved in next door, if only ... There was no point in looking back, Belinda knew, as she refilled the glass with water. No matter how much water she drank, she imagined that she could still taste the salt of her neighbour's sperm. This was a nightmare, she mused fearfully, as Desiree asked her whether she thought Tony would like her new skirts.

'I really don't know,' Belinda replied.

'I'll never know.' The girl sighed.

'What do you mean?'

'I won't be seeing him again.'

'Oh, right,' Belinda said, trying not to sound too pleased. 'So, when did you decide this?'

'He's made it clear that there's nothing between us.'

'If he chased after you ... I mean, if he changed his mind, would you see him?'

'Yes, I would. I know your thoughts about my seeing him ... I really like him, Mum. He's kind, caring. Perhaps, one day, he'll change his mind about me. When I'm a little older, he might want me. Right, I'll go upstairs and change. I'll be down in a minute.'

Gazing out of her bedroom window, Desiree waved at Tony as he worked in his garden. Finally looking up as she tapped on the window, he smiled at her. She held up her new skirts and tops, indicating that she'd change and then go round to his house. Putting his thumb up, he winked at her. He'd like her new clothes, she was sure. Her stomach somersaulted as she gazed at her new thong. She locked her door and changed into her new clothes. The skirt was very short, she observed, looking at her reflection in the full-length mirror. But she looked feminine, and she knew that Tony would like that.

The feel of the silky thong against her hairless pussy lips sent quivers through her young womb and she

85

hoped that Tony would like her new purchase. He'd specifically mentioned a thong, she reflected, lifting her skirt and gazing at the triangular patch of material swelling with her pussy lips. A short skirt, a thong ... Tony would be happy, wouldn't he? She left her room, slipped down the stairs and told her mother that she was going to meet a friend in town. She hated lying to her mother, but couldn't see that she had a choice.

'I'll only be an hour or so,' she said.

'Your skirt is ... is nice,' Belinda said, eyeing the girl's naked thighs.

'I'm glad you like it.'

'Well, I'll get on in the garden and see you later.'

'OK, Mum. See you later.'

Desiree left the house, walked past Tony's front gate and then stopped. She crept alongside the bushes, hoping that her mother wasn't looking out of the window, and slipped down the path to his front door. She didn't want to have to lie to her mother or sneak around behind her back. But she wanted Tony, and this was the only way. He opened the door and ushered her in before she'd rung the bell. Pleased that he'd been looking out for her, waiting for her, she followed him into the lounge and looked down at her skirt.

'What do you think?' she asked him.

'Wow,' he replied. 'You look terrific.'

'And I bought this,' she said, lifting her skirt and displaying her tight thong. 'I bought it to please you.'

'A thong,' he said, his wide eyes gazing at the bulging material. 'You look beautiful. Don't move,' he said, grabbing his camera. 'That's it, hold your skirt up high. I want a couple of shots of your tight little thong.'

'You and your camera.' She giggled as he took several photographs. 'You'll soon have dozens of me,' she said, finally lowering her skirt.

'What's wrong with taking photographs of the girl I love? I assume that your mum doesn't know you're here?'

'I told her that I was going into town.'

'Where did you get to last night? I didn't hear you leave.'

'I got dressed and then crept out,' she replied. 'I heard you in here with my mum. Why did you close the door?'

'I thought that you might sneak out and I didn't want her to hear you.'

'She thinks I'm in town, so we'll be all right. I like your shorts.'

'Oh, thanks. I've been clearing up the garden. It's pretty hot out there.'

'You said that I'd not touched you,' Desiree murmured, dropping to her knees. 'So, I'd better change that.'

She pulled his shorts down, stroked the flaccid shaft of his penis and fondled his heavy balls. Tony looked down, breathing heavily and grinning as his cock stiffened and finally stood to attention before the girl's pretty face. Determined to keep him, to please him, Desiree rolled his foreskin back and parted her full lips. Taking his ripe plum into her hot mouth, she closed her eyes and savoured the taste of his salt. Her first penis, she mused happily, surprised by the pleasant taste of his manhood. Now that she believed him to be a virgin, she liked the idea of sucking on his swollen knob. Now that she thought herself to be the first girl to do this to him, she decided that she'd not only suck his knob, but drink his sperm. Whatever pleased him would please her, she thought, as she suckled on his purple glans. Now that he had a proper relationship, she was sure that he'd not want to work abroad. He had a full relationship, she thought happily, as she kneaded his huge balls. But not quite a full relationship, she reflected. They'd not made love, yet. He'd not eased his virgin penis deep into her pussy and loved her fully.

'God, that's nice,' Tony said as she rolled her succulent lips back and forth along his veined shaft.

'You're the first, Desiree,' he lied. 'You're the first – and the only girl there'll ever be.'

Feeling happier than ever, Desiree instinctively moved her head back and forth, repeatedly taking his ballooning knob to the back of her throat as he trembled and gasped. There was no need for her mother to know anything, she mused dreamily, as she waited expectantly for his sperm to flow and bathe her pink tongue. That way, there'd be no lectures, no disagreements or arguments . . . All the time her mother thought that she was seeing a friend or going around town, everything would be fine.

Tony's sperm jetted from his throbbing knob and flooded over her tongue as he towered above her, gasping in his male pleasure. Desiree allowed her cheeks to fill before swallowing the creamy liquid. For the first time, she felt really close to Tony. Although they'd not yet made love, she felt at one with him as her mouth deluged with his sperm. This was love, she mused, again swallowing the fruits of his orgasm. They were learning together, experimenting, discovering . . . And loving.

Finally he slipped his knob out of her sperm-bubbling mouth as his shaft began to deflate and Desiree lapped up the spilled sperm running over his scrotum. Tony again gasped and trembled as her tongue snaked over the sac of his scrotum and lapped up the male milk from his glistening shaft. He was pleased with her, she was sure as she again took his knob into her pretty mouth and sucked out the remnants of his sperm. Finishing her job of cleansing, she sat back on her heels and looked up at him.

'You're amazing,' he said, smiling at her. 'God, you're just like your mother.'

'My mother?' she echoed, her smile turning into a frown. 'What do you mean?'

'Your looks, Desiree. Hang on, don't move.'

'What are you doing?'

'A photograph.' He chuckled and grabbed his camera from the mantlepiece. 'I want a photograph of you with sperm running down your chin.'

Smiling as he knelt before her and focused on her beaming face, he took several shots of her spermed lips, the white liquid running down her chin. Continually praising her, affirming his great love for her, he stood up and suggested that he take a shot of her with his cock in her mouth. Desiree complied, again sucking his knob into her mouth as he clicked the camera and took his photographs.

'That's great,' he said, his cock stiffening as she rolled her tongue over his inflating glans. 'I'll always have the pictures to remind me of our first time together.'

'You'll have to give me some copies,' she said, moving her hand back and slipping his cock out of her mouth.

'I will, but don't let your mother see them.' He laughed.

'God, can you imagine her reaction?' She giggled.

'Yes, I can. She'd go absolutely mad. I think this is going to work out well, Desiree. I know that you're having to lie to her, but at least we now have a proper relationship. So, did you like what we just did? Did you like the taste?'

'Yes, very much. Did you like it? I mean, did I do it properly?'

'You did it expertly, Desiree. We'll have to do it again.'

'Oh, yes,' she trilled. 'Every time I come round, we'll do it.'

Wondering when they'd make love, enjoy full-blown intercourse, Desiree climbed to her feet as Tony tugged his shorts up. Feeling horny, sexy, aroused as never before, she became aware of her wetting thong as she sat on the sofa. She desperately needed Tony to love her, to massage her clitoris and bring her the relief of orgasm. But, seemingly unaware of her feminine needs, he started talking about his garden.

'I hear that you're a bit of an expert in the garden,' he said. 'I told your mum that I might ask you to help me, give me some advice, but she didn't seem too keen on the idea.'

'Of course I'll help you,' Desiree said. 'I'll tell Mum that it was my idea.'

'All right. If I go out there and start work, you could happen to see me and offer to help.'

'Tony, I was hoping that you'd . . . Well, you know – love me.'

'I'll tell you what we'll do. It's a lovely day so you join me in the garden a little later and we'll go into the bushes. There's a secluded spot at the end of the garden. I'll love you in the warm summer air.'

'Yes, I'd like that,' she trilled eagerly. 'I'll go home now and look out for you.'

'OK. As it's so warm, don't wear your thong.'

'You mean, walk around with nothing on beneath my skirt? But . . .'

'That way, I'll be able to see your sweet pussy when you squat or sit down. And I'll be able to love you properly.'

'All right, I'll take my thong off before I come round.'

Desiree left Tony's house and felt her stomach somersault as she crept along his path to the street. To be loved in the bushes would be heavenly, she mused happily. She walked to her front door, let herself in and bounded up the stairs to her room. She could see her mother working in the garden as she slipped her wet thong off and stuffed the garment into her dressing-table drawer. There'd be no problem if she suggested helping Tony, she was sure, as she made her way downstairs. Just because she was helping Tony, it didn't mean to say that they had a relationship.

'Hi, Mum,' she said, emerging from the house. 'How are you getting on?'

'Oh, Desiree. You haven't been long.'

90

'It's too hot to walk around town. I thought I'd come back and –'

'Hi, Desiree,' Tony called over the fence.

'Oh, hi,' she said, walking towards him.

'I'm going to get this garden sorted out,' he said. 'Your garden puts mine to shame.'

'I'll come round and give you some ideas, if you want me to,' she offered, winking at him.

'Desiree,' her mother began, 'I ... I could do with some help.'

'I'll just give Tony some ideas and then I'll be back to help you,' Desiree replied.

'There's a gap in the fence behind those bushes,' Tony said, pointing to the end of the garden. 'If you'd like to come round now, I'd really appreciate your advice.'

Desiree walked past her mother, disappeared into the bushes and went into Tony's garden. Belinda wasn't at all happy as she watched the girl talking to Tony. Her skirt was far too short, she mused. Showing her naked thighs like that would only give Tony ideas. Keeping an eye on her daughter, Belinda carried on forking over the border. There was no way she could stop the girl from helping their neighbour, but she wished that Tony had declined her offer. They had a deal, she reflected. If he didn't keep his side of the bargain ...

'You'll have to start by digging these weeds out,' Desiree said, standing next to Tony. 'And that ivy will have to go.'

'OK,' Tony said, watching Belinda out of the corner of his eye.

'And these bushes need cutting back,' Desiree said, walking down the garden. 'The grass will be in permanent shade unless you cut them back.'

Watching Tony follow Desiree to the bushes, Belinda lost sight of him as he disappeared into the foliage. Trying to remain calm, she carried on working with the fork. Tony would hardly try anything in the garden, she decided. Recalling Desiree's words, she was sure that the girl would be safe enough. *He's made it clear that there's nothing between us.*

'You'll have to cut the branches back to here,' Desiree said, loud enough for her mother to hear.

'And I'll have to kiss your sweet little pussy,' Tony whispered, kneeling before her and lifting up her short skirt. 'You're beautiful, Desiree,' he said, planting a kiss on her swollen outer lips. 'Smooth, hairless, soft, warm and very wet.'

Remaining silent as she felt Tony's tongue running up and down the opening crack of her vulva, Desiree trembled uncontrollably. Her clitoris responded to his intimate licking and she held his head as he parted her fleshy labia and pushed his tongue deep into her creamy-wet vagina. As the warm summer air wafted between her parted legs and the fragrance of the garden filled her nostrils, she decided that the secluded spot in the bushes would become their secret meeting place. Their secret loving place.

'You taste beautiful,' Tony murmured. 'You're a little angel.'

'That's nice,' Desiree whispered, parting her feet further. 'Tony, I . . . I think I'm going to . . .'

'Stretch your pussy lips wide apart for me.'

'Yes, yes.' She gasped, holding her fleshy sex cushions open to allow him better access to her femininity.

Her orgasm exploded as Tony sucked her pulsating clitoris into his hot mouth and thrust two fingers deep into her teenage pussy. Desiree stifled her gasps of pleasure. Her young body shook wildly and her juices of orgasm flowed over his hand. She threw her head back and closed her eyes as her climax rocked her very soul. She could hear the squelching of her vaginal milk as he fingered her, the slurping and sucking of his mouth as he sustained her incredible pleasure. Oblivious to her surroundings, she drifted on clouds of orgasm, wallowed in her love for Tony.

'Desiree?' Belinda called as her daughter's whimpers disturbed the still summer air. 'Desiree, are you all right?'

'Yes, yes,' Desiree managed to reply as Tony sucked on her orgasming clitoris.

'Where are you? Are you sure you're all right?'

'I'm . . . I'm fine.'

'God, I love your beautiful little cunt,' Tony whispered. He lapped at Desiree's pulsating clitoris and repeatedly rammed his fingers deep into her vaginal sheath.

Her climax beginning to recede, Desiree swayed on her trembling legs as Tony slipped his fingers out of her sex-drenched vagina. He locked his lips to the pink cone of flesh surrounding her open sex hole and sucked out her orgasmic juices as she parted her outer labia to the extreme. Desiree trembled uncontrollably, her head dizzy as she heard her mother rustling the bushes. Lowering her skirt as Tony stood up, she did her best to calm herself and appear composed and relaxed.

'What are you up to?' Belinda asked, entering the small clearing.

'Wondering what to do with this area,' Tony replied, wiping his pussy-wet mouth on the back of his hand.

'Desiree, are you all right?' her mother asked. 'You look very hot and flushed.'

'I am hot,' the girl replied. 'I'll . . . I'll go and get a drink.'

Waiting until Desiree had gone, Belinda stared hard at Tony. 'What were you doing to her?' she asked him accusingly.

'Doing to her?' he echoed, his dark eyes frowning. 'We were talking about the garden. You're going to

93

have to trust me, Belinda. We have a deal, and I intend to stick to it.'

'I hope you do.' Belinda sighed. 'Because, if you don't . . .'

'I'm a man of my word, Belinda. Whatever you might think of me, I'm a man of my word. I can't ignore Desiree. She offered to take a look at my garden and give me some advice. Should I have told her that I didn't want her help?'

'No, I suppose not.'

'You don't trust your daughter, you don't trust me. Do you trust your husband? Or do you think he's wandering around Tokyo screwing Japanese girls?'

'How can I trust you, Tony? You're blackmailing me, for God's sake.'

'No, I'm not.'

'You said that it's either me or my daughter. If that's not blackmail, then I don't know what is.'

'I suppose it could be looked upon as a form of blackmail. But you enjoy sex as much as I do. Why don't you pull your knickers down and let me lick you to orgasm?'

'No. Not with Desiree around.'

'OK, I'll meet you here later.'

'I . . . I don't know.'

'This is our spot, Belinda. In the bushes, hidden from prying eyes, this is our spot. We don't want it to become Desiree's secret meeting place, do we?'

'Tony, if you . . .'

'I'll meet you here later. I have to go out and do some shopping, but I'll be back.'

'I don't know what Desiree will be doing later. I can hardly come out here and meet you in the bushes if she's around.'

'Throw a small stone at my kitchen window when you're ready. I'll be in town for an hour or so. Oh, and wear that short skirt – without your panties.'

'All right.' Belinda sighed, the fragrance of the bushes again reminding her of her school days. Sex in the woods. 'I'll see you later.'

'And I'll fuck you later,' he quipped as she walked away.

Six

'What are you doing this evening?' Belinda asked Desiree as she finished clearing away the dinner plates.

'It's a nice evening so I might see whether Tony wants any more help in his garden.'

'Er ... He's going out. When I was talking to him earlier, he said that he had to go and see a work colleague this evening.'

'Oh, in that case ... I might catch up with my college work.'

'Now, that is a good idea. I think I'll go out for a walk. To the park, perhaps.'

'I'll come with you,' Desiree said eagerly.

'Er ... No, you stay here in case your father rings. Besides, I think you got far too hot in the garden earlier. And there's your work to catch up with.'

'I am getting a little behind with my work.' She sighed. 'OK, I'll go and switch my computer on. I'll see you later.'

'I won't be very long. When I get back, we'll watch TV. There might be a film on later.'

Belinda waited until Desiree had gone up to her room, then she stepped out onto the patio and closed the door quietly behind her. She felt like a thief in the night as she looked up at her daughter's bedroom window. Her hands were trembling and her heart was racing. She wasn't looking forward to meeting Tony in the bushes. But this had to be done, she reflected, slipping her panties off and feeling incredibly guilty as she gazed at the brick barbecue her husband had built. Naked beneath her short skirt, she was going to meet another man in the bushes. Meet another man for a session of crude sex.

'God,' she murmured, clutching her panties as she grabbed a small stone and lobbed it at Tony's kitchen window. 'What the hell am I doing?' Walking across the lawn, she repeatedly turned and gazed at Desiree's open window. She crept into the bushes and recalled Tony's words as she waited. *We don't want it to become Desiree's secret meeting place, do we?* This was risky, she knew. If Desiree had seen her, if she saw Tony heading for the bushes ... Guilt swamping her, she reminded herself that she was doing this for her daughter's sake.

Waiting in the shade in the small clearing, Belinda took a deep breath. Her arousal was beginning to rise, but she didn't want this. She didn't want Tony to touch her, to finger her wet pussy and lick between her vaginal lips. As the thought of Tony's tongue snaking around the solid bulb of her clitoris roused her inner desires, she wondered where she'd gone wrong. Perhaps she shouldn't have interfered with Desiree's relationship, she mused. Perhaps she should have let things run their course.

'Hi,' Tony said, as he entered the small clearing. 'Everything all right?'

'Not really.' Belinda sighed. 'I've had to lie to Desiree. I said that I was going to the park for a walk.'

'That's a small price to pay.' He chuckled. 'A small price for hard sex. Are you wet?'

'Tony, don't start ...'

'I see you're holding your panties. Do you like the feel of the breeze cooling your cunny lips?'

'Shall we get this over with? I told Desiree that I wouldn't be long.'

Kneeling, Tony lifted her skirt and drove his tongue between the fleshy lips of her vagina. Belinda gasped and clung to a branch as she felt his tongue delve into the heat of her very wet vaginal sheath. Her breathing fast and shallow, she closed her eyes and tried to drive images of her husband out of her mind as she listened to the slurping of Tony's mouth. Her husband had built the barbecue, he was working abroad to earn money for his wife and daughter, Desiree was studying in her room, her mother had lied to her ... And Belinda, the loyal wife and good mother, was allowing another man to tongue-fuck her sex-starved vagina.

Tony was a bastard, she mused, as her juices of lust streamed from her gaping vaginal entrance. He knew that Belinda had to protect her daughter, he knew that she was feeling lonely without her husband, he knew that she needed sex ... And he was using her weakness, her predicament, to satisfy his lust for illicit sex. Parting her feet wider, allowing him better access to her gaping vulval gully, she felt her womb contract as her clitoris swelled expectantly. He was a bastard, and she desperately needed the relief of orgasm.

'God, you're very wet,' Tony whispered, parting the fleshy pads of her outer labia and exposing the solid nub of her clitoris. 'I'll bet you've been thinking about this for hours? Looking forward to a good cunny licking all afternoon.'

'No, I haven't,' she murmured softly. 'Look, I don't have much time.'

'In that case, bend over that branch and I'll ...'

'You'll what?'

'Give you one, Belinda. Fuck you senseless and ...'

'No, Tony. There's no way you're going to ...'

'Oh, is the deal off?'

'No, no. But I don't want to commit adultery. It's one thing ...'

'It's one thing having your pretty mouth fucked and spunked, but not your pussy?'

'Yes, if you have to put it like that.'

'So, the deal's off? In that case, I'll go and see whether Desiree wants to take another look at my garden.'

'I'll do anything you want, but not that.'

'OK, bend over the branch and I'll spank you.'

'Spank me? What the hell do you think I am?'

'A horny little bitch who's desperate to come. Bend over, Belinda. Bend over, or I go and see Desiree.'

Taking her position over the branch, Belinda closed her eyes as Tony yanked her short skirt up over her back. Trying not to listen to his crude words as he talked about her firm buttocks, her slender waist, her dark bush nestling between her shapely thighs, she imagined Desiree appearing and witnessing the illicit spanking. What would the girl think of her mother? Would she think her a slut? If Desiree ever discovered the shocking truth, she'd never understand that her mother had done this for her sake.

'God, no!' Belinda exclaimed as Tony brought his hand down across the tensed flesh of her bared buttocks with a loud slap. Crying out as his palm again landed squarely across the twitching flesh of her bottom, she hoped that her daughter wouldn't hear the spanking. Her bedroom window was open, she would be sitting quietly at her computer ... If she heard the slaps and cries of an illicit spanking, she'd be bound to come and investigate.

As Tony's palm met the reddening flesh of her buttocks again and again, Belinda tried to stifle her whimpers. Although her juices of arousal seeped between the engorged lips of her vulva and her clitoris was painfully hard, she tried to deny her soaring libido. Her naked buttocks were stinging, burning like fire and she thought that she wouldn't be able to sit down for several days. As the merciless thrashing continued, her bottom globes numbing, she realised that her arousal was rocketing to frightening heights. She was desperate to come, desperate to have Tony suck a massive orgasm from her swollen clitoris . . . Desperate to have him fuck her? Adultery.

'Disobedient little bitch,' Tony hissed, landing the hardest slap yet. 'You'll be spanked every day, Belinda. Spanked every day for your naughtiness.'

'Please, that's enough,' she implored. 'Desiree might hear and . . .'

'Beg me to fuck you,' he said, halting the thrashing.

'No, I . . .'

'Beg me, Belinda.'

'Please . . . No, no I can't.'

'In that case, I'll spank you until you scream.'

Again spanking her glowing buttocks, Tony held her down with his free hand. Realising that he was heavily into debauched sex, Belinda thanked God that she'd saved her daughter from his wicked ways. Desiree needed to be introduced to sex as part of a loving relationship, not crude satisfaction. Doing her best to stifle her cries, Belinda couldn't imagine Desiree in this humiliating and degrading position. She was now going to have to do everything in her power to shield her daughter from Tony's perverted ways.

'Please, no more,' Belinda cried as her vaginal muscles tightened, squeezing out her pussy-milk. 'I can't take any more.'

'Then, beg me to fuck you,' Tony ordered her, halting the thrashing.

'Tony, please be reasonable. My daughter is in the house and . . .'

'Beg me to fuck you, or I'll invite Desiree round to my place and offer her vodka.'

'All right, all right. Please . . . please, fuck me.'

'Beg me to fuck your tight cunt.'

'Please, fuck my tight cunt.'

Squeezing her eyes shut as she felt the swollen knob of Tony's penis slip between the dripping inner lips of her vulval slit, Belinda held her breath. This was full-blown adultery, she mused anxiously, as his glans began its journey along the tight sheath of her vagina. Gasping as he impaled her fully on his huge cock, she felt his knob pressing hard against the creamy-wet ring of her cervix. Her vagina stretched open to capacity, her inner lips hugging the root of his solid cock, she again hoped that Desiree wouldn't appear and witness the debauched act.

There was no turning back now, she knew, as she looked up between her parted thighs at his swinging balls. She'd sucked the sperm out of another man's knob, she'd endured a crude spanking, and now his cock was embedded deep within her pussy. *Let no man put asunder* ... Her marriage vows in ruins, she'd betrayed her husband, lied to her daughter, cheated and deceived ... She'd been a slut during her teenage years. Nothing had changed.

'God, you're a tight-cunted little whore,' Tony whispered, withdrawing his pussy-slimed cock and again ramming it into her. 'Tight, hot, wet ...'

'Just get it over with,' she whimpered as guilt again swamped her.

'I doubt that you're as tight as your sweet little daughter, but ...'

'Shut up,' Belinda hissed. 'Leave Desiree out of this.'

'I'll leave Desiree out, all the time I have you to fuck and spunk.'

Her body jolting as Tony found his rhythm, the branch hurting her stomach, she rested her hands on the ground and grimaced. She detested the way he continually referred to Desiree, coming out with his lewd innuendoes and threats. The situation was bad enough without Tony's quips, she reflected. She wondered whether the girl was still studying in her bedroom. To have Tony even mention Desiree's name as he fucked her mother was obscene. Was he thinking about the girl

101

now? she wondered, as he gasped and increased his vaginal-fucking rhythm. Was he picturing Desiree in her mother's place, imagining that he was shafting her young virgin pussy with his huge cock as she bent over the branch?

'Is that nice?' he asked her, the squelching sounds of her vaginal juices resounding around the bushes as he repeatedly drove his knob deep into her tightening vaginal duct. 'Is that hard and fast enough to please your adulterous little cunt?'

'God, yes,' Belinda answered, without thinking.

'You love a good cock-shafting, don't you? How many cocks have you had up your tight little cunt?'

'I ... I don't know,' Belinda said, his crude talk sending her arousal soaring.

'Ten? Twenty?'

Her vaginal muscles were spasming as the sensitive tip of her erect clitoris was massaged by his wet shaft. She knew that she was nearing her climax as he grabbed her hips. Breathing in the scent of the bushes, the decaying leaves strewn around her feet, she again recalled her teenage years. Taking boys into the woods and stripping off, allowing them to suck her ripe nipples, finger her young pussy and fuck her senseless beneath the trees ... What had become of her sex life? she reflected. Her husband had as good as neglected her feminine needs: oral sex was only a memory, foreplay was nonexistent ... And he'd never talked dirty.

With Tony's lower belly slapping her burning buttocks as he fucked her with a cruel vengeance, his swinging balls battering the gentle rise of her mons, she cried out as her aching clitoris erupted in orgasm. Her long black hair cascaded over the ground as the branch rocked and creaked and her body shook violently. She'd never known such an intense orgasm. On and on, tremors of sex rolled through her pelvis as Tony gasped and she felt his sperm flooding her vaginal cavern.

Ramming into her, his knob battering her cervix, pumping her full of creamy spunk, Tony sustained her incredible climax and she again cried out in the grip of her illicit coming.

Gazing up between her splayed thighs and watching Tony's sperm overflowing from her bloated vagina, hanging in a long strand from her outer lips and dropping to the ground, Belinda shuddered as her orgasm peaked. Never had she been used for crude sex like this; never had she been threatened, blackmailed and used purely to satisfy a man's lust for cold sex. Focusing on his wet penile shaft repeatedly emerging and driving deep into her spermed pussy, she thought that she was going to pass out with the incredible pleasure she was deriving from the adulterous act.

'You're going to get this every day,' Tony said, slapping her stinging buttocks and ramming his sperming knob deep into her sex-drenched pussy. 'A damned good fucking every day. That's what a slut like you needs.'

'I can't take any more,' Belinda cried, watching the sperm hanging in a long thread from his scrotal sac. 'Tony . . . Please, that's enough.'

'Of course you can take it.' He chortled, slowing his pistoning rhythm as his sperm-flow ceased. 'You're a dirty little slut, Belinda. You should be used to getting fucked.'

'God, no!' she exclaimed as he again slapped her burning buttocks before withdrawing his spent penis. 'Please, let me go now.'

'I needed that,' he said, hauling her shaking body upright and spinning her round. 'Was that good enough for you?'

'Yes, yes, it was,' she replied without thinking. Brushing her long black hair away from her flushed face, she leaned on the branch to steady her trembling body. 'Tony, that was . . . I have to go now.'

'That was what? Amazing?'

'Yes, no . . .'

'Before you go, I'd like to take a good look at your tits,' he said, tearing the front of her blouse open and lifting her bra.

'For God's sake,' she cried as he sucked her ripe nipple into his wet mouth. 'Tony, please . . . You've ripped my blouse to shreds.'

'You have nice tits,' he praised her. 'I hope your husband appreciates your tits?'

'No, he . . . he does. Leave me now. I have to go and see Desiree.'

'You really do have nice tits,' he repeated, squeezing her mammary spheres. 'Probably not as hard and firm as Desiree's, but . . .'

'If you mention my daughter once more, I'll . . .'

'Calm down,' he said, reaching between her thighs and scooping up a cocktail of sperm and vaginal milk. Massaging the warm cream into her breasts, her ripe nipples, he laughed. 'Spunk-glistening tits,' he quipped.

'God, you're vile,' she hissed, leaving the clearing.

'I'll see you tomorrow,' he called as she dashed across the lawn to the house.

Closing the back door behind her, she clutched her ripped blouse together to conceal her sperm-glistening breasts and crept up the stairs. With her clothes in tatters, her hair dishevelled and sperm coursing down her inner thighs, she daren't allow Desiree to see her. Slipping into her bedroom, she heard Desiree call out. She changed quickly into her dressing gown.

'Are you all right?' the girl asked, knocking on the door.

'Yes, yes,' Belinda replied. 'It's all right, you can come in.'

'I've managed to get some work done and . . .' Her words tailed off and Desiree frowned at her mother. 'There are leaves and twigs in your hair,' she said. 'What on earth have you been doing?'

'I . . . I tripped over when I was walking through the woods,' Belinda lied. 'I'm OK. Just a little mucky, that's all.'

'You look like you've been dragged through the bushes backwards.'

'Yes, I . . . I think I'll have a shower.'

When Desiree had left the room and closed the door, Belinda rested on her bed. She had never felt so guilty, so deceitful. This was a nightmare situation, she thought sadly. She'd now committed adultery, betrayed her husband, lied to her daughter . . . Drifting into an uneasy sleep, she dreamed of Tony's cock shafting her tight vagina, his sperm decanting from her inflamed sex hole. Spanking, mouth-sperming, vaginal-shafting, clit-licking . . . She dreamed of beautifully debased sex with her neighbour.

Desiree had showered, dressed and enjoyed her breakfast, and still her mother was sleeping. Deciding not to wake her, she opened the back door and stepped out onto the patio. The sun warmed her and she knew that it was going to be another beautiful day as she wandered across the lawn to the bushes. She was naked beneath her short skirt: naked, hairless and ready to be licked. But there was no sign of Tony. Her arousal rising fast as the cool breeze wafted around the hairless lips of her vulva, she wondered whether they'd meet in their secret place again later in the day.

Wandering into the small clearing, she noticed a pair of black panties lying amongst the decaying leaves. She picked them up and frowned. They weren't hers, that was sure. And they weren't dirty or grubby so they couldn't have been there for long. Had Tony taken another girl into the bushes? she pondered anxiously. The panties hadn't been there the day before, she knew that much, so . . . If Tony was seeing someone else, he'd have taken her into his house rather than the bushes. Sure that they had nothing to do with Tony, she emerged from the bushes and wandered back to the house.

Sitting on a patio chair, Desiree again examined the panties. There was a white stain in the crotch, she noticed. They were as good as new, so they couldn't have been beneath the bushes for long. Who had taken their panties off and dropped them there, she had no idea, she couldn't even hazard a guess. Hearing her mother in the bathroom, she recalled her saying that she'd been clearing the leaves from beneath the bushes. But, she wouldn't have taken her panties off and left them on the ground. Besides, they hadn't been there the previous afternoon.

'I overslept,' her mother said, finally emerging from the house. 'I've had a shower and . . . What have you got there?'

'Panties,' Desiree replied, holding the garment up. 'I found them beneath the bushes at the end of the garden.'

'Beneath the bushes?' Belinda echoed, forcing a laugh. 'What were your panties doing beneath . . .'

'They're not mine, Mum. They weren't there yesterday, so where have they come from?'

'I . . . I really don't know. Anyway, I wouldn't worry about it. Have you had breakfast?'

'I'm not worried about it. But I am intrigued.'

'Desiree, they've probably been there for ages. I might have unearthed them when I was raking up the leaves.'

'No, no. They're as good as new. After all that rain we had the other week, they'd be grubby and . . .'

'Perhaps the wind whipped them off someone's washing line?'

'They weren't there yesterday, and we've had no wind.'

'While you play at being Sherlock Holmes, I'm going to have some breakfast.'

'I'm going to take another look around the bushes.'

* * *

Belinda watched Desiree heading across the lawn, then stepped into the kitchen and filled the kettle. A fatal mistake, she mused, wondering whether there were any other signs of recent sex beneath the bushes. This was Tony's fault, she decided. Playing dangerous games, spanking and screwing in the bushes knowing that Desiree had been in the house . . . There was too much at stake to take silly risks, she thought, pouring herself a cup of coffee.

'A button,' Desiree said, walking into the kitchen. 'A button attached to a piece of white material.'

'That's from my blouse,' Belinda said. 'I caught it on a branch when I was clearing the leaves. But I don't lay claim to the panties,' she added with a giggle. 'Would you like some coffee?'

'No, thanks,' Desire murmured pensively. 'I'm determined to get to the bottom of this.'

'The bottom of what?'

'The panties, Mum. They weren't there yesterday.'

'Hang on a minute,' Belinda said, coming up with an idea. 'I got pretty hot yesterday and I went upstairs and changed my panties. Meaning to drop the old ones into the linen basket, I stuffed them into my pocket. They must have fallen out when I was clearing the leaves.'

'But, they weren't there later. After you'd cleared the leaves, I mean.'

'I was doing all sorts in the garden yesterday. They must have fallen out at some stage.'

'Oh, right. So, mystery solved.'

'Indeed it is. What are your plans for today?'

'I haven't got any plans.' Desiree sighed. 'I might just potter about in the garden. Oh, there's Tony,' she trilled, gazing through the kitchen window. 'Perhaps I'll help him in his garden.'

Before Belinda could say anything, Desiree had bounded across the lawn and was leaning on the fence chatting to Tony. Trying to remain calm, Belinda took her coffee out onto the patio and sat down. She listened to their conversation: Desiree's offer to help Tony in the garden, his eagerness to have her come round and get started. Tony was trying to rile Belinda, she was sure, as he winked at her and then rather loudly said how nice Desiree looked in her short skirt.

'Desiree, hadn't you better change if you're going to do some gardening?' Belinda called.

'It's only planning, really,' Desiree replied. 'I'll not be doing any work, yet.'

'How are you this morning?' Tony asked Belinda.

'Fine, thank you.'

'I'll go and put my shorts on and we'll get started,' he said, smiling at Desiree. 'I won't be long.'

'Desiree,' Belinda said, beckoning her daughter as Tony disappeared into his house. 'Desiree, I really don't think it a good idea to wear such a short skirt.'

'Why not?' the girl asked, joining her mother on the patio. 'It's hot today, Mum. I don't want to wear jeans.'

'I know, but ... it's hardly the way to dress when you're helping Tony in the garden.'

'I haven't got anything else, apart from jeans. Besides, you're wearing a short skirt.'

'Yes, but I'm not helping Tony. If you bend over or ... he'll see your panties, Desiree.'

'No, he won't. Don't fuss so much, Mum.'

'I'm not fussing. Would you like to borrow one of my summer dresses?'

'No, the skirt is fine. I won't be bending over, will I? All we're doing is planning the garden.'

'All right.' Belinda sighed, realising that she couldn't win. 'Oh, there's the phone.'

'I'll get it,' Desiree said and bounded into the house.

Hearing her daughter talking to one of the girls from college, Belinda wandered across the lawn to the fence and gazed at Tony's garden. She was sure that he had no interest in gardening. This was just a ploy to get

Desiree to spend some time with him, and to annoy Belinda in the process. As he emerged from his house wearing his shorts, he donned a huge grin. He knew that the situation was getting to Belinda as he approached her. But she was determined to remain calm.

'Where's Desiree gone?' he asked.

'She's on the phone,' Belinda replied, trying not to gaze at the bulge in his shorts. 'Tony, I don't want Desiree spending all her time in your garden. We have our own garden to do, and she has her studies to get on with.'

'She's only going to give me some advice,' he said, eyeing her cleavage revealed by her partially open blouse. 'Did you enjoy it last night? Did you enjoy a good, hard fucking?'

'No, I didn't.'

'Why don't you reach over the fence and give me a quick wank?' he whispered, lowering the front of his shorts and exposing his flaccid penis.

'For God's sake ... If you're going to keep on like this, then I'll take Desiree out somewhere and you'll see neither of us all day.'

'Feel it,' he said, running his hand up and down his stiffening shaft. 'Feel the hardness, Belinda.'

'No, I won't.'

'Imagine it gliding in and out of your wet pussy. You are wet, aren't you?'

'Tony, we have a deal. A deal that I don't want, but it's a deal. However, I'm not doing anything with you while Desiree is around. When she's at college or out somewhere, then I'll see you. It's too risky when she's around. I have a lot to lose, surely you understand that?'

'Yes, you do have a lot to lose. But you also have a lot to give.'

'What do you mean?'

'You're beautiful, Belinda. You're attractive, you have a perfect body ...'

'Don't try to flatter me.'

'I'm being honest. You're the most beautiful woman I've ever known.'

'Yes, well . . . I have things to do.'

'I'll see you later,' he called as she walked back to the house. 'We'll meet later.'

Filling the kettle again, Belinda felt her stomach somersault as she recalled Tony's words. *You're attractive, you have a perfect body . . .* He was only flattering her, she knew. But it made her feel good, all the same. His dirty talk had also made her feel good, she reflected. Her husband rarely complimented her these days, and he'd never spoken during love-making. The way Tony talked about her body, her pussy and breasts, the crude words he used . . . Her womb contracting, she poured another cup of coffee and tried not to think about sex with Tony.

'That was Jenny on the phone,' Desiree said, wandering into the kitchen. 'Right, I'm going next door.'

'Don't be too long,' Belinda said.

'Why, have you got something planned?'

'No, no. It's just that I'd like to spend some time with you.'

'OK, I'll see you later.'

Dashing across the lawn and slipping through the bushes, Desiree felt a wave of excitement roll through her young body as she imagined Tony licking her pussy crack and sucking her clitoris to orgasm. Her arousal riding high as she made her way across the lawn to his open back door, she felt her juices of desire seeping between the firm lips of her pussy. Stepping into the kitchen, she was about to call out when Tony emerged from the dining room clutching a pair of handcuffs.

'Oh, hi,' he said. 'Er . . . I was just sorting out some bits and pieces.'

'What are they for?' Desiree asked, frowning as she stared at the handcuffs.

'They were given to me years ago by a mate of mine. They were a joke birthday present. You look lovely, as always.'

'Thanks. Shall we go out into the garden?'

'In a minute. Desiree, I need to talk to you.'

'Oh?'

'I want you to tell your mum that I have a girlfriend.'

'Tell her about us?'

'No, no. You see, she worries about you. If she hears from you that I have a girlfriend, that'll put her mind at rest.'

'Oh, right.'

'To make it sound convincing, say that I told you all about her. Say that she's in her early thirties with long black hair.'

'That's a good idea,' Desiree said. 'You're right, she does worry about me.'

'If you tell her that all the time I'm seeing this woman I won't be interested in you, she'll be happy. Go home now and tell her.'

'Now?'

'I don't want her to worry, Desiree. She's a lovely lady, and I don't want her worrying about you. Besides, if she believes that I have another woman, she'll not mind you coming round here.'

'That's true.'

'Don't say that you've met this woman because she might start asking questions that you can't answer.'

'No, no, I won't.'

'I'll meet you in the garden in a while.'

'OK, I'll be back soon.'

Returning to her house, Desiree thought it nice that Tony was concerned about her mother. His idea was good, she mused. Her mother worried far too much and, hopefully, this would put her mind at rest once and for all. Finding her in the kitchen, she explained that Tony was about to have a shower as he was seeing his girlfriend later.

'His girlfriend?' Belinda echoed.

'Yes, he's seeing her later today. We're going to plan the garden once he's out of the shower.'

'Oh, I see,' Belinda said. 'Has he just met her or . . .'

'I suppose he must have done. He seems to like her very much. Apparently, she's in her thirties with long black hair. There's no way he'll be interested in me now that he has someone else.'

'No, no, he won't. So, how did the subject come up? I mean, why mention this woman to you?'

'I went round to help with the garden but he was about to have a shower. He told me that he wanted to be ready to meet his girlfriend later.'

'And, you're not unhappy about it?'

'Well, I suppose I was sort of hoping that one day we might . . . Anyway, all the time he has someone else, I might as well forget about it.'

'Right, well . . . That's that, then.'

'Yes, it is. I'll go and wait for him in his garden. I'll start planning.'

'OK, see you later.'

Belinda was pleased to think that Tony had kept to his side of the bargain and put Desiree off by mentioning a girlfriend. But there was a major problem: Belinda was the girlfriend. And she was going to have to keep Tony happy for quite some time. She knew only too well that if she stopped seeing Tony, he'd home in on Desiree and . . . The consequences didn't bear thinking about.

'Did you tell her?' Tony asked, walking towards Desiree as she hovered by the bushes at the end of his garden.

'Yes, I told her,' Desiree replied, her pretty face beaming. 'She's not worried about me now, I can tell.'

'I'm glad it worked. You'll have to keep the scam going, though. Every now and then, mention that I'm seeing my girlfriend. You did well, Desiree. Now, you'll be able to come round here whenever you want and she won't mind.'

'Dressed like this,' she whispered, lifting her short skirt up and exposing the hairless lips of her vagina.

'You are the most beautiful girl in the world,' he said, gazing longingly at her tightly closed sex crack. 'Let's slip into the bushes.'

Again lifting her skirt as she stood in the small clearing, Desiree closed her eyes as Tony dropped to his knees and kissed the fleshy swell of her vulval lips. The feel of his wet tongue running up and down her vaginal valley sent quivers through her pelvis. She parted her feet to the extreme to allow him better access to the sexual centre of her body. She held her pussy lips wide apart, exposing the ripe nub of her sensitive clitoris to his sweeping tongue, and let out a rush of breath as he drove two fingers deep into her creamy-wet vaginal duct.

'It's time we made love,' Tony whispered.

'Yes, yes,' Desiree said. 'Let's go into your house.'

'No, we'll do it out here.'

'But . . .'

'Bend over that branch,' he instructed her, rising to his feet. 'Bend over and I'll –'

'Tony, not out here,' she complained. 'My mum might come out into the garden. Can't we go into your house?'

'This is our secret place, Desiree. It would be nice to christen our secret place with our first love-making . . .'

'All right,' she conceded. 'I'd rather we were in bed, but . . . if that's what you want.'

'Good girl. Bend over the branch and, together, we'll move on and leave virginity behind us.'

Bending over the branch, Desiree thought how she would have wanted their first love-making to be in Tony's bed. Warm, loving, caring . . . As he lifted her short skirt up over her back and stroked the tensed flesh of her naked buttocks, she breathed in deeply. She could feel his fingertips moving down, running over the swell of her hairless vaginal lips. This was it, she mused, wondering whether her tight vagina could accommodate his massive penis. As his bulbous knob slipped between the engorged wings of her wet inner lips, she held her breath and closed her eyes.

'Desiree, are you there?' Belinda called.

'Fucking hell,' Tony hissed. 'Now what?'

'I said that we should have gone into your house,' Desiree whispered, standing and adjusting her skirt.

'Desiree, Jenny's here to see you.'

'Who's Jenny?'

'A friend of mine.'

'Go and get rid of her.'

'I can't get rid of her. She's come to see me ... I thought she'd be at least an hour.'

'At this rate, I'll never get to fuck you.'

'Never get to ... Don't you mean, make love to me?'

'Yes, yes, whatever,' he replied agitatedly.

Desiree left the bushes and walked across the lawn to the patio. She couldn't help but wonder about Tony's words as she stepped into the kitchen. *At this rate, I'll never get to fuck you.* Why had he put it that way? she reflected, finding her mother in the lounge with Jenny. *At this rate, I'll never get to fuck you.*

Seven

Belinda gazed at her reflection in the full-length mirror and smiled as she again recalled Tony's words. *You're attractive, you have a perfect body* . . . He was a charmer, she reflected, tossing her long black hair over her shoulder. With her blouse revealing her deep cleavage and her short black skirt displaying her slender thighs, she looked good and felt good. But, she reminded herself, as she left her bedroom, she was a married woman. And Tony was as good as blackmailing her.

Passing Desiree's bedroom door, she stopped and listened as she heard Jenny giggling. She was pleased that Jenny had come round. Desiree needed someone to take her mind off Tony, someone of her own age to chat and laugh with. Jenny was a nice girl, Belinda mused. She was studious and very keen to go on to university. Hopefully, her influence would put Desiree back on the rails.

'Spanking?' Jenny said as Belinda was about to descend the stairs.

'Yes,' Desiree replied. 'Bare-bottom spanking.'

'God. Tell me more.'

'Well . . .'

Unable to hear the girls' whispers, Belinda made her way down to the kitchen. Shocked, she hoped that she'd misheard her daughter. But the words had been clear enough. Bare-bottom spanking? she pondered, wondering what on earth Desiree had been up to. She could only have been talking about Tony, she decided, her stomach churning as she walked briskly across the lawn to the bushes. Spanking? What the hell had he done to Desiree? She called out as she approached his back door and then stepped into the kitchen.

'Oh, Belinda,' Tony said, emerging from the lounge. 'You look lovely, as always.'

'What's all this about spanking?' she asked him.

'Spanking?' he echoed, looking mystified. 'What do you mean?'

'Have you spanked my daughter?'

'*What*? Have you gone raving mad?'

'Far from it. What have you done to my daughter?'

'Done? I haven't done anything. Calm down and tell me what this is all about.'

'I think you know what it's about. I've just overheard Desiree talking to her friend about bare-bottom spanking.'

'And?'

'Well, I . . .'

'What does that have to do with me?'

'Where else would she learn about such debased things? You're into spanking, so . . .'

'So you came storming round here and . . .'

'You spanked me, didn't you?'

'Yes, I did. Look, girls of that age talk about sex. They talk about all aspects of sex.'

'Where would Desiree have heard about spanking?'

'From other girls, from a magazine . . . For God's sake, I've been keeping my side of the bargain. I've told her that I'm not interested in anything other than friendship and I've even said that I have a girlfriend. And yet, again, you come storming round here with your bloody allegations.'

'You've threatened to seduce my daughter often enough. All you talk about is Desiree and how you're going to . . .'

'I'm not going to threaten to seduce her again, Belinda.'

'I'm pleased to hear it.'

'I'm going to do it.'

'What? You'll keep away from her.'

'All along you've accused me of trying to seduce her, and now you're saying that I've spanked her. I think the time has come to strip young Desiree of her virginity.'

'Tony, if you dare to . . .'

'I've kept my side of the bargain, Belinda. But our deal isn't working, is it?'

'Yes, it is. I've committed adultery, for Christ's sake. If that's not keeping my side of the bargain, then I don't know what is.'

'Yes, we fucked in the bushes. But it's your constant allegations and accusations that rile me. You perpetually accuse me of doing this and that to Desiree. So, I might as well do it.'

'I'm sorry, Tony. It's just that, hearing Desiree talking about bare-bottom spanking . . . Please, forgive me.'

'Come with me,' he ordered. He closed and locked the back door.

'Where to?'

Following him up the stairs, Belinda wondered whether she was in for another spanking. He led her into the spare room at the back of the house. She'd enjoyed the feel of his palm meeting the smooth flesh of her naked buttocks when they'd been in the bushes. But, looking around the room as he closed the door behind her, she knew that she was in for more than a spanking. A wooden frame in the shape of an X stood in the centre of the room, handcuffs and bamboo canes were neatly laid out on a corner table, vibrators, candles, a leather riding crop . . .

'What the hell . . .' she said as he locked the door. 'Tony, what is all this?'

117

'This is my punishment room,' he enlightened her. 'I've been working hard to get the room ready. What do you think?'

'You're mad,' she said. 'To convert a room into a . . . a sex den is crazy.'

'I thought it rather a good idea. I'll show you what the frame is for.'

'I don't want to know what it's for. God, I knew that you were a pervert, but this is incredible.'

'Just allow me to show you what it's for,' he said, spinning her round and pushing her against the wooden frame.

As he pulled her arms high above her head, Belinda didn't realise what he was doing until he'd secured her wrists to handcuffs at the tops of the wooden posts. She struggled and cursed as he parted her feet wide and cuffed each ankle to the bottom of the X-frame, but was unable to halt the bondage of her trembling body. Ignoring her protests, he released a catch and lowered the top half of the hinged frame. Her body bent over, her long black hair fanning out across the floor, her rounded buttocks billowing her tight skirt, she begged him to release her.

'When you've been punished, I'll allow you your freedom,' he said, yanking her skirt up and tearing her panties away from her firm buttocks.

'Punished?' she exclaimed, unable to believe what he was doing. 'Tony, please . . . You're crazy. Unless you let me go, I'll . . .'

'This is the deal.' He chuckled. 'It's either you or . . .'

'My daughter?'

'You wouldn't want me to bring Desiree up to my punishment room, would you?'

'Of course I wouldn't.'

'Then, shut up. As I said, I've had enough of your accusations.'

'I won't say anything again, I promise. Let me go, and I'll . . .'

'You need disciplining, Belinda. You're rude, you answer back, you complain, you accuse me of spanking your daughter ... Once I've corrected your wicked ways, you'll be an obedient slave.'

'A slave?' she repeated. 'Tony, I don't want to be your slave. For God's sake, let me go.'

'If I let you go, then I'll not only seduce Desiree, which will be easy, but I'll pervert and corrupt her. She's hooked on me, Belinda. She'd do anything for me.'

'This has gone beyond a joke. Let me go and we'll talk about it.'

'This is no joke, Belinda. And it's gone beyond talking. We've talked again and again about this. We made a deal, and I kept my side of the bargain.'

'Let me go and –'

'One more word, and I'll be forced to gag you. Besides, a dirty little sex-starved slut like you should love a session of bondage and spanking.'

Gazing at her captor through her parted legs as he knelt on the floor and spread the firm globes of her buttocks, she tried not to picture Desiree cuffed to the wooden frame. Tony was a pervert, she thought, as she felt the tip of his wet tongue teasing the sensitive eye of her exposed anus. A complete pervert. But she reckoned that he was harmless enough. His punishment room, the wooden frame and handcuffs – all this was part of his perverted games. He probably spent hours flicking through dirty magazines and watching porn videos. He was a pervert and, more than likely, a harmless loner. But she didn't want Desiree anywhere near him or his punishment room. *A dirty sex-starved slut?*

Her womb contracted and her vaginal muscles tightened as he tongued her bottom hole. She felt her sex-milk oozing between the inner lips of her vulval crack. Looking back to the day Tony had moved in, Belinda reckoned that he'd never had any interest in Desiree. He'd said that he didn't want silly teenage girls, and she now believed him. His game wasn't designed to get his hands on Desiree's young body. His threats to seduce the young girl had been a clever ploy to seduce Mom.

Tony was good, she reflected, as his tongue entered the tight hole of her anus. He knew what to do to a woman, how to pleasure a woman – a slut. As long as he didn't do this to Desiree, she thought anxiously, again trying not to picture the girl tethered to the wooden frame. No, Tony wasn't after Desiree. He'd used the girl as a weapon, as a means to an end. He'd had his eye on mother from day one.

Pushing thoughts of her daughter aside, Belinda was horrified to think that she was actually enjoying bondage and an enforced anal-tonguing. Although she'd been a slut during her teenage years, she'd never dreamed of bondage. The closest she'd come had been when she'd gone to the woods with three boys. During their sex games, two of the boys had held her down while the third had shafted her tight vagina. Finally marrying, she'd settled down to a staid love life. Until now.

Gasping as Tony drove two fingers deep into the sex-wet sheath of her tight pussy, Belinda pondered on the idea of becoming his sex slave. There was no way she'd do that, she decided. Once her husband was home, the games would have to come to an end. Far from her master, Tony would be nothing more than her next-door neighbour. But, what about his punishment room? she pondered. He'd obviously prepared the room with Belinda in mind. What would he do when the crude sex games ended?

'Have you ever had a cock up your tight little arse?' he asked her crudely.

'No,' she whispered, her wide eyes staring at him between her splayed legs. 'And I'm not going to.'

'I'll decide whether or not you'll have your arse fucked,' he said firmly.

'Tony, I'm not prepared to . . .'

'I could always fuck Desiree's arse.'

'Desiree doesn't want you. Besides, there's no way she'd allow a pervert like you anywhere near her.'

'She doesn't want me? That's odd because she told me that she . . . No, it wouldn't be fair to tell you what Desiree said to me in private.'

'Tony, my back is aching like hell. Please, let me go now.'

'I will, just as soon as I've finished with you.'

Belinda watched as he took a huge vibrator from the table and drove it deep into the tightening sheath of her drenched vagina. She let out a rush of breath as he switched the device on. As the soft buzzing sound reverberated around the room and the vibrations permeated her trembling pelvis, she realised that her daughter's bedroom was the other side of the wall. If Desiree knew what her mother was doing, if she ever discovered her wanton adultery, her whoredom . . . Desiree had to be shielded from the debauchery. No matter what it took, Belinda knew that she had to protect her young daughter from the perverted acts.

'No,' she whispered as Tony pressed the tip of a second vibrator into the tight hole of her anus. Ignoring her, he pushed and twisted the plastic shaft, driving the buzzing phallus deep into her hot rectum as she gasped and trembled. Her sex sheaths bloated, the sensations driving her wild, she again thought of Desiree in her bedroom next door. With only a wall dividing the two rooms, she prayed that the girl wouldn't hear her whimpers of pleasure. Then Tony grabbed something else from the table. Her eyes widened as she gazed at a riding crop in his hand and she tensed her buttocks. This was depravity beyond belief, she knew, as he raised the crop above his head.

'I do believe that a light thrashing is in order.' He chuckled as he brought the leather loop down across the twitching globes of her bottom. Again, the leather met her tensed flesh with a loud crack. Crying out as he administered the merciless thrashing, she again prayed that her daughter couldn't hear the debauchery. What would Desiree think if she discovered the shocking truth? Her mother cuffed to a wooden frame with two vibrators forced into the depths of her most private holes, her naked buttocks whipped with a riding crop ... But, worst of all was the fact that Belinda was enjoying the gruelling thrashing.

'Are you going to be an obedient slave?' Tony asked, halting the lashing of her glowing buttocks.

'Tony, please ... I can't become a slave to you.'

'You can, and you will.'

'I'm married, for God's sake. How can I become a sex slave to another man?'

'Quite easily, Belinda. You'll give your body to me, your master, whenever I snap my fingers. If I need your mouth, you'll kneel and allow me to throat-spunk you. Whenever I need your hot cunt, you'll open your legs and ...'

'No, I can't agree to that.'

'Then, Desiree will become my slave. I didn't want to have to say this again, but you leave me no choice. It's either you, or your daughter.'

Tony resumed the cruel lashing of Belinda's crimsoned buttocks. He chuckled as the larger vibrator shot out of his victim's vagina like a bullet. Switching the device off, he slipped the second vibrator out of her stretched anal canal and again brought the riding crop down across her burning flesh with a deafening crack. Her buttocks numbing, her juices of lust streaming from her gaping sex hole and coursing down her inner thighs, Belinda knew that she couldn't take much more. Begging him to halt the punishment, she knew that she had no choice other than to become his slave.

'All right,' she finally said. 'All right, I'll be your slave.'

'I'm pleased to hear it,' he said, lowering the riding crop to his side. 'You swear to open your mouth and suck out my spunk at my command?'

'Yes, yes, all right.'

'You swear to allow me to fuck your beautiful cunt whenever I wish.'

'Yes, anything you say. Please, let me go now.'

'And you swear to offer me your tight little arsehole whenever I want . . .'

'No,' she said. 'No, I'll not do that.'

'In that case, I'll fuck your daughter's tight little bottom hole. She wants me to fuck her, Belinda.'

'Don't talk rubbish. Desiree would never . . .'

'You don't believe me?'

'Tony, I know your game. I've worked it out. All this nonsense about seducing Desiree, saying that it's me or my daughter . . . It was all a ploy, wasn't it?'

'A ploy? I'm not with you.'

'It was me you were after all along. I should have realised from the outset that you –'

'Take a look at this,' he cut in, pulling a photograph from his trouser pocket. 'See? Desiree lifting her skirt and showing me her thong.'

'A thong?' she echoed, gazing between her thighs at the upside-down picture. 'But . . . When do you . . .'

'You've got it all wrong, Belinda. Desiree is begging for it. Taking her thong off and fucking her tight little pussy would be the easiest thing in the world.'

'When did she . . . Did she allow you to take that photograph?'

'Of course she did. Can't you see the impish smile on her face? Can't you see the wicked sparkle in her eyes?'

'She's young and confused. She doesn't know what she wants.'

'Maybe not, but I know what I want. It's you or your daughter, Belinda.'

'Desiree isn't like that. I didn't know that she had a thong. I can't believe that she'd lift her skirt and . . .'

'Photographs don't lie. So, do you swear to offer me your tight little arsehole whenever I want anal sex?'

Stunned by her daughter's lewd behaviour as Tony stood behind her, Belinda couldn't rid her mind of the image. Desiree, lifting her skirt and allowing him to take a photograph of her thong . . . *Photographs don't lie.* Feeling the bulbous knob of Tony's cock slip between the juice-dripping petals of her inner lips, she realised that she'd have to become a slave to her neighbour, she'd have to be at his beck and call, agree to his every perverted whim. With his good looks and his charm, he'd have no trouble seducing Desiree. Belinda had to become his obedient sex slave.

This was cold sex for the sake of sex, she mused as his rock-hard shaft entered the tight duct of her pussy. No love, no strings . . . Just immensely satisfying sex. And blackmail. She daren't say anything to Desiree about the photograph, she decided, as her vaginal duct opened wide to accommodate her neighbour's solid cock. If she mentioned the thong, then the girl would realise that she'd been talking to Tony, trying to intervene in her private affairs. How wrong she'd been, Belinda reflected. Tony would have no qualms about stripping Desiree of her virginity.

'Is that nice?' Tony asked, breaking her reverie. 'Do you like the feel of my hard cock stretching your sweet cunt wide open?'

'You're a vulgar man,' Belinda said, watching his huge balls swinging between her thighs as he began his fucking motions. 'A vulgar, despicable –'

'Young man?' he quipped. 'How old is your husband?'

'He's forty-eight.'

'You should think yourself lucky, Belinda. A young man of twenty-seven shafting your pussy. You should think yourself very lucky.'

'Handcuffed to a wooden frame, forced to take your cock, thrashed, threatened, blackmailed . . . I don't call that luck.'

'Your female cravings satisfied by a virile young man while your ageing husband is away? If that's not lucky, then I don't know what is. And your pretty little daughter's virginity is safe. What more could you ask for?'

'My daughter better be safe,' she returned. 'Do you have other photographs of her?'

'No, only the one I showed you. Shall I tell you what she said when I took that photograph?'

'I don't want to know.'

'She said, "My body is yours, if you want it." '

'You're lying.'

'I don't lie, Belinda. But I did lie to her when I said that I only wanted to be friends. I want to be far more than friends with the sexy little bitch. But, all the time I have you, I'll not touch her. You're standing between me and your daughter's tight little virgin pussy. Give me what I want, and I'll not give Desiree what she wants. That's the deal, Belinda.'

He meant every word, Belinda knew, as her tethered body rocked back and forth with his crude vaginal shafting. Desiree was young, naive and stupid in her inexperience. But, worse, she thought that she was in love. Tony was playing games with her, keeping her hanging on, using her. Had he already touched her? Belinda wondered, as the squelching sound of her pussy-milk resounded around the room – the sex den. She was going to have to talk to the girl, she decided. Desiree would probably see it as intervention and may even rebel, but that was a chance Belinda was going to have to take.

As her solid clitoris was massaged by the pussy-wet shaft of Tony's thrusting penis, Belinda felt her womb contract. She tried not to enjoy the sensations, tried to deny the immense pleasure he was bringing her. The glowing flesh of her buttocks stinging from the riding crop, her clitoris pulsating in the beginnings of an orgasm, her sex-milk flowing freely from her shafted vagina: there was no denying the incredible pleasure. She'd been a slut during her teens, she reflected. Once a slut, always a slut? But she was only doing this for Desiree's sake. *You're standing between me and your daughter's tight little virgin pussy.*

Belinda was sure that once Brian was home things would be different. She'd make an effort to rekindle their sex life, do her best to please him in bed and ... But, as always, he'd have too much to do between his business trips to take an interest in sex. They'd almost got to the stage where they had a brother–sister relationship, she reflected, as Tony began gasping. But she'd do her utmost to change that. She'd ignore Tony, keep out of his way and concentrate solely on repairing her marriage.

Repairing? she mused, as Tony grabbed her hips and increased his vaginal pistoning rhythm. How could something that had been torn to shreds ever be repaired? *Let no man put asunder.* Lies, deceit, betrayal, adultery ... And, unless Belinda agreed to Tony's demands, Desiree would pay the price. Tony would dump the girl when he'd finished with her. A year, two years ... He'd soon tire of her and lure another young girl into his bed – into his sex den. Where would that leave Desiree? Soiled, sullied, distraught.

'Here it comes,' Tony said breathlessly, his bulbous knob battering Belinda's ripe cervix as he swung his hips and shafted her tight vagina with a vengeance. 'This is what you want, isn't it?'

'No, no.' She gasped as her clitoris exploded in orgasm. 'God, no.'

'Feel it,' he cried, his lower belly slapping her crimsoned buttocks, his swinging balls repeatedly meeting her mons. 'Feel the spunk, Belinda. Feel the spunk filling your beautiful little cunt. I'll bet your husband doesn't screw you like this.'

His vulgar words heightening her pleasure as she rode the crest of her orgasm, she again thought of her husband. Shuddering as her climax peaked, she knew that she'd never enjoy sex like this with the man she'd married. This was illicit sex. Crude sex without love. Hard-core sex. When she'd married, she'd thought that she'd remain ever-faithful to Brian, giving her body to no other man. Until death do us part. But now? As Tony's sperm flooded her spasming vaginal sheath, she knew that there was no turning back. She'd committed adultery.

All she could do when her husband returned was try to forget about Tony. Try not to think of the illicit sexual acts, the incredible pleasure he'd brought her. It wouldn't be easy, but she was determined to concentrate on the family home, her marriage and the family unit. When Tony demanded crude sex, as she knew he would, she'd have to be strong and decline his offer of amazing orgasms. His sex den, his vibrators and handcuffs, the wooden frame, the beautiful whipping of her naked buttocks . . . She'd resist temptation. And do her best to keep her daughter away from him.

Shuddering as her orgasm rocked her very soul, she prayed for Desiree to listen to her father. Once he was home and he discovered her so-called love for Tony, he'd talk to her, make her see sense. Desiree had always listened to him, taken his advice. She looked up to him, and would understand his concern. But, in the meantime, it was down to Belinda to safeguard the girl's virginity.

'Tight-cunted slut,' Tony said, making his final thrusts as his swinging balls drained. 'You must have gone for years without a good fucking.'

'Shut up,' Belinda snapped as her orgasm began to wane and guilt consumed her. 'I have a very good sex life with my husband.'

'That's not what Desiree said.' He chortled as he withdrew his deflating cock from her sperm-bubbling vagina.

'What? What the hell has she been saying?'

'I'd best not divulge our conversation.'

'Let me go, for God's sake,' Belinda said. 'Desiree knows nothing about my sex life. You're just trying to cause trouble, as usual.'

'I'll let you go after I've taken a couple of photographs for my collection.'

'Don't you dare take photographs of me,' she hissed through gritted teeth as he grabbed his camera. 'Tony, if you . . .'

'Too late.' He chuckled as he knelt behind her and focused on her sex-dripping vaginal lips. 'Give me a big smile.'

'Not my face, for Christ's sake.'

'Perfect. I like to have a little insurance.'

'Insurance? What the hell are you talking about?'

'Should you decide to go blabbing to your husband, I'll show him what sort of woman he's married to.'

'Let me go, you bastard.'

Finally Tony pulled the wooden frame upright and released the handcuffs. He stood back and watched Belinda straighten her trembling body. Adjusting her clothes and running her fingers through her dishevelled hair, she ignored his crude remarks about sperm running down her inner thighs. All she wanted to do was get home and take a shower, wash away the signs of her adulterous act. Grabbing her torn panties from the floor as he opened the door for her, she hoped that Desiree hadn't heard the debauchery – her mother's debauched whimpers.

'I'll see you later,' Tony said as she fled the room and bounded down the stairs. She left by the back door and slipped through the bushes at the end of the garden, hoping that her daughter wasn't looking out of her window as she headed for the safety of her house. Sperm streamed from her inflamed vagina, her bottom burned like hell, her clothes were crumpled . . .

'God,' Desiree said as Belinda slipped into the kitchen. 'Are you all right? What happened to you?'

'I . . . I got caught up in the bushes,' Belinda lied. 'I was clearing up and . . . It's all right, I'm OK.'

'You're a right mess. You'd better get cleaned up.'

'Yes, I will. Has Jenny gone?'

'She's just left. I didn't realise that you were gardening.'

'I thought I'd make the most of the fine weather. Desiree, we need to talk.'

'Oh? What about?'

'Things, everything.'

'What things?'

'I know that you think you're in love with Tony.'

'I don't think that at all. I've already told you, he has a girlfriend.'

'Desiree, I don't quite know how to put this. Tony has made several passes at me.'

'Passes at you?' She giggled. 'Mum, be serious.'

'I'm not unattractive, Desiree.'

'I know, but . . .'

'I'm telling you for your own good. He's only after sex.'

'Here we go again.' Desiree sighed, raising her eyes to the ceiling. 'Another lecture.'

'No, not a lecture. This is a serious talk. I'm only a few years older than Tony. Why you should laugh when I say that he's made passes at me, I really don't know.'

'Because you're my mum. I'm not saying that you're old or anything, but . . .'

'But what? I'm a woman, Desiree. Why shouldn't a man fancy me?'

'Yes, but not Tony.'

'Why not?'

'Because . . . Firstly, in case you've forgotten, you're a married woman.'

'Of course I haven't forgotten.'

'Since the day Tony moved in, you've been weird. You've changed, Mum.'

'*Me*? Desiree, you're the one who's changed.'

'You know that Tony likes me and you know how much I like him. You're jealous.'

'Jealous? Desiree, I'm far from jealous. I'm anything but jealous. We used to do things together, talk to each other. The garden, shopping, housework, going for walks . . . We hardly see each other now. You help Tony with his garden and –'

'That proves it,' Desiree cut in. 'You're jealous. Shall I tell you what I think? I think that *you* have been making passes at Tony.'

'For God's sake, Desiree.'

'To keep him away from me, you've been chasing after him. That is right, isn't it?'

'That's ridiculous.'

'That's why your clothes are all crumpled. You've been trying to get off with Tony. Is that what your panties were doing in the bushes? Had you pulled them off for him?'

'Desiree, please,' Belinda called as the girl stormed out of the room. 'Desiree . . .'

Holding her hand to her head as Desiree slammed her bedroom door shut, Belinda couldn't believe how close to the truth her daughter was. This was worse than a nightmare, she reflected, acutely aware of sperm running down her inner thighs as she climbed the stairs. She'd made a complete mess of attempting to talk to Desiree, she thought sadly, as she closed and locked the bathroom door. And she'd made things ten times worse.

After a shower, Belinda slipped into a summer dress and went out into the garden. There was no point in trying to talk to Desiree again. The girl was locked in her room, and would no doubt stay there for several hours. Her buttocks still stinging from the riding crop as she sat on a patio chair, Belinda tried to comprehend the incredible situation. Her husband hadn't been gone for more than a week and Tony had only just moved in ... And her life had been turned upside down and inside out.

Although she'd committed adultery for Desiree's sake, she knew that she'd harboured a yearning for sexual satisfaction for many years. The odd shafting from Brian as he'd snuggled up behind her in bed had left her full of sperm, but empty inside. She realised now that she'd craved real sex, gratifying sex, for a long time. Perhaps she was using Desiree as an excuse? she pondered. Screwing Tony to preserve her daughter's virginity was the ideal excuse to enjoy rampant sex. But, whatever the reason for her adultery, she knew that she was drifting away from Desiree. A wedge was being driven between them. And Tony was that wedge.

Pondering on the future, Belinda wondered where the path she was treading would take her. She was now moving away from her twee marriage, her insular world, but where to? Could she enjoy crude sex with Tony and yet remain with her husband? Could she live a double life? The loyal, faithful and loving wife when her husband was around, and the common sex-starved slut when he was away. Two lives, two men ...

'I'm going out,' Desiree announced, leaning on the back-door frame.

'Oh, er ... Where to?' Belinda asked, smiling at the girl.

'I don't know. Just out.'

'All right,' Belinda said, noticing Tony hovering in his garden. 'I'll see you later.'

'Maybe,' Desiree said, turning and disappearing into the house.

'Everything all right?' Tony asked.

'No, it's not,' Belinda replied as the front door slammed shut.

'Is Desiree in a bad mood?'

'I'm the one who's in a bad mood,' Belinda snapped, walking across the lawn. 'Do you realise just what you've done?'

'Fucked your sweet little –'

'To me, to my family. You've ruined my relationship with my daughter and –'

'*Me*?'

'Yes, you. Until you turned up, everything was fine.'

'How can you blame me? Just because you're screwing your life up . . .'

'Screwing my life up? You're the one who's screwing my life up. And my daughter's life.'

'I think you need a hard screw,' he quipped.

'Keep your voice down. I've given you my body, Tony. To save Desiree from your perverted ways, I've allowed you to . . . She found my panties in the bushes.'

'You shouldn't have left them there.'

'I had a hell of a job explaining how they got there. She now thinks that I'm after you, making passes at you and . . .'

'Aren't you?'

'No, I am not. All right, my sex life with my husband isn't up to much. But that doesn't mean to say that I want sex with you.'

'Don't you?'

'Look, I'll do anything to keep you and Desiree apart. If you want sex, then . . .' Her words tailing off as she heard Desiree's bedroom window close. She bit her lip. 'God, she's been listening.' She sighed. 'I thought she'd gone out.'

Belinda dashed into the house, climbed the stairs and tapped on her daughter's bedroom door. Wondering what the girl had heard, how much of the conversation

132

she'd heard, she knew that she couldn't put things right now. She called out, asking Desiree to let her in, and said that she could explain everything. Hearing soft cries, whimpers of despair, she hung her head. Desiree obviously believed that her mother was a jealous slut who was prepared to have sex with Tony in order to keep him away from her. That was partly true, Belinda reflected. But Desiree would never understand.

Eight

'You're up early,' Belinda said, wondering whether Desiree was going to talk to her as she walked into the kitchen.

'I didn't sleep very well,' the girl said coldly. 'My mind was cluttered with images of you and . . .'

'We'd better talk.' Belinda sighed.

'You're the one who needs to talk,' Desiree returned. 'You're the one who needs to explain.'

'Yes, well . . . The thing is . . .'

' "I'll do anything to keep you and Desiree apart." That's what you said to Tony, isn't it?'

'Yes, but . . .'

' "My sex life with my husband isn't up to much." How come you're discussing your sex life with your next-door neighbour?'

'Desiree, listen to me for a moment. You obviously heard snippets of my conversation with Tony, and you've got the wrong end of the stick. You've taken the bits you heard out of context.'

' "She found my panties in the bushes." Why were you telling Tony that I'd found your panties in the bushes?'

'If you'd just listen to me and allow me to explain . . . I was talking about sex because I've been trying to protect you. God, I don't know where to begin. Tony is a highly sexed man. When I said that I'd do anything to

134

keep you and him apart, I was trying to explain that you want to go on to university and shouldn't be distracted.'

'He's not distracting me.'

'Isn't he? How much work have you done since he moved in? How many days have you taken off college?'

'OK, so I've had other interests, but . . .'

'Tony has been taunting me, Desiree. He's been saying that you're young and beautiful and he could easily get you into his bed.'

'He has a girlfriend. He's told me that he's not interested in anything other than friendship with me. Why are you lying?'

'I'm not lying. To him, all this is a game. He knows how protective I am towards you, and he enjoys taunting me.'

'Why tell him about your sex life with Dad? Why tell him intimate details about your marriage?'

'I wasn't telling him intimate details. He was saying that I should be having fun while Dad's away. He said that things go stale after years of marriage and all I said was . . . I admitted that my sex life wasn't up to much. Had you listened, you'd have then heard me say that the passion might die off but the love grows.'

'And your panties? Why tell Tony that I found your panties in the bushes?'

'Because he'd seen them there. He made some joke or other about someone leaving a pair of panties in the bushes. I said that the wind had blown them off the line and you'd found them. There was nothing dark or mysterious about our conversation, Desiree. You over-heard bits and pieces, put two and two together and . . .'

'Why are you still trying to keep us apart when I've told you that he has a girlfriend? He's not interested in me, so why keep on like this?'

'He said that you showed him your thong. I didn't even know that you had a thong. And as for lifting your skirt up and showing it to Tony . . .'

'I . . . There was nothing wrong with that. I'd bought it in town and decided to show him, that was all.'

'Didn't you think that you'd turn him on by doing that? An attractive sixteen-year-old girl lifting her skirt up and showing her thong to a man . . . That's an invitation if ever there was one.'

'OK, maybe I shouldn't have done that. Why was he telling you about it?'

'He was taunting me. He's always taunting me, Desiree. That proves it, doesn't it? He was making lewd jokes about the panties in the bushes, saying that you'd lifted your skirt up and –'

'Hang on, I don't understand. Why would he want to taunt you?'

'As I said, this is all a game to him. He'll obviously deny it. He'll probably say that I'm trying to stir up trouble.'

'Aren't you? I mean, you said that you'd do anything to keep us apart so . . . Does that include having sex with him?'

'God, no.' Belinda gasped, shocked by her daughter's insight. 'How can you say such a thing?'

'Quite easily, seeing as you told him that your sex life is no good and he said that you should be having fun while Dad's away. Anyway, Tony is a virgin.'

'What?' Belinda giggled. 'Tony? A virgin? God, he's had more women than . . .'

'He told me that he's a virgin, and I believe him.'

'Desiree, if you believe that you'll believe anything. Can't you see that I'm trying to protect you? When I was your age, I made some very big mistakes. I don't want to stand by and watch you make the same mistakes.'

'What mistakes did you make?'

'I . . . I went with boys. Neglecting my studies, I had lots of boyfriends and . . .'

'You put it about?'

'Well, yes.'

136

'How many boys?'

'Oh, I don't know.'

'Ten? Twenty? Fifty?'

'No, no. I can't remember how many.'

'You lost count, you mean?'

'No, of course not.'

'At sixteen years old, you fucked around and lost count.'

'Don't use that word, Desiree.'

'Why not? It's the right word, isn't it? So, you were a slut during your teens? What changed you?'

'I wasn't a slut. Marriage changed me and . . .'

'You've been after Tony, haven't you?'

'Of course not. That's the last thing I'd do.'

'Just like you were during your teenage years, you want to fuck around. With Dad away and Tony next door . . . I was right, you're jealous. You want Tony for yourself, that's why you'd do anything to keep us apart.'

'That's not true, Desiree.'

'I overheard other things, you know.'

'Such as?'

'Does Dad know that you fucked around before you met him? Does he know that you were a slut?'

'Desiree, please . . .'

'I'm going to talk to Tony,' Desire said, opening the back-door. 'I'll ask him what you said.'

'Desiree, wait.'

Belinda sighed as she watched her daughter run across the lawn and disappear into the bushes. She knew that she'd made things worse than ever. She should never have mentioned her teenage years, she reflected. But she'd only been trying to explain why she was overly protective, why she didn't want her daughter going off the rails. Desiree now thought her a slut who fucked about. What the hell was Tony saying to Desiree? If the girl went blabbing to her father . . . Could this get any worse? Belinda pondered.

* * *

137

'She's lying,' Tony said firmly. 'I've never come out with lewd jokes or taunted her.'

'Why was she telling you about her sex life with my dad?' Desiree sighed. 'That's not the sort of thing married women discuss with other men. And why did you say that she should be having fun while Dad's away?'

'She's taken it out of context. All I was saying was that she should relax a little and not worry so much about you. I said that she should be having some fun rather than spending her time checking up on you.'

'What I don't understand is why you told her that I'd lifted my skirt up and shown you my thong. That was taunting her, Tony. There's no other word for it.'

'Again, she's taken it out of context. I was saying that I only want to be friends with you. I mentioned that we're more like brother and sister and you showing me your thong ... Look, this is crazy. Aren't you going to college today?'

'Yes, I suppose I should. I'll see you later this afternoon. Are you going to work?'

'I'm waiting for a phone call.'

'Oh, right. Well, I'll see you later.'

After breakfast, Belinda decided to have another talk with Tony. With Desiree at college, she'd have time for a proper discussion, and not be overheard. Wearing her summer dress, she called at his front door rather than go sneaking through the bushes. Things were going to change, she decided. Desiree was stuck in the middle, used as a pawn in some horrendous adult sex game. The girl should be enjoying her studies, mixing with girls of her own age and living her life. This nightmare was going to end. And the fence panel was going back in place, dividing the gardens and keeping the pervert at bay.

'I thought you might come round,' Tony said, closing the door as Belinda walked past him into the hall. 'Why have you been trying to cause trouble?'

'*Me?*' Belinda said. 'You're the one who ... Look, we're not going to get anywhere by arguing. Desiree is caught up in the middle of this nightmare and I want it to stop. At her age, she shouldn't be going through this. She should be enjoying her life, Tony. Not having to play these ridiculous mind games.'

'Mind games? She's not playing mind games, Belinda. Look at the simple facts. Desiree wants a relationship with me. I don't want to be anything more than friends with her. But I do want a relationship with you.'

'So, you use her as a pawn in order to get what you want from me?'

'No, not at all.'

'You've threatened to screw her, Tony. You've said many times that it's either me or my daughter. You've blackmailed me into having sex with you.'

'Be honest with yourself. You want sex with me, don't you?'

'No, no I don't.'

'Oh, come on. You love a good shafting. You love sucking the spunk out of my cock, feeling my spunk flooding your tight little pussy and –'

'Stop it, Tony. For God's sake, stop it.'

'The truth hurts? Is that it? As you said, we'll get nowhere by arguing. I know that you think I'm a bastard, and you're probably right. The thing is ... I'm a normal man, Belinda. And Desiree is an extremely horny sixteen-year-old girl. I live alone and, at times, I need company. I also need physical contact, as you do. Your husband is away for weeks at a time. All I want is for us to enjoy sex together.'

'Yes, but ... Had you not dragged Desiree into this, things might have been different.'

'You'd have opened your legs for me?'

'No.'

'There you are, then. Had it not been for Desiree, we wouldn't be enjoying a sexual relationship.'

'We're not enjoying –'

'I can read you like a book, Belinda. You love cold, hard, crude sex with me. Admit it.'

'I will admit that I get lonely at times. And I do enjoy sex. But I'm married, Tony. Where will this lead? Where will my adultery take me? Inevitably, to the ruination of my marriage.'

'Why should it? You're making this unnecessarily complicated. I need sex, Belinda. I either have sex with you, or Desiree. It's as simple as that.'

'Blackmail.'

'Call it what you like. Desiree wants me. I want her to carry on with her studies and get somewhere in life. However, if you're not going to give me what I want, what I need, then . . .'

'Then you'll ruin Desiree's life? I've already agreed to have sex with you, Tony. All I'm asking in return is that you stick to your side of the deal.'

'I am sticking to it. Good God, I could lure Desiree into my bed at the drop of a hat. Why haven't I done that? Because I'm sticking to my side of the deal. As I said, you're the one who's causing trouble, making things difficult and creating problems. Now, as Desiree is at college, I'd like you to strip naked.'

'I can't, I have things to do.'

'Yes, you do have things to do. You have your master to . . .'

'Later, maybe. I have to go into town and . . .'

'Strip naked, Belinda. Show me that you're an obedient slave, and I'll promise to keep Desiree out of this.'

Unbuttoning the front of her summer dress, Belinda hoped that Tony would at last leave Desiree out of the equation if she did as he asked. If he stopped his lewd jokes, his taunting and threats . . . But, at what price? Adultery. Maybe he was right, she mused, tossing her dress onto the sofa. Perhaps her adultery wouldn't lead to the ruination of her marriage. Why should it? If she only saw Tony when her husband was working abroad, if Desiree's suspicions were allayed, why should her adultery come to light and destroy her marriage?

But, still a question nagged Belinda. Was she agreeing to become Tony's sex slave to preserve Desiree's virginity? Or was she doing it because, at heart, she was a slut? If only Brian had been a little more adventurous in bed, she mused as she stood before her master in her bra and panties. If only he'd paid a little attention to her feminine needs, her inner desires. But he hadn't, and there was no point in looking back. Her sex life with Brian was boring, staid and completely unsatisfying. Unable to recall when she'd last enjoyed an orgasm with her husband, she knew that nothing would change. Sex with her husband was bland. But, with her next-door neighbour . . . Tony had no idea how to treat a lady. But he certainly knew how to treat a common slut.

Her full breasts tumbled from the cups of her bra as she unhooked it. Then she slipped her panties down and kicked the garment aside. Tony looked her up and down, his huge grin showing his obvious appreciation for her curvaceous body as she stood naked before him. *You love a good shafting. You love sucking the spunk out of my cock, feeling my spunk flooding your tight little pussy . . .* Once a slut, always a slut, she reflected, as she recalled Tony's words. Why try to deny it? She'd lusted after boys during her teens and had successfully quashed her darker side throughout her marriage. Perhaps the time had come to allow her true character to surface once again.

'I want you to get into the role of a sex slave,' Tony said. 'Get on all fours and crawl around for me.'

'Tony, I'm not going to . . .'

'Just do it, Belinda,' he said, raising his eyes to the ceiling.

'I'm not going to crawl around on the floor like an animal. I've agreed to have sex with you, but I'm not going to be treated like an animal.'

'Is it love you're looking for?' he asked, stroking her erect nipples.

'I have love with my husband,' she returned.

'In that case, it's sex you're looking for.'

'No, I . . .'

'Belinda, we both know that you want cold, crude sex. There's nothing you'd like more than to be treated like an animal and used for hard sex.'

'I'm not just a lump of female flesh to be used and abused.'

'That's what you really want, isn't it? I've told you before to be honest with yourself. Let yourself go and enjoy your body. Once you get into the role of my sex slave, you'll be gagging for a hard fuck.'

Taking her position on the floor, she knew that her vaginal lips were bulging below her bottom, nestling alluringly between her slender thighs. Although humiliated and degraded as Tony stood behind her and commented on her firm buttocks, she realised that she was also highly aroused. Crawling around on the floor like a dog, her sex crack crudely displayed to her master, she felt her pussy-milk oozing between the fleshy cushions of her swelling labia. She could lead two lives, she mused. The loving wife and mother, and the common whore.

The excitement, the danger, the humiliation and degradation – all combined to send Belinda's arousal soaring to frightening heights. Tony had no idea how to treat a lady, she again reflected. But he knew how to treat a sex-starved slut. Did she really want to be treated like an animal? she pondered. A lump of female flesh to be used and abused by her next-door neighbour? She'd known only too well of her darker side during her teenage years: her lusting for boys' cocks, her yearning to suck purple knobs, her craving to drink fresh sperm. But, to be treated like a dog?

Slipping his trousers off and sitting on the sofa, Tony ordered her to crawl across the floor and settle between his feet. As Belinda made her way across the carpet on her hands and knees, she realised that she was behaving like an obedient dog. The notion excited her and she gazed at his heaving balls, the veined shaft of his erect penis. He'd want her to suck on his swollen knob and bring out his creamy spunk, she was sure, as she watched his full balls heaving and rolling. He had a big penis, she observed, far broader and longer than her husband's cock.

'Lick my balls,' Tony instructed her, parting his legs wide and moving forward on the sofa until his buttocks were over the edge of the cushion. 'Lick my balls and make me nice and wet. Do it properly, and you'll have your prize. You'll have what you crave, Belinda. A mouthful of creamy spunk.'

Sweeping her pink tongue over his hairy ball sac, Belinda breathed in his aphrodisiacal male scent. Her juices of lust streaming from her opening vaginal entrance and running down her inner thighs, she knew that her darker side was surfacing once again. She'd been known amongst a group of boys at school as the oral tart. Using her hot mouth, her wet tongue, she'd sucked many a boy's cock to orgasm. She'd loved knob-sucking and swallowing creamy spunk. Barely able to wait until school was over so that she could spend time in the local woods with several boys, she'd got a reputation as a cock-loving slut. But marriage had come and had taken her pleasure away.

Lapping at Tony's rolling balls, Belinda followed her master's orders and squeezed his shaft as hard as she could. Realising that it must be rather painful, she wondered what other perversions he was into as he told her to sink her teeth into the base of his cock. Complying, she forced his thighs wider apart and bit into the root of his solid penis. He gasped and trembled on the sofa, obviously enjoying the pain as she gripped his cock hard and sank her teeth deeper into his fleshy rod.

'That's good,' he murmured, his thighs twitching. 'When you get home later, I want you to shave your pussy.'

'No way,' Belinda said firmly, raising her head and staring hard at him. 'There's no way I'm shaving, Tony.'

'You'll do as you're told,' he returned. 'As my obedient slave –'

'What the hell do you think my husband will say if I shave? It's bad enough having to come here and have sex with you behind his back, but to shave my pubes off . . .'

'Bad enough having to come here and have sex? Don't make me laugh. You love it.'

'Yes, but . . .'

'I don't want to argue with you, Belinda. You'll shave, and that's the end of the matter. Besides, your husband might like it.'

'No, you don't understand. We don't have that sort of sex life. He'd think me . . . God only knows what he'd think of me. He'd probably think me a slut. I can't do it, Tony. I won't do it.'

'Now that really is disappointing.' He sighed, running his hand up and down his solid shaft. 'I didn't want to have to cane you, Belinda. But you leave me no choice.'

'For God's sake –'

'Suck out my spunk,' he snapped. 'You'll give me a decent blow job before I cane you.'

Taking his swollen knob into her wet mouth, Belinda knew that she couldn't shave her pussy even if she wanted to. Running her tongue around the rim of Tony's glans, savouring the salty taste of his purple globe, she imagined her husband's reaction to her shaving. He wouldn't understand, she was sure, as she gripped the root of Tony's cock and took his solid knob to the back of her throat. He'd never believe her if she said that she'd shaved for him. Far from liking her without pubic hair, he'd think she'd gone mad. And, if

Desiree came out with the odd remark about the man next door ... No, she asserted mentally. There was no way she was going to shave her pubic hair off.

Wanking Tony's cock and sucking hard on his purple plum as he quipped about her looking like a schoolgirl without her pubes, she knew that he wasn't going to give up. Tony would threaten her, goad her, until she agreed to shaving. Although her sex life with her husband was virtually non-existent, he often saw her naked. She'd not be able to conceal her hairless vulva, she knew. Dressing in the morning or getting ready for bed at night ... She'd never be able to keep her dirty little secret from her husband.

As Tony began to gasp and tremble, Belinda bobbed her head up and down and repeatedly took his bulbous knob to the back of her throat. Although desperate for his creamy sperm, she couldn't stop thinking about his unreasonable request. Realising that, if he caned her, her husband would notice the weals fanning out across the taut flesh of her buttocks, she decided to lay down some rules. No shaving, no marks on her body, nothing to rouse her husband's suspicion. She could probably get away with committing adultery, but only if she was extremely careful.

'Don't swallow,' Tony instructed. 'Let it fill your mouth and run down my cock. Then you can lap it up like a dog. You can lick my balls clean, suck up my spunk and stiffen me again ready to fuck your tight little arsehole.'

His sperm flooded her mouth. Belinda did as he'd asked and allowed the milky liquid to stream down his cock shaft and flow over his hairy scrotum. There was no way he was going to push his penis into her bottom, she thought, as she savoured the salty taste of his fresh spunk. No matter what punishment he threatened her with, she wasn't going to shave or take his cock into her bottom hole. Repeatedly thrusting his hips forwards, pumping her mouth full of sperm, Tony uttered his words of crude sex. *Cock-sucking slut, mouth-fucking tart, sperm-guzzling whore* ... Turned on by his lewd comments, Belinda bobbed her head up and down faster and sucked out his fresh cream. This was crude sex, she mused. Crude, cold, hard, loveless ... But beautiful. Slipping his knob out of her mouth as his sperm-flow finally ceased, she began lapping up the spilled cream from his ball sac.

'Clean me up properly,' he ordered her, his body trembling in the aftermath of his coming. 'Lap it all up like a good dog. And then I'll give you a good caning.'

A dog? Belinda reflected. If Desiree knew how Tony was treating her mother ... A good caning? This was going to have to remain a carefully guarded secret, Belinda thought anxiously, as she sucked the sperm out of Tony's sex-matted pubic curls. Desiree had already unwittingly ventured too close to the truth. If she discovered her mother's shocking whoredom ... The outcome didn't bear thinking about. Finishing the job of cleansing Tony's balls, Belinda sat back on her heels and stared at him. He was good-looking, she mused. Good-looking, as horny as hell, virile ...

'You're doing well,' he praised her. 'Learning to become an obedient slave.'

'Do I have a choice?' she asked him, looking down at his stiffening cock.

'Of course you have a choice. It's either you or Desiree. OK, knees wide apart and rest your head on the sofa cushion. The time has come to break in your sweet little bottom hole.'

'Tony, no ... I don't want anal sex, or the cane or ...'

'Wait a minute. It's not what you want that concerns me. It's what I want, Belinda.'

'God, Desiree must be home,' Belinda whispered, hearing her front door slam shut. 'I'd better get back.'

146

'Not until you've had your arse spunked.'

'Tony, I . . .'

'Lean on the sofa,' he ordered her, taking his position behind her.

'No, Tony.'

'All I'm going to do is give you a light spanking.' He chuckled.

'Are you sure that's all?'

'Of course I'm sure. It's either you, or your . . .'

'Yes, I know.' She sighed. 'Spank me, if you have to. And then I must go home.'

Resting her head on the sofa cushion, she parted her knees wide and thought about Desiree. Why had the girl come home early? she wondered. As Tony's palm landed across the tensed flesh of her rounded buttocks with a deafening slap, she let out a yelp. If Desiree heard the cries of crude sex emanating from Tony's house . . . As his palm repeatedly met the quivering flesh of her naked buttocks, Belinda buried her face in the sofa cushion to muffle her yelps. The pain permeated her bare bottom, sending quivers of pleasure through her contracting womb, and she again thought what a dirty little slut she was.

'You love a damned good spanking, don't you?' Tony quipped, landing the hardest slap yet across her crimsoned bottom orbs. 'You've been sex-starved for years. But I'm going to change that.'

He was right, she reflected, as he continued with the gruelling spanking. She'd been sex-starved for years, starved of sexual gratification throughout her entire marriage. Tony *had* changed that, she mused, as he halted the spanking and yanked her burning buttocks wide apart. The feel of his wet tongue teasing the delicate tissue of her anus sent ripples of sex through her pelvis. She could never imagine her husband committing such a debased act. Brian was hardly into straight sex, she reflected, let alone oral or anything out of the

147

ordinary. Had he been more like Tony, then things would have been very different. Had he been as horny as Tony, then she'd never have committed adultery. Or would she?

Reaching behind her back and stretching her bottom orbs wide apart as she felt Tony's tongue enter her rectum, she let out a gasp. 'God, yes,' she murmured as he licked deep inside her anal duct. 'Tongue-fuck my arse as hard as you can.' Her crude words shocking her, she again wondered whether she could live two separate lives: the tart and the loving wife? Could she keep the two very different sides of her character apart? Could she keep Tony and her husband apart? If they became friends and Tony came out with his lewd remarks and quips . . .

'No,' Belinda cried as she felt the bulbous knob of Tony's solid cock pressing hard against her well-salivated anal ring. 'Tony, please . . .'

'What's the matter?' He chuckled. 'Have you never had your sweet arse fucked?'

'For God's sake, what the hell do you think I am?'

'A sex-starved little whore. Are you ready for this?'

'No, I . . .'

'I'll bet that Desiree would love my cock up her arse.'

As he drove his knob deep into the tight sheath of her rectum, Belinda again cried out. He was an evil man, she thought, as his swollen glans journeyed along her hot duct to the depths of her bowels. She could feel her anal tube opening, her pelvic cavity bloating, as he pushed his solid shaft deep into the core of her naked body. Her anal ring stretched tautly around the root of his huge penis as he impaled her completely. She dug her fingernails into the sofa cushion and grimaced as he slapped her tensed buttocks. To even suggest doing this to Desiree was disgusting, she reflected. He was an evil pervert, a despicable man . . . And he had to be kept away from Desiree at any cost.

'There's nothing I like more than the feel of a girl's tight arse gripping my cock,' he said, again slapping her bare bottom.

'I've never known a man like you,' Belinda said as he withdrew his rock-hard cock and rammed his bulbous knob deep into the dank heat of her bowels. 'You're evil.'

'In that case, you're lucky to have met me.' He chortled. 'It's high time you had your arse fucked, Belinda. A slut like you should be arse-fucked regularly, don't you agree?'

'I'm not a slut,' she returned.

'You're a slut, and you know it.'

He was right, she thought dolefully. Even Desiree, her own daughter, had called her a slut. Once a slut, always a slut. *At sixteen years old, you fucked around and lost count.* Desiree's harsh words battered her tormented mind as Tony found his anal pistoning rhythm. Belinda's naked body rocked back and forth with the crude rectal pumping. Even though she was a slut, she'd never dreamed about anal sex. And she'd certainly never thought that she'd experience the forbidden act. The brown tissue surrounding her stretched anus rolling back and forth along Tony's solid shaft, she closed her eyes and tried not to think of her husband or her daughter. This was her secret life, she mused. Her dark and very dirty secret.

Unable to deny that the amazing sensations were driving her wild, she began whimpering as her vaginal milk seeped between the engorged wings of her inner labia. This was real sex, she mused dreamily, her clitoris becoming painfully solid. Losing herself in her arousal, she clung to the sofa cushion and breathed deeply through her nose as her neighbour committed the illicit act. Tony reached beneath his swinging balls, drove two fingers into the tightening sheath of her drenched vagina and massaged her hot inner flesh. Dizzy in her sexual delirium, lost in her crude act of adultery, Belinda shook violently as she neared her climax. Her inflamed anal duct tightening around Tony's thrusting cock, she hoped that his sperm would soon fill her and lubricate the forbidden union.

'Like it?' Tony asked, quickening his thrusting motions.

'God, yes,' Belinda murmured, rocking her hips to meet his penile thrusts.

'You're a tight-arsed little bitch, Belinda. If your husband doesn't fuck your arse, then he doesn't know what he's missing.'

Wishing that Tony wouldn't continually refer to her husband and Desiree, Belinda felt her anal muscles tighten around his shafting cock as her neglected clitoris swelled. Again his fingers thrust deep into her vaginal cavity and his knob repeatedly drove deep into the heat of her bowels. She couldn't imagine her daughter consenting to anal sex: Desiree needed a warm, loving relationship with a caring man, not crude anal sex with a pervert. Again trying not to think about her daughter, she parted her knees wider and jutted her bottom out to allow Tony deeper access to the core of her abused body.

'Are you ready for your first arse-spunking?' Tony asked his slave.

'Yes, yes, do it,' Belinda said, squeezing her eyes shut as her inflamed anal duct gripped his pistoning cock tighter. 'Fuck my arse hard and spunk me.'

Again, her crude words of lust shocked her. Was this her true character surfacing? she pondered. Forcing at least three fingers deep into her spasming vaginal sheath, Tony let out a gasp of pleasure as his sperm jetted from his orgasming knob. His male cream lubricated her anal cylinder and eased the pistoning of his granite-hard cock. She shuddered and whimpered in the grip of her adulterous act. The squelching sound of his spunk resounded around the room, the warm liquid spurting from her overflowing rectum. She reached between her thighs and massaged her clitoris to a much-needed orgasm.

'Harder,' she cried as he repeatedly rammed his throbbing knob deep into her sperm-flooded bowels. 'Fuck my arse harder and fill me with your spunk.'

'Filthy slut,' he said, his lower belly slapping the crimsoned globes of her bottom. 'Dirty, filthy, little whore slut.'

'God, you're so big,' she whimpered as her clitoris pulsated beneath her vibrating fingertips. 'I'm . . . I'm coming.'

Her orgasm erupted within the painfully hard bulb of her clitoris and Belinda cried out in the grip of her illicit shafting. Throwing her head back, her curtain of long black hair veiling her flushed face, she screamed as her climax peaked and rocked her very soul. Never had she known an orgasm of such intensity and duration, never had she realised the immense pleasure derivable from her tight bottom hole. Her bloated sex holes burning and inflamed, she couldn't help but cry out as she rode the crest of her multiple orgasm. Tony's fingers massaged his thrusting cock through the thin membrane dividing her lust ducts and she again let out a scream of debased pleasure. Never had she been so beautifully used and abused in the name of depraved sex. Never had she been arse-fucked in the name of adultery.

'You're bloody good,' Tony praised her as he finally withdrew his deflating penis from her sperm-drenched anal duct. 'You're the best arse-fuck I've ever had.'

'God, I feel dizzy,' Belinda said. 'That was incredible.'

'I'm glad you enjoyed your first arse-fucking.' He chortled. 'This is only the beginning. From now on, you're going to have your tight little bottom fucked and spunked every day.'

'I have to go now,' she murmured, hauling her sated body upright. 'Desiree will be wondering where I am.'

'I'll allow you to go, but you'll come back later.'

'Yes, yes all right.'

'And when you come back, you'll show me your shaved pussy.'

Deciding not to argue with him, Belinda grabbed her clothes and dressed. Pulling her panties up her long legs and veiling her inflamed sex holes, she knew that she was going to have to compose herself before facing Desiree. Running her fingers through her tousled hair, she decided to tell the girl that she'd been out for a walk in the park. Hoping that Desiree wouldn't be suspicious, she felt Tony's sperm seeping from the burning eye of her anus and soaking into her tight panties. A dog, she reflected. A lump of female flesh used and abused . . .

'I'll see you later,' Tony said as Belinda headed for the door.

'Don't tell Desiree that I've been here,' she said as he followed her into the hall. 'Say nothing to her, all right?'

'I'll say nothing at all, Belinda. If you shave, that is.'

'Tony . . .'

'I'll see you later.' He chuckled, opening the front door for her. 'Shaved and ready for another arse-fucking and a damned good caning.'

Nine

Opening the front door and stepping into the hall, Belinda called out for Desiree. Her hair dishevelled, her face flushed, she knew that she couldn't make out that she'd fallen over again. What could she say? she pondered. Reckoning that the girl had gone back to college, she breathed a sigh of relief. She was about to go upstairs and take a shower and change into some clean clothes when the phone rang. Should she answer it? she mused. Was it Tony calling to remind her to shave her pussy?

Sperm oozed from her inflamed bottom hole, wetting her tight panties as she walked into the lounge, and she was pleased that Desiree wasn't around. The girl would only become suspicious and start asking searching questions. Lifting the receiver, she knew that she couldn't keep coming home looking as though she'd been dragged through the bushes backwards. Things were going to have to change, she decided.

'It's me,' Brian said as Belinda pressed the receiver to her ear.

'Oh, hi,' she said, acutely aware of her sperm-drenched panties. 'Er . . . How are you?'

'I'm fine. It's you I'm concerned about.'

'Me? What do you mean?'

'Desiree rang me at the hotel. She seemed concerned.'

'Concerned? About what?'

'She said that you've been spending a lot of time with the man next door.'

'Oh, our new neighbour?' Belinda said shakily, wondering what on earth Desiree had been saying. 'I wouldn't say that I've spent a *lot* of time . . .'

'You've had a drink with him?'

'A glass of wine, yes. I've been helping him to choose curtains, that sort of thing. What did Desiree say, exactly?'

'It wasn't so much what she said but the impression I got.'

'Which was?'

'Are you sure that everything's all right? I mean, spending time with this man and . . .'

'Everything's fine, Brian. Tony, that's our new neighbour, is a very nice young man. I've been advising him about curtains and Desiree has been helping him to plan his garden.'

'You're well in with him, then?'

'I wouldn't say that. The truth of the matter is that Desiree has fallen for him. I've been trying to steer her away from him and encourage her to get back to her studies. He's twenty-seven and . . .'

'I got the impression that *you* were the one who needed to be steered away from him, Belinda.'

'*Me!*' she exclaimed, her hands trembling. 'Why would I need to be steered away from him?'

'You must get very lonely.'

'Brian, what the hell are you suggesting?'

'A single man moves in next door, you're on your own for six weeks . . .'

'Yes, I do get very lonely. But not so lonely that I'd have an affair with the man next door. Or any man, for that matter. What on earth do you think I am?'

'I didn't mean it that way.'

'What did you mean, then? Look, I've been going next door with Desiree to make sure that she isn't alone

154

with him too often. You've got the wrong end of the stick, Brian.'

'Yes, well ... I'm sorry. It's just that Desiree seemed concerned.'

'If she's concerned about anything then it's because I'm always around when she wants to be alone with Tony. I'm just trying to protect her, Brian.'

'Yes, I can see that. OK, I'd better be going. I'll ring tomorrow, if I can.'

'All right. And don't worry.'

'I won't, love. I'm sorry.'

'There's nothing to be sorry about. Just don't go getting any silly ideas.'

'I'd hate to think that you're going with another man.'

'Don't be so silly,' she said, forcing a giggle. 'Another man, indeed.'

'When we first met, you said that you were a virgin.'

'Yes, I ... I remember.'

'To think of you with another man ... Sorry, now I *am* being silly.'

'I'll talk to you tomorrow, Brian.'

'OK, bye for now.'

Belinda replaced the receiver and held her hand to her head as guilt swamped her. Desiree had gone too far, she thought angrily. Her heart banged hard against her chest as she pondered on lying to her husband, betraying her husband. She recalled Tony's cock shafting her tight bottom hole. Adultery. The word battering her tormented mind, she knew that it was too late to change things now. *You said that you were a virgin.* She'd lied to Brian from day one, she mused. But, had she told him that she'd been with dozens of boys, allowed two boys to spunk in her mouth simultaneously ... And now, she was still lying to him.

Desiree was obviously trying to cause trouble, Belinda reflected. But why? Did she really believe that her mother wanted her out of the way so that she could have an affair with Tony? If she did believe that, then she was right, Belinda thought anxiously. Desiree's suspicions were bad enough without Brian adding to the horror by asking awkward questions. This was a nightmare situation, and it was getting worse.

Making her way up to the bathroom and slipping out of her clothes, Belinda decided not to say anything to Desiree. Having quelled Brian's suspicions, it was best to leave it at that. But, if Desiree started blabbing again Belinda knew that there was nothing she could do, other than be very careful. Her visits to Tony's house would have to be planned in advance. Then again, if Desiree was going to come home from college in the middle of the day ... This needn't be a nightmare, Belinda decided. With careful planning, things would be fine.

Stepping into the shower, she pondered on Tony's request, his demand. *You'll shave, and that's the end of the matter.* Massaging shampoo into her long black hair, she wondered how long it would take for her pubic hair to grow. Two weeks? Four weeks? By the time her husband had returned from Tokyo, she was sure that her pussy would once again sport a good covering of dark curls. If Tony didn't cane her bottom, if her curls grew back ... Brian would be none the wiser.

She took the shaving foam from the shelf, turned the shower off and massaged the cream into her vulval mound. She knew that Desiree would be horrified if she discovered that her mother had shaved her pussy for another man. But the girl would never discover her secret, she mused, as she took the razor from the shelf. To shave just this once would be all right, she decided. Desiree must never discover the shocking truth about her mother's filthy whoredom.

Dragging the razor over the gentle rise of her mons, Belinda again recalled her early teenage years. When she'd first explored the intimate folds nestling within her crack and discovered her ripening clitoris, her tight vaginal sheath, she'd woken her inner desires. From that fateful day forwards, she'd looked at boys in a new light. She'd wondered about their cocks, their balls, and had wasted no time in getting her hands inside a lad's trousers. The hardness of his young cock, the feel of his silky-smooth knob, the taste of his creamy spunk ... From that day of sexual discovery, she was hooked on sex. And then marriage came.

Working the razor over the fleshy swell of her vulval lips, she finished the job of depilation and washed away the foam and curls with the shower. Her clitoris swelling as she dried her naked body with a towel, she became acutely aware of her nude pussy. Feeling the soft flesh of her swelling pussy lips, the smoothness of her sensitive vulval flesh, she gazed at her reflection in the mirror and grinned. Far from horrified by the sight that met her wide eyes, she felt a quiver of excitement run through her womb.

Finally leaving the bathroom, she slipped into her summer dress and went downstairs. Her silk panties caressed her hairless vulval lips as she made a cup of coffee and she wondered when to show Tony her denuded pussy. He'd be delighted, she mused. He'd bury his face between her thighs, lick deep inside her cream-flooded vagina and suck hard on her swollen clitoris. Her juices of arousal oozing between the pink petals of her inner lips, her clitoris yearning for attention, she again pondered on her husband's reaction. He'd never understand, so there was little point in hoping to keep her vulva free of hair.

'Where did you get to this morning?' Desiree asked accusingly as she closed the front door and walked into the kitchen. 'I came home and you weren't here.'

'I went for a walk in the park,' Belinda lied. 'Why did you come home?'

'We had a free period so I thought I'd come home for an hour. I've finished early because I have some work to do on my computer.'

'Desiree . . . When we talked earlier . . .'

'Yes?'

'I'm not a slut. I've never been a slut. Admittedly, I had several boyfriends. But I've never been a slut.'

'How can you say that when you can't even remember how many boys you went with? Anyway, I don't care whether you're a slut or not.'

'What do you mean by that?'

'It doesn't affect me, does it? If you want to fuck around, that's your business.'

'Desiree, I am not . . . I'm not going with anyone. Look, we have to settle this once and for all. We used to get on so well together. Now we're distant. I feel that we don't know each other at all.'

'You're right there. I thought I knew you but, obviously, I was very wrong. I now realise why you didn't like Kathy.'

'What do you mean?'

'Kathy's a slut. I suppose you saw yourself in her and didn't like it.'

Pondering on her daughter's uncanny knack of hitting the nail on the head, Belinda didn't know what to say. What could she say? she wondered. There were no words that would change Desiree's mind. Deciding to say no more on the subject, she refilled the kettle and took another cup from the shelf. It was best to let the girl simmer down, she thought, spooning coffee into the cup. Hopefully, now that Tony had his obedient sex slave, he wouldn't stir up trouble with his lewd remarks. Was it possible to get back to some kind of normality? she reflected. Would Desiree enjoy gardening and shopping with her mother once again? Or would she go blabbing to her father?

'Do you fancy going out for a meal this evening?' Belinda asked.

'I'm going round to a friend's house,' Desiree replied coldly. 'I might stay overnight.'

'Oh, right. Your father rang earlier.'

'Oh? What did he say?'

'Nothing much. He just asked how we were.'

'He didn't mention me then?'

'He asked how college is going. Oh, and he wanted to know how we're doing with the garden.'

'So, he didn't mention Tony?'

'No, why should he?'

'No reason.'

'As you're going to work on your computer, I think I'll sit in the garden for a while.'

'I'm just going to see whether Tony went to work,' Desiree said, stepping out of the back door.

'Oh, er . . . I thought you were going to study? And, what about your coffee?'

'I'll be back in a minute. I just want a quick word with him, that's all.'

Biting her lip as Desiree walked across the lawn to the bushes, Belinda wished that the girl hadn't come home early. There seemed to be no privacy, she mused, sipping her coffee. There seemed to be no time to . . . spend with Tony? Again acutely aware of her silk panties brushing against the hairless lips of her pussy, she was horrified as she realised that she was jealous of Desiree. The girl was next door with Tony, talking to him and . . . Why the hell had she come home early?

Belinda slipped her panties off and walked out into the garden. The sun warming her back, the breeze cooling her naked pussy, she felt a quiver run through her womb as she thought about Tony's cock. She shouldn't have taken her panties off, she knew. But she wanted to be ready for Tony, naked beneath her dress and ready for his beautiful cock. Unable to think of anything else as her clitoris again called for attention, she decided to do some more work in the garden to take her mind off sex. Walking across the lawn and staring down at the flowers lining the border, she knew that she couldn't concentrate. Sex was beginning to rule her life.

She was going to have to quell her libido, but how? Masturbation. The word playing on her mind, she again realised that she had no privacy. Desiree would be back any minute; there was nowhere to go, nowhere to masturbate and appease her yearning clitoris. Finally she walked down the garden and crept into the bushes. She slipped her hand up her dress and ran her fingertip up and down her sex-wet crack. Breathing heavily as her clitoris responded, she again recalled her times in the woods with boys after school. They'd loved to pull her knickers down and examine her sex slit: finger her there; kiss and lick her there. She'd not realised how lucky she'd been at the time. Sex every day with as many boys as she'd liked . . . Why had she met Brian? Why had she married? She'd thought that she'd found love, she reflected, easing two fingers into her hot vagina. Was Desiree thinking that she'd found love?

'My mum hasn't been here, then?' Desiree asked Tony as he pulled her T-shirt up and lifted her bra clear of her breasts. 'Tony, has she been here or not?'

'No, she hasn't,' he replied abstractly, gazing at the ripe teats of her nipples. 'How many times do I have to tell you?'

'She said that she went for a walk in the park, but I don't believe her.'

'You have wonderful tits, Desiree. Small and hard with nice puffy nipples.'

'That's nice,' she murmured as he sucked her sensitive nipple into his hot mouth. 'God, you really do turn me on.'

'Enough to slip out of your clothes and allow me to make love to you?'

'Why don't we go up to your bedroom?'

'No, in here,' he said, pulling her T-shirt over her head. 'I want you in here, on the sofa.'

Desiree had known that this moment would come. She unhooked her bra and dropped her skirt. She was ready for sex now, she mused dreamily as Tony slipped his trousers and shirt off. Stepping out of her panties, she stood naked before the man she loved and looked down at his erect penis. She spied his purple knob through the small opening in his fleshy foreskin and watched his huge balls heave and roll. Then she sat on the sofa with her thighs wide apart.

No words passed their lips as Tony knelt between her feet and kissed her hairless mons. Breathing deeply, heavily, Desiree watched as he licked her sex crack, wetting her there in readiness to penetrate her and strip her of her virginity. Her clitoris swelling, her juices of lust flowing freely from the opening entrance to her vagina, she let out a rush of breath as he tweaked her erect nipples and drove his tongue deep into her hot pussy. Gasping, shuddering, she gripped the sofa cushion and arched her back as he sucked out her sex-milk.

'That's nice,' she whispered, parting her thighs wider to allow him deeper access to her vaginal duct. 'I've waited for this moment.'

'So have I,' he said through a mouthful of vaginal flesh.

'Our first time, Tony. Your first time, my first time . . .'

'You're my first and last girl,' he said, straightening his body and smiling at her. 'Are you ready?'

'Yes, yes, I'm ready.'

Gazing at the purple crown of his solid penis as he fully retracted his foreskin, she moved forwards on the sofa. Parting the fleshy lips of her hairless vulva, he pressed his swollen glans hard against the virgin hole of her teenage pussy. His knob slipped into her hot duct, entering her vaginal tube, and she closed her eyes and held her breath. She could feel his glans entering her, opening her virgin sex duct as he pushed his cock slowly into her young body. Trembling, gasping, she dug her fingernails into the sofa cushion as he impaled her fully on his rock-hard penis.

'Yes,' she said, her virginity finally stripped. 'God, that feels nice.'

'Our first time, Desiree.'

'Yes, yes.'

'The first of many times.'

'Oh, yes. The first of many, many times.'

'I'm twenty-seven, and you're my first girl. I've waited for this for years.'

'You'll never have to wait again. I'll always be here for you.'

Withdrawing his rock-hard cock until her engorged inner lips hugged his pussy-wet knob, he slid gently into her pussy again. Her lower stomach rising and falling as he found his pistoning rhythm, she arched her back and opened her eyes. Watching the wet shaft of his solid penis repeatedly emerging from her bloated vagina and driving into her young body again, she swivelled her hips and pressed her erect clitoris against his sex-creamed shaft. Hoping that they'd come together, she wasn't sure how long she could hold back as the birth of her orgasm stirred deep within her contracting womb. To feel his sperm flooding her tight vagina as she reached her orgasm would be heavenly, she knew, as her head lolled from side to side and her eyes rolled. Lost in her ecstasy, quivering uncontrollably in her sexual delirium, she knew that she'd found true love.

Sure that she'd been mistaken about her mother chasing after Tony, she decided to make things up with her. She'd been unfair, unreasonable. It was now obvious to her that Tony had no interest in her mother. Making love, losing their virginity together, there was no way Tony wanted anyone else – least of all her mother. Listening to the squelching of her pussy-milk as Tony quickened his thrusting motions, she threw her head back as she teetered on the brink of her first penis-induced orgasm.

'Here it comes,' Tony said, repeatedly ramming his rock-hard cock deep into her tight pussy.

Her orgasm erupted within the solid nub of her pulsating clitoris as her young vagina swallowed its first deluge of fresh sperm and Desiree cried out in the grip of her pioneering climax. She'd done it, she mused dreamily, her young body rocking with the penile thrusting. Her virginity stripped, she'd not only found love, but womanhood. Nothing would ever come between Tony and her, she swore, as her orgasm peaked. They'd make love every day, announce to the world that they were a couple . . . And she'd tell her mother.

'God, you're a tight-cunted little bitch,' Tony murmured, making his last penile thrusts into her spasming vaginal duct. 'Hot, tight, wet . . . You're the best fuck ever.'

Her orgasm receding as his crude words careered around the confusion littering her mind, Desiree felt empty inside. *A tight-cunted little bitch. You're the best fuck ever.* Shuddering as the last ripples of sex emanated from her swollen clitoris and transmitted deep into her young womb, she hoped that Tony had breathed his harsh words in the heat of the moment. Cold words, crude words . . . Loveless.

'God, that was brilliant,' Tony murmured, slowing his pistoning. 'You're great, Desiree. You're amazing. Not only that, but you're no longer a virgin.'

'Neither are you,' she said softly, focusing on her inner lips encompassing the root of his deflating penis. 'You do love me, don't you?'

'Of course.' He chuckled, finally withdrawing his cock from her sperm-bubbling sex sheath. 'You've got a beautiful little pussy. Hot, and bloody tight.'

'I'd better be going.' Desiree sighed.

'Already?'

'I told my mum that I wouldn't be long.'

'You'll come back later? We can fuck again, Desiree. Again and again.'

'Yes, I . . . I will.'

Grabbing her clothes and dressing, Desiree knew that she should feel awash with happiness. She'd made love, given her virginity to the man she loved . . . Wondering why she wasn't elated, she tossed her long black hair over her shoulder and moved to the door. Tony tugged his trousers on and buttoned his shirt as she hovered by the doorway. That was it, she reflected. Her first time. Frowning as Tony quipped about her tight pussy and said that they'd fuck every day, she wondered where the love was. Surely they should have hugged, kissed, their bodies entwined in passion after having sex?

'My mum reckons that you've had loads of women,' she finally said.

'How would she know?' he returned.

'Instinct, I suppose. Tony, I am the first, aren't I?'

'Of course you are. Do you think I've lied to you?'

'No, no . . . It's just that . . .'

'I could ask you the same question, Desiree. Was it your first time? Or have you screwed around?'

'You know very well that it was my first time.'

'Do I? You're young and attractive. You must come into contact with hundreds of boys at the college. Perhaps you told them all that it was your first time?'

'Tony, that's a terrible thing to say. I was a virgin.'

'And so was I, Desiree. I don't know why you bother to listen to your bloody mother. All she does is try to cause trouble between us. I'll see you later, OK?'

'OK.' She sighed, leaving the room.

Making her way to the bushes, Desiree felt more confused than ever. Tony had seemed cold after they'd made love. Cold and loveless. Hovering in the bushes, she recalled lifting her skirt and allowing Tony to lick her sex crack. This was their special meeting place, she reflected dolefully as she felt his sperm streaming from her inflamed vagina and soaking into her tight panties. She'd bought a thong, sucked the sperm from his knob, allowed him to make love to her ... Why did this feel so very wrong?

'You were a long time,' Belinda said as Desiree stepped into the kitchen. 'Are you all right?'

'Yes, I'm fine,' Desiree said softly, averting her gaze.

'What's happened, Desiree? Something's wrong, I know it.'

'Nothing's wrong, Mum,' she returned agitatedly.

'It's Tony, isn't it? What's he said to you now?'

'He hasn't said anything. I'm fine, OK?'

'I don't like you going round to see him.'

'You've made that crystal clear. Every day, you make it crystal clear. I don't know why you don't mind your own bloody business.'

'You *are* my business, Desiree. You're sixteen and, while you're living under my roof ...'

'God, not another lecture?'

'We need to talk, Desiree.'

'What about?'

'About you, Tony, your college work, the situation ... Since Tony moved in next door, you've neglected your work, you've called me a slut and –'

'I don't want to talk about it, Mum.'

'I know you don't, but I do. We can't go on like this. Before Tony arrived on the scene, you were happy. You helped me with the garden and ... No, *I* helped *you* with the garden. We went for walks and went shopping together. We enjoyed cooking, watching TV and ...'

'I know, I know.' Desiree sighed. 'I'm sorry I called you a slut. I don't know what's happened to me. I feel ... I don't know how I feel. When you met your first ever boyfriend, how did you feel? After you'd had sex for the first time, I mean.'

'My first time?' Belinda said, wondering whether Tony had got his hands on her virgin daughter. 'Well, it was nice, warm and loving ... I felt very close to him after that. It didn't last, of course. First boyfriends

165

never seem to last. I told you that I had several boyfriends. I was looking for something. Looking for something in someone. I now realise that I didn't know what I was looking for.'

'I suppose that's how I feel,' Desiree confessed. 'I'm looking for something, but I don't know what it is.'

'Has Tony ... I mean ...'

'No, Mum. Tony is a friend and nothing more.'

'Do you want more?'

'Yes, I do. But, all the time he has a girlfriend, I don't stand a chance.'

'Why not look around for someone of your own age? There are lots of boys at the college. Surely there must be one that you like?'

'Yes, I like several of them. But I wouldn't want to go out with them. Boys of my age are inherently stupid and childish. Tony is ... He's understanding, caring, and good company.'

'And he has a girlfriend. Someone will come along, Desiree. You'll just have to be patient. Of course, all the time you're wanting Tony, you'll not find anyone else.'

'Do you really think that he's been with a lot of women?'

'You say that he has a girlfriend, so there's one for starters. Look at it this way. For a good-looking man of twenty-seven to still be a virgin ... There must be something very wrong with him.'

'Not all men have sex.'

'No, they don't. But Tony has his own house, a good job, he travels around the world ... You can't believe that he's a virgin, Desiree.'

'I'd better get on with some work. I'll see you later.'

'OK. I'll be in the garden.'

Stepping out onto the patio as Desiree went up to her room, Belinda felt relieved to think that she'd at last been able to talk to her daughter. The notion that Tony was a virgin was ridiculous, and she hoped that Desiree could now see that. But, what had caused the girl to talk about first-time sex? she wondered. Why had she talked about first-time sex the minute she'd returned from Tony's house? Feeling that she was at last winning her daughter over, she wondered whether she could cut her ties with Tony. Although she'd enjoyed hard sex with him, she knew that it couldn't last. If Desiree lost interest in him, then his threats would be empty.

Belinda grabbed a fork and started digging over the flower border. After her self-induced orgasm in the bushes, she felt relaxed and calm, and was able to think of things other than sex with Tony. Perhaps that was the answer, she mused: resort to masturbation every time her libido hit the roof. Desiree would never discover that her mother masturbated, and Brian would be none the wiser. Hoping that the nightmare was coming to an end, she looked up and smiled as Tony walked across his lawn to the fence.

'Nice day,' she said, forking around the flowers.

'It was particularly nice this morning.' He chortled. 'Hot, tight . . .'

'Isn't it about time you started on your garden?' Belinda interrupted him. 'This weather won't last forever.'

'All in good time,' he said. 'Have you shaved your pussy yet?'

'No, Tony,' she returned. 'And I'm not going to. I'm a happily married woman. I don't want you, I don't need you, and neither does Desiree.'

'Really? In that case, why has she been begging me for sex?'

'Don't delude yourself, Tony.'

'Not more than fifteen minutes ago, she begged me to have sex with her. Seeing as I have you to fuck, I sent her packing.'

'You live in a fantasy world, don't you? Trying to play one off against the other when the truth of the matter is that neither of us wants you. I reckon that

167

Desiree took a mild interest in you at first, but she soon discovered that –'

'A mild interest?' he echoed mockingly. 'Would you call dropping her panties taking a mild interest in me?'

'Don't be ridiculous. Desiree would never do such a thing.'

'Wouldn't she? Perhaps I'll invite her round this evening and –'

'She's going out this evening. In fact, she's staying at a friend's house overnight.'

'I have influence over Desiree. I have power over her.'

'Of course you do.' Belinda chuckled.

'I'll prove to you how I have her under my thumb. I'll invite her to my place this evening, and she'll cancel whatever arrangements she's made.'

'You do that, Tony. You go and play your games and I'll get on with the garden.'

Stabbing at the ground with the fork as Tony went back into his house, Belinda was fuming. Again, Tony was riling her, trying to cause trouble. After all they'd talked about, after their agreement, he was still harping on about Desiree, making lewd comments about the girl. Belinda reckoned that the only way forwards was to keep working on Desiree, keep drumming into her head the fact that Tony has had hundreds of women and is only interested in yet another sexual conquest.

Doing her best to forget about Tony and carry on with the garden, Belinda again became acutely aware of her knickerless pussy, her hairless vaginal lips. Recalling Tony's solid cock shafting her tight rectum, she felt a quiver run through her womb. This was ridiculous, she thought agitatedly. Sex was continually playing on her mind, beginning to rule her. Wishing that she'd not shaved her vulval flesh, she gave up with the garden and went back into the house.

'Tony just rang,' Desiree said, joining her mother in the kitchen.

'Oh?'

'He's invited me out this evening.'

'That figures.'

'What do you mean?'

'I was talking to him in the garden just now. He was saying that some girl or other has let him down. He invited me round for a drink, but I declined.'

'He invited you round?'

'Yes, but I don't really want to become too friendly with him. He's all right as a neighbour, but that's about as far as it goes.'

'You don't like him, do you?'

'It's funny to hear you say that. Particularly after you accused me of chasing after him. To be honest, no, I don't like him. He's not truthful, he leches after women . . .'

'How do you know that?'

'He has no idea how to treat a lady, Desiree. From certain things he's said, I reckon that he has no respect for women. He uses them, it's as simple as that. Anyway, I thought you were staying at a friend's house tonight?'

'Yes, I . . . I am. I haven't accepted Tony's invitation.'

'No doubt he'll find some woman or other to keep him company.'

'I think I'll go to Jane's house now. I've packed my things. She said to turn up whenever I was ready.'

'All right. I'll see you tomorrow, then. After college.'

'OK. Bye, Mum.'

Feeling triumphant as Desiree grabbed her bag from her room and left the house, Belinda was positive that this was the way to play things. The more she dropped derogatory hints and comments about Tony, the more Desiree would doubt the man. Again aware of her hairless pussy, Belinda knew that she was going to have to deny herself the pleasure of Tony's solid cock. If she could push all thoughts of sex from her mind and get back into gardening ... Was that possible? she pondered, as she felt her sex-milk flowing. Her clitoris rousing, again calling for her intimate attention, she knew that she had to fight her overwhelming desire for her neighbour's penis.

Ten

Waking to the sun streaming in through her bedroom window, Belinda was pleased to think that Desiree had spent the night at her friend's place. Tony had phoned and knocked on the front door several times during the evening, but Belinda had ignored him. Things might be changing at long last, she mused. She wondered, as she lay on her back and slipped her hand between her parted thighs, whether Desiree could stay at her friend's place for a few days. Also, she thought it odd that Tony hadn't yet been to work. He was supposed to have been going to Ireland, she reflected, her fingertips running up and down the hairless valley of her vulva.

Belinda pictured Tony's erect penis as she slipped her free hand beneath her thigh and drove two fingers deep into her yearning vagina. She imagined his swollen knob bloating her mouth. Massaging her solid clitoris and breathing deeply as her arousal soared, she licked her succulent lips. She could almost taste the salt of his purple glans as she imagined probing his knob-slit with her wet tongue. What was it about Tony? she pondered. He was crude, arrogant, obnoxious ... And yet she couldn't stop thinking about him.

Desiree had obviously seen something in Tony, Belinda reflected as she massaged the wet inner flesh of her tightening vagina. At least the girl wasn't thinking about his cock, she mused dreamily, as her clitoris

171

swelled. At least Desiree wasn't imagining Tony's purple knob bloating her pretty mouth; his sperm bathing her darting tongue. Sure that her daughter didn't even masturbate, let alone have lewd thoughts about the man next door, Belinda found herself thinking about her husband.

Brian was hard working, caring, loving ... But he seemed to have no sex drive at all. Many times when they were first married, Belinda had woken in the mornings and grabbed his cock. She'd attempted to wank him, but he'd always leaped out of bed and complained that it was getting late. She'd often slipped beneath the quilt and taken his knob into her sperm-thirsty mouth, but his only response was to push her away and talk about getting to work on time.

'Good morning,' Tony said, appearing in the doorway and almost giving Belinda a heart attack.

'God!' Belinda exclaimed, staring wide-eyed at him. 'What the ... How the hell did you get into my house?'

'I slipped the catch on your front door,' he replied. 'With Desiree away, I thought you might be having a lie in.'

'Get out,' Belinda snapped, eyeing his shorts, his naked chest. 'How dare you break into my house and walk into my bedroom. What if my husband had ...'

'He's in Tokyo, Belinda. Don't you want me to attend to your feminine needs and satisfy your sexual desires?'

'No, I don't.'

'So, this is the marital bedroom where it all happens? Or, doesn't happen.'

'Get out, Tony. Desiree might be back at any time.'

'The marital bed.' He chortled. 'Is this where you get fucked senseless every day?'

'I don't know who the hell you think you are,' Belinda hissed, 'but you're not welcome in my house. And certainly not my bedroom.'

'I don't know about you but, when I wake up in the mornings, I always feel really horny.' Lowering his

172

shorts and displaying his erect penis, he grinned at her. 'There, see what I mean?'

Although Belinda couldn't believe his audacity as she gazed at the solid shaft of his erect penis, she knew that she was going to have one hell of a battle denying herself the pleasure of his rock-hard erection. Imagining him walking into Desiree's bedroom and dropping his shorts, she knew that she was going to have to be strong. Unless she won this battle, he'd be marching into the house whenever he wanted sex. If she happened to be out and Desiree was in her bedroom ... He wouldn't dare, would he?

'I'm your dream come true,' he quipped, standing by the bed with his massive penis pointing to the ceiling.

'My nightmare come true, don't you mean? Please, Tony, I want you to leave.'

'Leave? You mean, you don't want my hard cock sliding deep into your wet and very tight little cunt?'

'No, I don't. This is my bedroom, for God's sake. This is the bed I share with my husband. I'm not going to –'

'How often does he fuck you, Belinda? How often does he spunk down your throat or cream your tight little arsehole?'

'He ... Get out, Tony.'

'Does he lick and suck your clitoris to multiple orgasms? Does he drink the girl-juice from your tight cunt?'

'That's enough. Get out of my house, and stay out.'

'All right, if that's what you want.'

'It is what I want.'

Watching him pull his shorts up and walk to the door, Belinda felt her vaginal muscles contract, a quiver run through her womb. She had to let him go, she knew, as he turned in the doorway and faced her. His shorts were bulging with his manhood, his balls would be full ... She had to lay down some rules. To have him wandering

173

into her bedroom with his hard cock exposed and his heavy balls rolling was despicable. Who the hell did he think he was? she ruminated. What the hell did she think she was? A common slut? A horny housewife desperate for a quick fuck?

'Desiree will be coming to see me after college,' he said, adjusting his rampant cock through his bulged shorts. 'Perhaps she'll be a little more accommodating than her mother.'

'Desiree will be away for a few days,' Belinda lied. 'So much for your influence over her. She didn't want to see you last night. She said that she'd rather spend the night at her friend's house.'

'She's away for a few days? So, you'll be all alone in the house. You'll be desperate for sex, won't you? What will you do?'

'Get on with the garden and –'

'And frig your clitty off? Are you sure that you don't want this?'

'Perfectly sure,' she said as he lowered his shorts and rolled his foreskin back.

'It's yours for the taking, Belinda. All you have to do is ask.'

'I . . . I can't,' she stammered, fighting to resist temptation. 'This is my bedroom. My husband and I . . .'

'Just say, yes, and this is yours,' he said, running his hand up and down his veined shaft. 'Look at it, Belinda. It's rock hard, desperate to slide deep into your hot cunt, desperate to pump you full of sperm. Are you thirsty? Are you thirsty for spunk? Look at my balls. Rolling, full . . . Just say, yes.'

'Yes,' she whispered, the word tumbling from her lips without her thinking.

Again standing by the bed, he retracted his fleshy foreskin and offered his purple plum to her sperm-thirsty mouth. Belinda sat upright, parting her full lips as she gazed longingly at his swollen glans, his spunk-slit. She knew that this was wrong. Another man in the marital bedroom, his cock standing to attention, his balls in dire need of draining ... But, weak in the powerful grip of her arousal, she'd lost the battle. She was a slut, she reflected, as she took his sex globe into her mouth and savoured the taste of his salt. Once a slut, always a slut.

Kneading his heaving balls, she gripped his hard shaft with her free hand as took his ripe plum to the back of her throat. Sinking her teeth gently into his fleshy rod, closing her eyes and savouring the moment, she did her best to blot out haunting images of her husband. This was their bedroom, she ruminated. The marital bedroom. They'd made love in this very bed, they'd loved, argued, dreamed ... *Let no man put asunder*.

'You're a cock-sucking little slut,' Tony said softly as she suckled on his purple knob like a babe at the breast. 'A dirty little spunk-guzzling whore. Is your cunt nice and wet? Is your tight little cunt ready for a good cock-shafting? The marital bedroom,' he quipped, clutching her head and rocking his hips. 'An adulterous mouth-fucking in the marital bedroom.'

His harsh words hurting her mind, she felt dirty: wanton in her lechery; guilty in her adulterous betrayal. This was Desiree's fault, she tried to convince herself. This was her husband's fault. Had Desiree not taken an interest in Tony, had Brian treated his wife like a whore ... She was hooked on Tony now, she knew, as he continued to talk dirty to her. *Spunk-loving slag, mouth-fucking little tart* ... There was no way she could live without hard, cold sex.

When her husband returned to the marital home, Belinda knew that she'd have to sneak round to Tony's house for crude, satisfying sex. If Brian was at home when she needed sexual gratification, she'd creep into the bushes at the end of the garden and allow Tony to fuck her. She'd stand in the garden chatting to her neighbour with her arm over the fence. She'd wank him, bring out his spunk and then lick her fingers clean and savour the taste of his orgasmic cream. Brian would be none the wiser. Dangerous games; exciting games of illicit sex. It wasn't Desiree's fault, she concluded. It wasn't her husband's fault. She was a wanton whore, and only had herself to blame for her sluttish adultery.

'Want it in your spunk-thirsty mouth or your cock-hungry cunt?' Tony asked her, his body trembling as she gobbled on his penis-head. 'Or maybe you want your sweet arse fucked rotten?' Yanking the quilt back, he gazed in awe at her hairless pussy lips rising alluringly either side of her vulval crack. 'Good girl,' he praised her. Slipping his cock out of her hot mouth, he grinned. 'Clean shaven and ready for my cock. I'm pleased to see that you're an obedient sex slave. Now, I want you to open your legs as wide as you can.'

Lying on her back with her legs spread, she closed her eyes. He kicked his shorts aside and settled between her thighs. He grabbed his solid member by the root and stabbed at her gaping vaginal hole with his purple knob. It had been so long since Brian had positioned himself on top of her in the marital bed, so long since she'd felt the solid rod of his cock penetrate her, shaft her, fuck her and spunk her. Was it any wonder that she'd invited another man into her bed? she reflected. After years of a virtually asexual marriage, she needed a real man, a hard cock to satisfy her.

Tony eased his knob into her contracting vaginal duct, thrust forwards and impaled her fully on his rock-hard penis. Belinda gasped, her fingernails digging into the mattress as he withdrew and again rammed his bulbous glans deep into her hot sex sheath. Brian should have been doing this, she mused. He should have been more attentive, more sexual, crude in his love-making. Her lower stomach rising with every thrust of Tony's cock, Belinda arched her back and breathed deeply.

'I'll do your tight arse next,' Tony said, his grinning face looking down at Belinda. 'You'd like that, wouldn't you?'

'Yes,' she murmured, her eyes rolling as she lost herself in her sexual frenzy.

'I'll force my hard cock deep into your hot bum and spunk you.'

'Yes, yes,' she again murmured, her head lolling from side to side. 'Fuck my cunt, my mouth, my arse ... Fuck all my holes, hard.'

'What do you fuck yourself with when your husband's away? Bananas, a cool cucumber, a candle? I'll bet you have a vibrator. Do you vibrate your clitty and bring yourself off?'

Saying nothing as she listened to the squelching of her pussy-milk, Belinda knew that she was going to be masturbating regularly from now on. Even with Tony to satisfy her lust for orgasm, there would be times when she needed to relieve her sexual tension. A cucumber? she pondered, as he increased his shafting rhythm. Desiree must never be exposed to her mother's crudities, she reflected. The problem was that the girl came home at different times. Calling home at lunchtime, finishing early some afternoons ... To have Tony in the marital bed might turn out to be a fatal mistake.

Again pondering on leading two lives – the dirty tart and the loving wife – she knew that Brian would be working abroad even more in the future. In line for promotion, he'd be spending a lot more time in Tokyo, leaving Belinda wanting, yearning. Her naked body rocking with the illicit shafting of her tightening vagina, she imagined Desiree bounding up the stairs, calling out and walking into the bedroom to discover ... Tony's house would be safer, she decided. They'd be safe in his bed or his sex den.

'Turn over and lie on your front,' Tony instructed her as he yanked his penis out of her sex-drenched pussy.

177

'No, I –' Belinda began.

'Turn over, for God's sake. I want your hot arse.'

Complying, Belinda buried her face in the pillow and jutted her buttocks out. Tony spread her legs, holding her bottom orbs apart and stabbing at her tight brown hole as she gripped the edges of the pillow. Recalling her initiation to anal sex the day before, she'd enjoyed the feel of his rock-hard cock penetrating her there. The stretching and bloating of her rectum had sent delightful quivers running through her womb. But it was the thought of being used and abused that had sent her arousal to frightening heights. The very notion of committing the crudest possible sexual act had woken sleeping desires, sleeping monsters.

Tony's crude words resounded around the marital bedroom as his bulbous glans journeyed along the tight duct of her rectum. Belinda breathed deeply into the pillow. *Anal whore, tight-arsed little slut* . . . The delicate brown tissue surrounding her anus stretched to capacity, gripping the root of his massive cock as he impaled her fully. She spread her legs wider and raised her bottom to allow him deeper access to the very core of her naked body.

'Fuck me hard,' she murmured into the pillow.

'I will.' He chortled. 'You can be sure of that.'

'Ram your cock deep into my arse and fuck me senseless.'

'You need me, Belinda. Even when your husband is back, you'll need me, won't you?'

'Yes, yes. I need your cock, your spunk. Fuck me, now. Fuck my arse hard.'

The true nature of her character had finally surfaced, she knew, as Tony began his illicit thrusting motions. Sexually used and abused, her once-sacrosanct bottom hole shafted by her neighbour's solid cock, she wallowed in the forbidden union of adulterous sex. She could no longer suppress her craving for debased sexual

178

gratification, no longer pretend to be happy and satisfied in her marriage. Although she could no longer use Desiree as an excuse for committing adultery, preserving the girl's virginity was still in her mind. Two birds with one stone, she mused dreamily, as Tony grabbed her hips and pulled her up onto her knees.

Watching his balls swinging between her thighs as he shafted her rectal canal, she slipped her fingertips into her valley of desire and massaged the solid nub of her insatiable clitoris. Her sex-milk streamed from her neglected vagina and ran over her slender fingers. She rocked her hips to meet his thrusts as he quickened his anal pistoning rhythm. She was going to come, she knew, as her breathing became fast and shallow and her heart banged hard against her chest. She was going to reach a massive orgasm in the marital bed . . . with another man.

'Yes,' Tony cried, his sperm, jetting from his throbbing knob and lubricating her anal cylinder. She could feel his creamy spunk filling her, flooding and cooling her hot bowels as he drained his heavy balls. Reaching her own climax, she massaged her pulsating clitoris faster and harder and drifted on clouds of orgasm as her naked body shook uncontrollably. This was real sex, she mused in her sexual craze. Her orgasm peaking, sending shock waves of pleasure throughout her glowing body, she lifted her head off the pillow and let out a scream of pleasure.

Catching a glimpse of her wedding photograph on the bedside table, she realised that she no longer felt guilty. She was a good wife and mother, she decided. She looked after the house, cooked nice meals and cared for her husband and daughter. What she did in her own time, her private time, had nothing to do with her family. It would be possible to lead two completely separate lives, she concluded. There was no reason that her two lives should interfere with each other. As long as she was very careful.

Yelping as Tony's palm met the taut flesh of her rounded buttock with a deafening slap, she felt her anal sphincter muscles tighten and grip his thrusting cock like a velvet-jawed vice. Again, he slapped her naked bottom hard. The spanking becoming a severe thrashing, and she cried out as the pain and pleasure mingled and rocked her very soul. Massaging her pulsating clitoris, sustaining her incredible orgasm, she again caught sight of her wedding photograph. Brian looked content, she looked happy. Their big day. *Let no man put asunder*.

'You're the best arse-fuck I've ever had,' Tony said, breaking her reverie. 'If your husband doesn't fuck your tight little bottom, there must be something very wrong with him.'

'There's nothing wrong with him,' Belinda said in his defence. 'He loves me, and this sort of thing isn't part of our loving.'

'You're a lucky little cow.' He chuckled, slowing his penile thrusting to a gentle shafting. 'You have your husband to love you, and me to fuck you. The best of both worlds.'

'Take your cock out now. I feel as though I'm on fire inside.'

'I'll leave it there for a while, Belinda. Leave it deep inside your bum for a while longer so you can enjoy every last moment. Does Desiree have the best of both worlds?'

'What do you mean?'

'She has a loving mother and a good home. But does she have sexual satisfaction?'

'I don't want you talking about Desiree. Leave her out of this.'

'But, she's very much a part of this.'

'She'll never be a part of such sordid . . .'

'What would you say if I told you that I've already fucked her?'

'I'd call you a liar. Please, take your cock out of my bum.'

'You're not very astute or intuitive, are you?' he asked her, finally sliding his cock out of her sperm-bubbling rectum. 'Haven't you noticed the change in Desiree?'

'Change?' Belinda echoed, deciding not to allow him to rile her. She rolled over onto her back and looked up at him. 'She's forgotten about you now, Tony. She was infatuated at first, but now –'

'Now, she's no longer a virgin.'

'In that case, you can forget about blackmailing me,' she returned nonchalantly. 'If you and Desiree have made love, then –'

'I didn't make love to her, Belinda. I fucked her.'

'You're off on your dreams again,' she said, forcing a giggle.

'I like your shaved cunt,' he murmured, yanking her thighs wide apart. 'Smooth, soft ... But Desiree is far more obedient than you.'

'What are you talking about?' she asked him as he drove two fingers deep into the hugging sheath of her vagina. 'Desiree is obedient? What do you mean?'

'She shaved her cunt without question. Whereas you –'

'Please, don't talk about my daughter like that,' Belinda cut in. 'How many times do I have to tell you not to bring Desiree into this?'

'The proof of the pudding is in the eating,' he quipped, forcing a third finger deep into her spasming sex duct. 'And the proof of her shaving is in her panties.'

Saying nothing as Tony lay full length on the bed and licked her swollen clitoris, Belinda knew that he was trying to cause trouble again. His fingers slid in and out of her tightening vagina, sending ripples of sex deep into her contracting womb. She knew that Desiree would never shave her pubic hair. Why did he have to try to cause trouble all the time? she pondered, as her insatiable clitoris swelled beneath his snaking tongue. He was a dreamer, she mused as he sucked her solid clitoris into his hot mouth. A dreamer, a troublemaker . . .

'You love having your cunt fingered and your clitty sucked, don't you?' Tony said. His wet tongue lapped at her solid sex button. 'You don't have to pretend with me, Belinda. I'm not your husband, so you can be your real self, behave like the slut that you really are.'

'I wish you'd shut up and get on with it,' she snapped.

'You want another orgasm?'

'Yes, very much.'

'Beg me, Belinda. Beg me to make you come.'

'Please, make me come.'

'Beg me to finger-fuck your tight cunt and suck your clitty to orgasm.'

'For God's sake . . . Please, finger-fuck my tight cunt and suck my clitty to orgasm.'

She closed her eyes as he stretched her fleshy outer lips apart to the extreme, and then let out a rush of breath as he again sucked hard on her painfully erect clitoris. His fingers bloated her vaginal cavern and his sperm squeezed out of the inflamed eye of her anus, as she tweaked her erect nipples to add to her incredible pleasure. Pulling on her milk teats, pinching and twisting her brown nipples, she shook fiercely as he managed to force a finger deep into the inflamed duct of her rectum.

He certainly knew how to pleasure a woman, she mused, again losing herself in her heightening arousal. He also knew how to rile her. Desiree would never shave her pubic hair, would she? *I didn't make love to her, Belinda. I fucked her.* He was lying, she was sure. Desiree was a good girl, a studious girl . . . She was sixteen years old, and her hormones would be rousing, stirring. Why had she talked about first-time sex? She'd not allow a man almost old enough to be her father to make love to her. *I didn't make love to her, Belinda. I fucked her.*

The proof of Desiree's shaving would be in her panties, Belinda reflected, recalling Tony's words. He was lying, he had to be. But there was no way Belinda would be able to find out. Desiree never walked around the house naked. And, if she *had* shaved, she'd make sure that her mother didn't glimpse her young pussy. Tony was a bastard, Belinda mused, as he stirred her vaginal cream with his fingers and repeatedly swept his tongue over the sensitive tip of her erect clitoris. A lying, troublemaking bastard. But she needed him, she knew. She needed his cock.

'I love shaved pussies,' he said, painfully stretching her vaginal lips further apart as he massaged the inner flesh of her rectum.

'You haven't touched my daughter, have you?' Belinda asked him, immediately wishing she hadn't brought up the subject.

'I've fucked her.' He laughed. 'I've fucked her shaved cunt.'

'I've never met anyone as coarse as you. It's no wonder you never married. No one would marry a man like you.'

'I have no wish to get married, Belinda. I'm single and free. Free to fuck sweet little sixteen-year-old girls. And their sluttish, sex-starved mothers.'

'Only in your dreams, Tony.'

The birth of her orgasm stirring deep within her contracting womb, Belinda threw her head back and pinched her erect nipples harder. This was heaven, she reflected, as he fingered her tight sex holes simultaneously. Her husband working away, her naked body expertly attended by another man, she knew that she could never say no to Tony. Whenever he wanted her, whenever he needed to use her for cold sex, she'd go running to him.

Wondering what she'd become as her naked body became rigid, she reckoned that Tony didn't stand a chance of getting anywhere near Desiree. Belinda was a slut, but her daughter certainly wasn't.

'Don't stop,' she cried as her clitoris exploded in orgasm. Her pussy-milk gushing from her finger-bloated vaginal sheath, her sex button pulsating wildly, she tossed her head from side to side and again cried out in the grip of her forbidden climax. 'God, my . . . my beautiful cunt.' Her orgasm rocking her naked body, her eyes rolling, she grabbed Tony's head and ground the wet flesh of her open sex valley hard against his mouth. Barely able to breathe as she locked his head between her thighs, he sucked on her pulsating clitoris and double-fingered the burning sheath of her vagina and her tightening rectal duct.

Again and again, tremors of sex crashed through her naked body, tightening every muscle and reaching every nerve ending. Her inflamed rectum burning like fire as he crudely fingered her there, she convulsed wildly on her bed in the grip of her debased pleasure. Desiree should never experience this, she mused in her druglike state. Both holes fingered, a massive orgasm sucked out of her painfully swollen clitoris . . . The girl should never be subjected to such crude and immense sexual pleasure. Tony didn't want Desiree, did he? Was jealousy rearing its ugly head?

Her pleasure finally subsiding, she released Tony's head and allowed him to pant for breath. Was jealousy surfacing? Belinda again wondered in the aftermath of her mind-blowing climax. Did she want to keep her daughter away from Tony because she wanted him for herself? Confused in her dizziness, she dreaded to think that Tony would want to pleasure her daughter like this. Desiree was young, attractive, slim with rock-hard tits and a tight little pussy and . . . Belinda was sure that she wasn't jealous of her young daughter. The very idea was ludicrous, wasn't it?

'God, that was the front door,' Belinda whispered, propping herself up on her elbows. 'Desiree must be back.'

'Lock the door,' Tony said, leaping off the bed.

'There's no lock. I'll go down and take her out into the garden. You leave by the front door once we're outside.'

'I might stay here, naked in the marital bedroom.' He chuckled softly.

'Don't be stupid,' Belinda snapped, slipping into her dressing gown. 'This is no time for your crazy games. Get out as soon as it's safe.'

Belinda bounded down the stairs, her hands trembling, adrenalin coursing through her veins, and slipped into the kitchen. Relieved to see Desiree hovering on the patio, she hoped that Tony wouldn't do anything stupid as she brushed her long black hair back with her fingers. If he hung around and Desiree discovered him in the house . . . This was a nightmare, she thought, joining her daughter beneath the summer sun. Another close shave. This time, too close for comfort.

'No college?' she asked the girl nonchalantly.

'Oh, hi,' Desiree said, turning and facing her mother. 'I've got some work to do at home today. It's OK, they know about it. I'm not bunking off.'

'I . . . I was about to have a shower,' Belinda lied, again hoping that Tony had left. 'If you'd like to sit out here, I'll make you some coffee.'

'No, I think I'll go up to my room and start work.'

'Er . . . I was going to ask you about the garden.'

'Oh?'

'I thought we might get a couple of shrubs and –'

'Mum, I'm not really in the mood to discuss the garden.'

'Oh, all right. Did you sleep well?'

'No, I didn't. I have things on my mind.'

'Do you want to talk about it?'

'I don't know.' Desiree sighed, finally sitting on a patio chair. 'I was talking to a couple of friends last night. We were chatting about relationships and ... I told them about Tony.'

'And?'

'They don't think he's too old for me. I know that you're not happy about it, but ...'

'Desiree, do you have a relationship with Tony? I think it's time that you were honest with me.'

'Well ...'

'Talk to me, Desiree. You used to be able to talk to me.'

'Yes, we have a relationship,' she finally confessed. 'You make some coffee, and we'll talk about it.'

'All right,' Belinda said, her hands trembling again as she stepped into the kitchen.

Her mind swirling with a thousand thoughts as she filled the kettle, Belinda prayed that Tony hadn't touched the girl. If they had sex and ... Was he screwing both mother and daughter? she wondered anxiously. Had that been his intention from day one? He was a bastard, she knew. But would he really play one off against the other. Had he driven his cock into Belinda's vagina and then screwed Desiree? Had he slipped his cock into Desiree's vagina and then commanded Belinda to suck it? Dreading her daughter's confession as she poured the coffee, she knew that she had to remain calm. This wasn't Desiree's fault, she reminded herself.

'Coffee,' she said with a smile, placing the cups on the patio table. 'So, you and Tony ... you have a proper relationship?'

'Yes, we do.'

'What about his girlfriend? You said that ...'

'He hasn't got a girlfriend,' Desiree confessed. 'I ... I made that up so you wouldn't worry about me.'

'Oh, er ... I see. What's been playing on your mind, then?'

186

'Tony says that he's a virgin, you say that he's had loads of girls . . . I'm confused.'

'This relationship . . . How far have you gone?'

'We . . . Well, only touching.'

'So, you've not actually . . .'

'No,' Desiree lied. 'Not yet.'

Breathing a sigh of relief, Belinda knew that it was only a matter of time before Tony sank his penis into Desiree's vagina. How long did she have to put a stop to this? she wondered. How long did she have to save her daughter's virginity? At least the girl was talking about it, she mused, as she sipped her coffee. Turning her thoughts to Tony, again thinking what a bastard he was, she reckoned that she was going to have to have Desiree catch him in the act. Another woman in his house, a naked woman . . . But, how the hell was she going to set it up? The idea was a non-starter, she decided. All she could do was talk to Desiree, keep working on her and hope that she could preserve her virginity. Had Tony fingered the girl?

'The reason that I didn't want you and Tony to get together was because I didn't want to see you get hurt,' Belinda said, toying with her coffee cup.

'I won't get hurt, Mum,' Desiree returned.

'Won't you? Tony is twenty-seven years old. He's been around the world, met women, no doubt gone into bars and clubs . . . Do you honestly believe that he's never touched another woman?'

'Well, I . . . That's why I'm confused. I agree with you that it seems rather odd that a man of his age hasn't done anything. He swears that he's a virgin, but . . .'

'But, you don't believe him?'

'I want to believe him, Mum. But I can't. I know that you don't like him, I know that he's twenty-seven, I know that he's been around the world . . . But I love him. If he's not a virgin, if he's lying, then it's because he doesn't want to hurt me.'

'But, he *is* hurting you. Can't you see that? You're confused, you didn't sleep properly . . . He *is* hurting you, Desiree.'

'I'd better get on with my work.' Desiree sighed, finishing her coffee and leaving the table.

'My advice is . . . don't do anything yet. Don't lose your virginity yet.'

'Yes, well . . . I'd better do my work.'

Fuming as the girl went into the house, Belinda decided to have this out with Tony. He'd touched her, probably fondled her breasts and fingered her vagina and . . . Had she touched him? she wondered fearfully. Had he taught her how to wank his cock and bring out his spunk? If she'd sucked his knob, swallowed his spunk and . . . Recalling her teenage years, she knew that she'd have been only too eager to suck a cock and drink the creamy spunk. How many boys had come in her mouth? she wondered. How much sperm had she swallowed?

Anger welling in the pit of her stomach, she went up to her room and slipped into her summer dress. The time had come to deal with Tony once and for all. No more lies or threats or deals. No more stupid games. The time had come to put a stop to his nonsense. Hearing Desiree tapping on her computer keyboard, she slipped downstairs and left by the back door. Desiree was so young and innocent, she mused, as she crossed the lawn to the bushes. To think that Tony had had his hand inside her knickers, to think that he'd squeezed her breasts . . . If she'd gripped his cock, wanked him and brought out his sperm, then it would not be long before he was shafting her virgin pussy.

Eleven

'Tony rang while you were in the shower,' Desiree said excitedly as she finished her breakfast. 'He's home this afternoon.'

'Oh, right,' Belinda murmured, her stomach churning. 'The week has gone so quickly.'

'It's dragged by for me. He said that Spain was too hot. At least the computer room he was working in was air conditioned.'

'I still think it odd that he went off to Spain for a week without saying anything.'

'I've already told you that he had a phone call and had to rush off.'

'Without so much as a goodbye?'

'His company sent a taxi for him. There was no time for anything.'

'You've done really well with your studies during the week. I hope you'll continue to work hard.'

'Of course I will. Right, I'm off to college. I'll see you later.'

'All right.'

As Desiree left the house, Belinda again thought it odd that Tony had rushed off without saying anything. He'd sneaked out of her house after that fateful episode in the marital bed, and had dashed off to Spain without a word. At least the week had been quiet, she mused, as she cleared away the breakfast things. Desiree had spent

all her spare time studying, Belinda had enjoyed gardening – things had been back to normal. But, now? Tony
was like a dark cloud, she reflected. The sun had shone
for a week, but now the black cloud was looming on the
horizon.

Pacing the lounge floor for hours, Belinda repeatedly
looked out of the window. She hoped that Tony would
arrive home before Desiree got back from college. She
had to speak to him, make him understand that things
were going to change from now on. No more crude sex,
no more adultery, threats, blackmail, lies and deceit.
Things were going to change. Sex, she mused dolefully,
imagining his hard cock shafting her tight pussy. The
feel of his knob battering her cervix, the taste of his
fresh spunk . . .

Hearing a noise next door, she knew that Tony was
home. She must have missed him arriving, she mused,
as she left the house by the front door. Walking briskly
up his front path, she didn't want to waste any time.
Desiree might come home early, she thought, ringing
the bell. The first thing the girl would do was to visit
Tony, and Belinda didn't want that. This was going to
end, here and now.

'Ah, it's the little slut,' Tony said as he opened the
door. 'Come in.'

'You can cut that out,' Belinda snapped, walking into
the hall and closing the front door. 'We need to talk.'

'I'd have thought that you'd need to fuck after a
whole week without my cock?' he quipped leading her
into the lounge. 'Have you been fucking yourself with a
cucumber or . . .'

'I had a long talk with Desiree the day you went
away.'

'Oh?'

'She admitted that you've touched her, done things to
her.'

'I told you that I'd fucked her.'

'I know that you haven't gone that far, yet. Desiree is an honest girl. She wouldn't lie to me.'

'OK, so I've fingered her tight little pussy.'

'Has she touched you?'

'No, not yet.'

'Tony, this has got to stop.'

'Why?'

'Because ... You fuck me, and then finger my daughter? Obviously, you plan to have both of us. Is that your kick? Is that your plan: to fuck mother and daughter?'

'I've told you all along that it's you I want.' He sighed. 'You push me away, and I'll go to Desiree for sex.'

'I didn't push you away, for God's sake. I kept to my side of the deal.'

'The day I fingered Desiree's hot little cunt was the day you said that you wanted nothing more to do with me. You seem to be suffering from short-term memory loss.'

'I wanted this to end, Tony. Can't you see that?'

'And I don't want it to end. What we did in your bed was amazing. And I want more. If I don't get it from you, then I'll get it from your daughter. I don't know why you can't accept that.'

'I had accepted it and was going along with you. What I didn't realise was that you were touching my daughter, fingering my daughter. You lied to me.'

'You turned me down, so I went to Desiree. I didn't lie to you, Belinda. I told you what I'd do if you turned me down. I've said all along that it's either you or Desiree. I didn't lie to you. Perhaps you'll believe me now when I tell you that it's either you or Desiree?'

'I ... Please, keep away from her. I'll do anything ...'

'I know you will, Belinda. You'll do anything and everything I tell you. Do you understand?'

'Yes, but you must swear to keep away from Desiree. She'll be round to see you later. Please, tell her that it's over. Tell her that ...'

'All right, I'll do that. Now, I want you to strip naked and go up to my sex den.'

'Yes, yes, anything. But, first, swear on your life that you'll not touch Desiree again.'

'I swear on my life, Belinda. But, the minute you mess me about, then I fuck the girl. So, you'll do as I ask when I ask. Agreed?'

'Agreed.'

Slipping out of her dress, Belinda knew that she was in for a session of sexual abuse. But, as long as Tony kept his word, she'd do anything. To keep him away from Desiree was of paramount importance. He'd already violated her young body by pushing his finger into her young vagina. That was bad enough, she thought anxiously, as she unhooked her bra and pulled her panties down. But it could have been a lot worse.

'Stubble?' Tony remarked, eyeing the hairs sprouting on her vaginal lips. 'This won't do, Belinda. You'll shave the minute you get home. Do you understand?'

'But, my husband . . .'

'That's your problem, not mine. Now, get upstairs.'

Climbing the stairs with Tony following, she knew that he was eyeing the bulge of her pussy lips nestling between her slender thighs. With her womb contracting and her stomach somersaulting, she also knew that she was desperate for crude sex. She'd masturbated every day since he'd been away, sometimes twice a day. She'd thought about his cock, imagined his sperm bathing her tongue, splattering her cervix, filling her bowels . . . But she'd sworn not to succumb to her inner desires and have sex with him. Again, she'd lost the battle.

But she was doing this for Desiree's sake, she reflected as she entered the sex den. No, she mused. The reason was twofold: to keep Desiree safe, and to enjoy hard, cold sex with her neighbour. Brian would notice her shaved pussy, she knew. But she'd come up with some excuse or other. Whether he believed her or not didn't matter. She'd rather have to try to explain her shaved pussy to her husband than to think that Desiree had shaved for Tony.

Following Tony's instructions and standing against the wooden frame, she allowed him to cuff her wrists and ankles. Her naked body bent over as he folded the frame and her long black hair cascaded over the floor. She looked up between her thighs as he knelt behind her and parted the firm cheeks of her bare bottom. This was her life now, she thought, as she felt his wet tongue teasing the sensitive eye of her anus. Crude sex, adultery, lies, deceit, betrayal . . . She was nothing more than a lump of female meat to be used and abused by her master.

'You've been a naughty girl,' Tony said, standing up. 'You haven't been shaving. I told you to keep your pussy shaved for me, and you deliberately ignored my order. That, in my opinion, isn't the way an obedient slave should behave. You leave me no choice, Belinda. I'll have to cane you.'

Saying nothing as he took a thin bamboo cane from the small corner table, Belinda squeezed her eyes shut. He would have caned her whether she'd shaved or not, she knew, as he ran the end of the cane up and down her anal gully. He didn't need an excuse or a reason to thrash her. The first strike of the thin bamboo across her tensed buttocks jolted her naked body and she let out a deafening yelp. Again, the cane bit into the tensed flesh of her naked bottom. She couldn't take too much of this, she knew, as the thin bamboo repeatedly landed across her burning buttocks. Her taut buttocks stung like hell and she felt dizzy. Six lashes, seven, eight . . .

'Please, no more,' she finally cried as the cane flailed her glowing bottom with a deafening crack. Ignoring her, Tony continued with the merciless thrashing. The pain permeated her glowing buttocks and her juices of arousal streamed down her inner thighs. She knew that she was in for an anal shafting the minute Tony had finished thrashing her. No one would know that she'd had anal sex with her next-door neighbour. But the weals fanning out across her crimsoned bottom would remain for at least a week. Evidence of her crude and illicit debauchery.

Breathing a sigh of relief as Tony finally dropped the cane to the floor, she watched as he then took something from a shelf and knelt behind her. He parted the fleshy pads of her outer labia and attached two metal clips to the sensitive wings of her inner lips. Fixing chains to the clips, he chuckled as he explained that she was going to be stretched. Her eyes widened as he hung weights from the chains and she watched the delicate petals of her inner labia pull away from her vaginal valley.

Leaving the heavy weights swinging between her thighs, painfully stretching the engorged petals of her inner labia, Tony grabbed a jar of Vaseline from the shelf. He smeared the grease over her anus, working it deep into her rectum with his finger, and then forced something hard and cold into the tight sheath of her bottom hole. Belinda said nothing as he twisted the shaft and pushed it fully home. This was the crude treatment she was saving her daughter from, she mused, as he rammed a huge vibrator deep into her vaginal canal. This was the crude treatment she'd longed for while Tony had been away. With her sex holes bloated, painfully stretched wide open, she knew that she was a common slut.

'What the hell are you doing?' she asked him as he blindfolded her.

'I'm going to take some photographs,' he replied. 'You don't want to be recognised, do you?'

'God, no,' she said. 'You're a bloody pervert. You have no idea how to treat a –'

'You're no lady,' he cut in. 'I'll remove the blindfold, if you like?'

'No, no. Just get it over with and let me go.'

Hearing movements as she peered into the darkness of the blindfold, she imagined her husband discovering the incriminating photographs. Hoping that the blindfold was enough to conceal her identity, she listened to the camera shutter as Tony took his pornographic pictures. If Desiree saw the evidence of her debauchery, she'd never understand. No one would understand, she knew, as Tony yanked the object out of her rectal canal.

'I'll take a few shots of my cock up your arse,' he said, chuckling. The burning globes of her bottom rudely yanked apart, she felt his bulbous knob pressing hard against her well-greased anus. He was a pervert, she again thought, as his glans slipped past her defeated anal sphincter muscles and peered into the depths of her rectum. But, what was she? Her vaginal sheath bloated by the huge vibrator, she gasped as he forced his solid cock deep into her bottom hole until his knob came to rest in the dank heat of her bowels. He was a pervert. And she was a slut.

The heavy weights swinging between her thighs, painfully stretching the pink wings of her inner labia, she grimaced as he began his thrusting motions. Never had she known such perversity, such degradation and humiliation. The camera shutter clicked as her tethered body rocked with the anal shafting. She thanked God that her face wasn't in shot. At least Tony had had the decency to blindfold her and conceal her identity, but what did he intend to do with the photographs? Sell them to a porn mag? Put them on the internet for all to see?

'Are you ready for my spunk?' Tony asked. Belinda could feel his lower belly slapping her crimsoned buttocks as he increased his shafting rhythm. Remaining silent, she felt her vaginal muscles tighten around the vibrator as her rectal duct flooded with creamy sperm. She knew that, apart from the incredible physical sensations permeating her tethered body, it was the thought of the crude shafting of her bottom hole that was sending her arousal sky-high. Bondage, a naked-bottom caning, the weights stretching her inner lips, a hard anal shafting . . . It was the very idea of the crude sexual abuse of her naked body that was driving her libido to hitherto unknown heights.

'I'll take a few shots of my spunk oozing out of your arsehole,' Tony said. Gasping as she felt his cock slide out of her rectum with a loud sucking sound, Belinda again heard the camera shutter clicking. She needed her freedom now. Her limbs were aching, her buttocks were stinging like hell, her rectal sheath was burning. She needed to go home and take a shower and rest. But Tony had other ideas. Amazed as he again drove his solid cock deep into her bottom, she let out a cry.

'No more,' she pleaded. 'God, please, not again.'

'Again and again.' He sniggered, driving his swollen knob deep into the fiery heat of her bowels. 'Again and again.'

'I don't know how you manage it,' she said. 'You must be some kind of sex machine.'

'I am, Belinda. I am.'

Unable to comprehend his amazing staying power, Belinda listened to the squelching of sperm as he again shafted her inflamed rectal canal with a vengeance. Brian was a wimp in comparison to this sex maniac, she reflected, as the weights swinging from her rubicund inner lips painfully stretched her intimate sex flesh. Brian with his excuses, his weekly shafting and sperming from behind followed by his snoring . . . He was no match for Tony.

Over the years of staid sex, Belinda had forgotten what it was like to enjoy a hard shafting. Tony's dirty talk and his virility had roused her sleeping lust, woken her inner desires. Now, she knew that she couldn't live without Tony and his magnificent cock. Although Brian had done nothing wrong, she realised that she was beginning to dislike him. He was boring, a stick-in-the-mud, unadventurous, he lacked spontaneity ... But he was her husband, she mused. And he was Desiree's father. The marital home, the family unit ...

'More spunk, Belinda.' Tony chuckled. 'That's what you want, isn't it? You want your arse overflowing with spunk.'

'Yes, yes,' she murmured, her rectal duct again tightening around his veined shaft.

Her caned buttocks still stinging, her rectal duct burning, her vagina painfully gripping the vibrator, Belinda felt the second load of orgasmic cream flooding the fiery depths of her bowels. She'd never dreamed that such crude abuse of her naked body could bring her such immense pleasure. Then again, her dreams of hard sex had melted over the years. Everything had melted over the years, she reflected. Her life had become mundane, monotonous ... Until now.

'Your brown ring is dragging along my cock,' Tony announced with a chuckle. 'I can see it pulling away and then disappearing into your bum as I fuck you. Can you feel my knob driving into your bowels?' he asked her. 'Can you feel the spunk filling you?'

'Fuck me,' she said. 'Fuck me senseless.'

Listening to his running commentary, Belinda let out a rush of breath as his balls drained and he finally withdrew his cock from her sperm-brimming rectal sheath. He'd not be able to shaft her again, she was sure, as she heard movements behind her. She hoped that she'd finally be allowed her freedom as the wooden frame was moved to the upright position. She squinted as Tony removed the blindfold. Shaking her head, her long black hair cascading down her naked back, she clung to the frame to support her sagging body as he released the handcuffs.

'That'll be enough for now,' he said as she turned and faced him. 'I'll give you another arse-fucking this evening.'

'I have to go home,' she said shakily, pulling the metal clips off her distended inner lips and tugging the vibrator out of her inflamed vagina. 'I need to rest and –'

'And shave the stubble off your pussy,' he cut in.

'Yes, I will.'

'You enjoyed that, didn't you? You enjoyed an arse-fucking.'

'Yes, I did. Tony, I . . .'

'You what? What's the problem?'

'Nothing.'

'I'll show you the photographs when you come back this evening.'

'I don't want to see them,' she returned, opening the door. 'I have some thinking to do. I'm confused and . . .'

'There's no reason to be confused,' he said. 'You want my cock up your arse. There's nothing confusing about that. I'll see you later, slave,' he called as she left the sex den.

Belinda made her way downstairs and hurriedly dressed in Tony's lounge. She didn't think that she'd be able to sit down for a week. Her buttocks stung like hell as she tugged her panties on. She headed for the back door and made her escape into the garden. Sperm oozed from the inflamed iris of her anus and soaked into the tight material of her panties as she slipped through the bushes and walked across the lawn to the patio. She needed a shower; she needed to rest. If Desiree came home and found her mother in this state . . . She dashed into the lounge and answered the phone and her heart leaped into her mouth as Brian asked her how she was.

'Fine,' she replied. 'I . . . I've been out for a walk.'

'Good news,' he said excitedly. 'I'll be home next week.'

'Next week?' Images of her shaved pussy filled her tormented mind. Pictures of her weal-lined buttocks. 'But . . .'

198

'My promotion is going ahead so I have to get back to the London office.'

'Oh, I see.'

'You don't sound very pleased.'

'No, no ... I'm delighted, Brian. Desiree will be so pleased.'

'I'll be back in Tokyo the week after next, but at least I'll have some time at home. How's that new chap next door? Settled in, yet?'

'I ... I don't know. I've not seen much of him.'

'We'll have to invite him to a barbecue.'

'Yes, that's a good idea.'

'Right, I have to go. I should be able to call tomorrow.'

'I'll tell Desiree the minute she gets home from college. She'll be delighted.'

'OK, love. Bye for now.'

'Bye.'

Replacing the receiver, Belinda felt panicky. Her heart banging hard against her chest, her hands trembling, she paced the lounge floor as anxiety gripped her. At least Brian was going back to Tokyo the following week, she thought. But he was bound to notice her shaved vulva and her crimsoned buttocks. Trying to calm herself, she had a quick shower and changed into a T-shirt and short skirt. She reckoned that, if she didn't shave again, the stubble covering her vulva might grow enough for Brian not to notice. She could say that she'd trimmed her pubes, she mused. Perhaps trimmed them a little too much.

To her horror, she found herself thinking that it would be best if her husband never came back. Life would be a lot easier and far more exciting, she thought in her rising wickedness. Sex with Tony, bondage and spanking, massive orgasms ... Trying to think straight, she made herself a cup of coffee and wandered out into the garden. She'd changed, she knew, as she placed her coffee on the table and eased her stinging bottom onto a chair. It was incredible to think that, in such a short space of time, she'd committed adultery, enjoyed anal sex, bondage and the cane . . . and was now wishing that her husband would never return. Her relationship with her daughter had also changed. In such a short time, her life had been turned upside down and inside out. Had she really changed? she mused. Once a slut, always a slut.

Images of Tony fingering Desiree's young vagina loomed in her mind as she sipped her coffee. The very fingers that had delved into her own pussy, she mused. Had Tony set out from day one to seduce both mother and daughter? The threats and taunts, his jibes about Desiree's young body . . . He'd been playing one against the other, she knew. Desiree was confused, thought that she was in love. But, once her father was home . . . Would she listen to him? Belinda wondered. She always used to listen to him and take his advice. Would she listen now?

Sperm still oozing from her abused bottom hole, Belinda felt her clitoris stir as she pictured Tony's knob stretching her anal ring wide open. This was all a game to him, she thought. What was it to her? Adultery, deceit, lies . . . One thing was for sure, she decided: the times she'd spent with Tony had been incredibly sexually gratifying. But her massive orgasms had only served to fire her libido and she now thought about sex constantly. Her pussy-milk was flowing into the tight crotch of her cotton panties, but she didn't want to have to masturbate yet again. But she knew that she had no choice as her vaginal muscles tightened.

'Hi, Mum,' Desiree trilled, skipping through the back door onto the patio. 'Is Tony back yet?'

'I . . . I don't know,' Belinda lied. No privacy, no time to masturbate. 'I'm sure that I would have heard him if –'

200

'I'll go and see,' the girl said excitedly, heading towards the bushes.

'Desiree, wait a minute. I want to talk to you.'

'What, now?'

'Yes, now. It's about your father.'

'Oh?'

'He'll be home next week.'

'Really?' Desiree cried, her pretty face beaming. 'But, why? I mean . . .'

'He rang and said that his promotion is going ahead and he has to come back to the London office.'

'When? Which day?'

'He didn't say. The thing is –'

'I can't wait to see him. That's great news, Mum.'

'Yes, it is. Desiree, the thing is that I don't know what he's going to say when he finds out about Tony.'

'Tony? What do you mean?'

'You know what your dad's like. You're only sixteen, Tony is twenty-seven and . . .'

'And what?'

'What do you think your dad will say when he discovers that you're seeing a man of his age?'

'Well, I . . . I don't know. I hadn't thought about it.'

'In that case, you'd better give it some serious thought.'

'He won't mind, will he?'

'Mind? I think he'll go mad. As you know, I'm not happy about it. What your dad will say, I dread to think.'

'I won't tell him,' Desiree said. 'Will you promise not to say anything to him?'

'Desiree, I won't lie to him. Besides, what will he think if you keep going out? You're bound to see Tony in the garden and . . .'

'It'll be all right. Once dad realises that I'm in love, he'll understand.'

'He might understand if you were in love with someone of your own age. But, a man of twenty-seven? Tony is almost as old as me.'

'I hadn't looked at it that way.'

'That's the way your dad will see it. His daughter's boyfriend is almost as old as his wife.'

'So, what shall I do?'

'Ideally, finish it now.'

'I can't, Mum. Why don't you talk to Dad? Explain that ...'

'Explain what? There's nothing I can say, Desiree. Tony is eleven years your senior. Nothing's going to change that. Even if it was possible to keep it secret, your dad would notice the change in you. When he left, you wore baggy jeans and tops and didn't bother about make-up. Now, you wear miniskirts, you have a thong, you're always doing yourself up ... And you're always going out. You've only just this minute got in, and you're rushing round to Tony's house.'

'I know, but I haven't seen him for a week.'

'Desiree, you were round there every five minutes before he went away. You either finish with Tony, or lie to your father. And lying won't work.'

'I'll be back in a while,' the girl said, ambling across the lawn to the bushes.

'You'd better give it some thought.'

'Yes, I will.'

Praying that, at last, she was beginning to make her daughter see sense, Belinda decided to keep on about her father and what his reaction would be. The problem was that Desiree was growing up fast. She might not listen to her father any more. If she rebelled ... Realising that the girl could move in with Tony, Belinda held her hand to her mouth. What was to stop her? she wondered. She was old enough to leave home. Dreading the idea, she wondered what the girl was up to next door. Had she seen Tony's sex den? Was she handcuffed to the wooden frame with Tony's cock embedded deep within her bottom hole?

'You have a lovely bum,' Tony praised Desiree, kneeling behind her as she pulled her short skirt up and leaned over the back of the armchair. 'I've really missed you.'

'And I've missed you.' She sighed as he pulled her panties down to her thighs and parted the firm orbs of her naked buttocks.

'I've missed your sweet bum,' he said with a chuckle, licking the sensitive tissue surrounding her anal hole. 'Mmm, you taste heavenly.'

Worrying about her father as Tony drove a finger deep into the dank heat of her rectum, Desiree knew that her mother was right. He'd never understand, let alone accept that his daughter was seeing a man of 27. But, what could she do? It would be impossible to leave Tony. Living next door, she'd see him in his garden and . . . No, she could never leave him.

'That hurts,' Desiree complained as Tony forced a second finger into her tight bottom hole. 'I thought that we were going to make love?'

'We are,' he said, biting on the firm flesh of her naked buttock. 'I want to love your bum first.'

Grimacing as Tony twisted his fingers, painfully stretching the delicate walls of her rectal duct, she again wondered about his intentions. Was this love? she mused anxiously. She'd not seen Tony for a week, and all he wanted to do was lick and finger her bottom hole. There'd been no passionate kiss, no embrace . . . *I want to love your bum first.* Desiree instinctively knew that this wasn't right as she felt Tony's tongue sweeping over the stretched tissue of her anus, licking around his fingers.

Slipping his free hand between her parted thighs and burying more fingers in the wet sheath of her vagina, he repeatedly thrust deep into her hot sex holes. Her young body rocked with the crude violation of her rectum and vagina and she again pondered on her father's reaction to her falling in love with an older man. Her mother was right, he'd go mad. But, if this was true love ... Was Tony in love? she reflected. He'd been to Spain and obviously had not thought about bringing her a little present. A small trinket from a market would have been nice. Anything, just to show that she was in his thoughts while he was away.

Slipping his sticky fingers out of her rectal duct, he pushed his tongue deep into her bottom hole. She could feel his lips locked to her brown ring as he licked inside her. Did he like the taste? she mused, again wishing that they'd gone up to his bed and made love properly. To have cuddled up to him in his bed, their naked bodies entwined ... Tony obviously wasn't the warm and loving type, she thought sadly. Not once had they been out for a walk, held hands and wandered through the park, enjoyed a coffee in town ...

'You taste great,' he said, his fingers squelching her vaginal juices. He tongued her hot rectum. 'There's nothing I like more than tongue-fucking a young girl's arse.'

How many girls had he done this to? she wondered. Was he a virgin? *There's nothing I like more than tongue-fucking a young girl's arse.* Dripping with confusion, Desiree didn't know what to think. She wasn't sure how she felt about Tony any more. It seemed that he only wanted her for sex – for crude, cold sex. Perhaps this was his way of showing his love for her? she pondered. Some couples walked in the countryside holding hands, embracing, kissing and making love beneath the summer sun. Tony wanted Desiree over the back of an armchair with his tongue embedded in the hot depths of her rectal canal.

'Tony, you do love me, don't you?' she asked as he yanked his pussy-wet fingers out of her vagina and stood behind her.

'You know I do,' he replied, matter-of-factly.

'You haven't told me about Spain.'

'There's nothing to tell. Too bloody hot, too much booze and the beaches littered with half-naked girls.'

'What did you do in the evenings?'

'Went to nightclubs. What else is there to do in Spain? Right, you wanted me to make love to you. Are you ready?'

'Can't we go up to your bedroom?'

'I want you here, over the armchair.'

Desiree felt the bulbous globe of his cock slipping between the engorged petals of her inner lips. She let out a rush of breath as he rammed the entire length of his solid penis deep into her teenage body. Her hair cascading over her face, her head resting on the armchair cushion, she listened to the slapping of his lower belly meeting her naked buttocks with every thrust of his huge cock. No embracing, no kissing. Just cold, loveless – as Tony would put it – fucking.

'No,' she cried as he slipped his juice-dripping cock out of her tight vagina and pressed his bulbous knob hard against her anal ring. 'Tony, please . . .'

'There's nothing like an arse-fucking.' He chortled, managing to force his purple crown past her defeated anal sphincter muscles.

'No, I . . . I don't want you to do that,' she whimpered.

'We're learning together, remember? Two virgins discovering sex together.'

'Yes, but . . .'

'This is the closest two people can be. The closest, most intimate loving two people can share.'

His knob glided along her tight rectal sheath, his shaft stretching her open to capacity. He managed to impale her fully on his rock-hard penis. Desiree gasped, her knuckles whitening as she gripped the arms of the chair. Feeling as though her pelvic cavity was about to explode, she couldn't believe that he'd managed to sink his huge penis deep into her tight bottom hole. His fingers reached beneath his heavy balls, delving into the wet depths of her vagina, and he massaged his cock through the thin membrane dividing her sex ducts.

'Like it?' he asked shakily.

'No, no, I . . .'

'Tighten your muscles and squeeze my cock,' he instructed. 'Squeeze the spunk out of my knob.'

'Tony, I . . .'

'Yes, that's it. God, you're so tight and hot.'

Doing her best to comply with his crude request, Desiree knew that the debased act was far removed from the loving relationship she'd dreamed of having with Tony. Was her mother right? she again wondered. Had Tony been with lots of women? Was he capable of loving? Slipping his pussy-slimed fingers out of her vagina, he gripped her hips and withdrew his solid cock until the sensitive brown tissue of her anal opening hugged the rim of his helmet. With a crude vengeance, he rammed his knob deep into the meat of her bowels. Again and again, he propelled his swollen knob into the very core of her young body. Gasping with every thrust of his hard shaft, he muttered his words of crude sex. *Tight-arsed schoolgirl, horny little bitch . . .*

The pain fading, her pleasure heightening, Desiree was beginning to enjoy the experience. She still wondered about love, holding and kissing. But the feel of Tony's cock sliding in and out of her tightening rectum was sending her arousal sky-high. Her clitoris now solid, yearning for attention, she recalled Tony's words: *We're learning together, remember? Two virgins discovering sex together. The closest, most intimate loving two people can share.*

As his sperm jetted from his throbbing knob, lubricating her anal cylinder and flooding her bowels, Desiree did feel close to him. No two people could have had a closer physical relationship, she mused dreamily. Her anal tissue dragging back and forth along his veined shaft, the squelching of his sperm resounding around the room, she knew that she'd found love. This was Tony's way of proving his great love for her, she was sure as his swinging balls battered the hairless flesh of her swollen pussy lips.

Repeatedly ramming his orgasming glans deep into the fiery heat of her bowels, his lower belly slapping her naked buttocks as he filled her with his seed, he reached between her thighs and massaged the solid nub of her sensitive clitoris. Desiree gasped, her breathing deep then shallow as she neared her climax. Tony was good, she mused in her sexual delirium. He knew exactly how to please a girl. Was this from experience? Or was he learning? They were learning together, weren't they?

'Coming,' she said, her young body trembling. 'Don't stop. I'm . . . I'm coming.'

'God, you've got a tight arsehole,' he said, swinging his hips as he massaged the solid bulb of her ripening clitoris.

'Please . . . Don't stop. I'm . . . I'm coming.'

Her orgasm erupted within the solid nub of her pulsating clitoris and she cried out in the grip of her climactic pleasure. Again and again, shockwaves of pure sexual bliss rolled throughout her body as her lover shafted her rectal duct and deluged her bowels with his creamy sperm. His vibrating fingertips working on her swollen clitoris, sustaining her multiple orgasm, he continued to shaft her anal canal until his swinging balls had drained and Desiree begged him to stop.

'No more,' she said, her young body shaking fiercely. 'God, I can't take any more.'

'You're amazing,' he said, slowing his clitoral mass-aging rhythm as her orgasm receded. 'We're perfect together.'

'Yes, yes we are,' she whimpered, her eyes rolling in the aftermath of her forbidden pleasure.

'I'd like to spank you now,' he said, bringing her back to reality. 'I want to spank your bare bottom.'

'No, I don't want that,' she said shakily as his knob slipped out of her anus with a loud sucking sound.

'Why not?'

'Because ... because I'd better get home. I need to rest, Tony. That was absolutely incredible.'

'We'll do it again,' he said, slapping her naked buttock. 'We'll do it every day.'

'Yes, we will,' she agreed readily, hauling her trembling body upright. 'I have some college work to do. I'll come back later.'

'I've got someone coming round this evening,' he said, pushing the armchair back into place. 'And I've got to unpack my things.'

'Who's coming to see you this evening?'

'A work colleague. A young lady by the name of Sarah. She's going to tell me where the company are sending me off to next.'

'Abroad, you mean?' she asked him, adjusting her clothing.

'More than likely.'

'Oh, right. Well, I'll see you tomorrow.'

'I enjoyed our time together,' he said, kissing her cheek. 'We'll do it again tomorrow, OK?'

'Yes, er ... OK.'

Leaving the house with sperm oozing from her abused bottom hole, Desiree wondered why he'd not kissed her passionately. He just wasn't that sort of person, she concluded, heading across the lawn to the bushes. He'd forced his cock into her bum and spermed her bowels and ... And that was it. That was his way of showing his love for her. Wondering where he'd be working next, she recalled his words about Spain. Nightclubs, booze, half-naked girls ... *A young lady by the name of Sarah.* She *was* a work colleague, wasn't she? Tony wouldn't lie to her, would he?

Twelve

Pulling the quilt over her head as her mother drew the curtains back, Desiree didn't want to go to college. After a sleepless night worrying about Tony and pondering on the illicit sex act she'd allowed him to commit, she couldn't face anything or anyone, let alone college lectures. Her bottom hole was sore, dried sperm glued her buttocks together: a stark reminder of the crude act. A loving act? Or loveless?

'You'll be late,' Belinda said.

'I'm working at home today,' Desiree murmured.

'Not another day off, surely?'

'I'm working at home,' the girl repeated agitatedly. 'I'm not taking a day off.'

'Why did you keep looking out of the lounge window last night? You seemed moody, so I didn't like to ask.'

'Tony had someone from work calling on him. I thought I'd see what she looked like.'

'Did you see her?'

'No, I must have missed her.'

'That explains it,' Belinda said mysteriously, coming up with an idea.

'Explains what?'

'The girl I saw leaving his place early this morning. Would you like some tea or coffee?'

'How old was she?'

'I didn't really take much notice,' Belinda replied nonchalantly as she left the room. 'I'll make some tea.'

As her mother went downstairs, Desiree sat upright and checked the time. Eight o'clock. Whoever it was had obviously stayed overnight with Tony, she mused angrily. So, he *had* lied to her. Deciding to have it out with him, she leaped out of bed and went into the bathroom. The time had come to sort this out, she thought, as she turned the shower on. The time had come to find out exactly what Tony was up to.

Massaging soap into the sperm-sticky valley between her firm buttocks, Desiree felt that the worst thing was how stupid and naive she'd been. To have shaved her pubic hair off was bad enough, but to have allowed Tony to have anal sex with her? Her mother had tried to tell her about Tony, what sort of man he was, but she'd not listened to her. Imagining Tony sinking his solid penis into another girl's rectal canal, pumping his sperm deep into her bowels, she finally stepped out of the shower and dried her curvaceous young body.

She'd been used and abused, she reflected angrily as she went back to her bedroom and dressed in a miniskirt and T-shirt. She'd fallen for his charm, believed his lies – and given her naked body to him in the name of love. Drying and brushing her long black hair, she finally went downstairs and informed her mother that she was going to see Tony.

'I've made you a cup of tea,' Belinda said.

'I won't be very long,' she murmured, leaving by the back door. 'I have to discuss a serious matter with Tony.'

'Is everything all right?' Belinda asked, following the girl out onto the patio.

'I don't know, yet. I'll be back in a while.'

Concealing a grin as Desiree headed for the bushes, Belinda was pleased with her plan. But, she also felt guilty. She didn't like lying to her daughter in order to ruin her relationship with Tony. But she was doing this for the girl's own good, she tried to convince herself. Or, was it that she wanted Tony for herself? Her guilt mingling with confusion, she hoped that she was winning the battle with her daughter as she went back into the kitchen.

'Your mother's lying again,' Tony said as Desiree confronted him in the lounge. 'I told you that Sarah was coming round last night. But she didn't stay more than an hour or so. And she certainly didn't stay all night.'

'My mother wouldn't lie to me,' Desiree said dolefully. 'She saw someone leaving your house early this morning.'

'Perhaps someone called and I didn't hear the bell. It could have been anyone walking down my path.'

'You wouldn't lie to me, would you?' Desiree asked, hanging her head.

'Why would I lie to you? Had I wanted Sarah to stay overnight, I'd not have told you that she was coming round.'

'You might have told me in case I saw her arrive.'

'I see your point, but how far do you want to take this?'

'What do you mean?'

'I could have said that she came back this morning to drop off some papers or something. One lie to cover another, and then more lies . . .'

'I'm sorry, Tony.'

'You don't have to be sorry. But I do think it's a shame that you don't trust me. You seem to believe that I'm cheating on you, lying to you . . . If you're going to become paranoid every time someone from work calls to see me –'

'I'm not paranoid,' she cut in. 'Surely, you can understand my concern? You said that a girl was coming round last night, and my mother said that she saw a girl leaving your house early this morning. I put two and two together, that's all.'

211

'And came up with five. If there's no trust, then I don't see how we can carry on. Relationships are built on trust and loyalty, as well as love.'

'Yes, I know. I'm sorry.'

'Are you going to college today?'

'No, I don't feel like . . .'

'I think you should, Desiree. Come round this afternoon, when you get home.'

'Yes, you're right. I'll go to college and . . . and I'll see you later.'

'OK, and don't go getting any silly ideas.'

'No, I won't.'

Pleased to see Desiree going off to college, Belinda wondered what Tony had said to her. She seemed a lot happier, which Belinda found disappointing. But things were going according to plan, she concluded. Desiree was obviously concerned about Tony, his intentions, which could only serve to weaken their relationship. Once lies reared their ugly head and trust began to fade, then the end of the relationship was in sight.

Was her relationship with her husband coming to an end? Belinda pondered. Was her marriage coming to an end? Things could certainly never be the same again. Every time Brian snuggled up behind her in bed and sank his penis into her vagina, she'd think about Tony. Would Brian notice the change in her? she mused. He'd certainly notice her weal-lined buttocks and her shaved vulva. But she'd come up with some excuse or other, some lie or other. She fell over in the bushes and landed on her bum. She'd trimmed her pubes and had gone too far. Lies and deceit. Betrayal.

'I want to talk to you,' Tony called, leaning on the fence as Belinda went out into the garden.

'Oh?' Belinda said, eyeing the envelope he was clutching.

'What's all this about a girl leaving my house this morning? You've been trying to cause trouble again, haven't you?'

'I really have no idea what you're talking about,' she returned. 'I just happened to mention to Desiree that I saw a girl leaving your house.'

'But, it's not true.'

'Tony, I saw a girl walking down your path early this morning. When I mentioned it to Desiree, I wasn't suggesting anything. I wasn't trying to imply anything. It was merely a passing comment.'

'Why you deliberately try to upset your daughter, I can't think. You'd better get yourself up to my sex den.'

'I'm busy this morning,' she returned.

'You'd better take a look at these,' he said, pulling several photographs out of the envelope.

Belinda gazed at a shot of Tony's cock embedded deep within her bottom hole and grimaced. 'I don't want to see your porn pics,' she snapped angrily.

'Perhaps Desiree would like to see them?' he said.

'There's no saying that it's me in the pictures, so don't start –'

'What about this one of you over the frame?' he cut in. 'There's a mole on your hip, you can see your long black hair trailing over the floor, and there's a small scar on your leg . . .'

'What the hell . . .' she said shakily, snatching the photograph. Gazing at an unknown man shafting her bottom hole, she leaned on the fence to steady herself on her sagging legs. 'Who, who . . .' she stammered.

'That's Ian, a mate of mine,' he enlightened her.

'You bastard,' she said, gazing at the young man. 'You fucking bastard.'

'That's what the blindfold was for.' He sniggered.

'You fucking . . .'

'Bastard?'

213

'I knew that you were a vile little man,' she hissed, ripping the photograph up. 'But to sink this low . . .'

'Come on, Belinda. You loved every minute of it. I fucked and spunked your arse, and then Ian had a go. And you loved it.'

Belinda staggered across the lawn to the patio, sat down and held her hand to her head. Stunned, she couldn't believe what Tony had done. He was despicable, she reflected angrily. To blindfold her and sneak another man into the room . . . To invite another man to shaft her rectum, and then take photographs of the vulgar act . . . Recalling the mole, the small scar, she knew that Desiree would recognise her instantly. And her husband, she thought fearfully. If he saw the incriminating photographs . . .

'Are you all right?' Tony called.

'No, I'm bloody not all right,' she retorted. 'How dare you . . .'

'A cock is a cock, Belinda. What does it matter who it belongs to?'

'What does it matter? For Christ's sake, Tony. What the hell do you think I am?'

'I didn't charge him for the pleasure of your tight arse.' He chuckled.

'You didn't charge him? My God, you're a vile man.'

'I do believe you're right.'

'I never want to see you again, do you understand?'

'You'll be seeing a lot more of me. And a hell of a lot more of my cock.'

'No, Tony. This has gone too far. I agreed to have sex with you on the understanding that you'd keep away from my daughter.'

'Which I've done. Well, almost.'

'I did *not* agree to have strangers fuck my . . . my bum.'

'Ian's not a stranger. He's a very good mate of mine.'

'You know what I mean. How dare you . . .'

214

'Calm down, for God's sake. You've had a couple of cocks spunk your arse. What of it?'

'What of it?'

'You must have had dozens of cocks, Belinda. Don't go all moralistic on me. You're a slut, and always have been.'

He was right, Belinda knew, as she twisted her hair nervously around her fingers. But to have one man after another sink his penis into her bottom hole and ... Recalling her teenage years, the two boys she'd taken to the woods, she remembered sucking on their purple knobs simultaneously. They'd come together, pumping their fresh spunk over her tongue as she'd gobbled on their orgasming plums and swallowed their teenage cream. But she'd been young and stupid, she reflected. Now, she was a married woman with a teenage daughter and a lovely home and ...

'You'd better get yourself up to my sex den,' Tony said, breaking her reverie.

'No,' she spat. 'If you think –'

'In that case, I'll invite Desiree up to my sex den,' he cut in. 'She's coming round after college. I wonder whether she'd like to see the photographs of her mother getting her arse fucked by two men?'

'You're a bastard.'

'So you keep saying.'

'I don't want anything more to do with you, Tony. Blackmail me, do what you like, but –'

'I'll do exactly what I like. And the first thing will be to initiate Desiree into the crude art of anal sex. The choice, as always, is yours. It's either you, or your daughter. I'll be waiting upstairs for you.'

As he went into his house, Belinda recalled Tony driving his cock deep into her bottom hole. He didn't have staying power after all, she mused, recalling the second man's solid penis gliding into her sperm-bubbling anal sheath. Although she tried to deny that the notion of two men taking turns to shaft her bum was sending her arousal rocketing, she felt her stomach somersault, her clitoris swell. Once a slut, always a slut.

Tony had no morals whatsoever, she thought. He was an unscrupulous bastard, a cheating, lying . . . The man was a sex-crazed pervert, she concluded. And she was nothing more than a lump of female meat to be used and abused, she decided, as her clitoris called for her intimate attention. Tony was a first-rate bastard. But there was something about him, something irresistible. His cock, she thought, imagining his purple knob bathing her tongue with spunk.

Leaving her chair and heading across the lawn to the bushes, she knew that she had no power to fight her inner desires. She also knew that, at any cost, she had to keep Desiree away from Tony. He'd have no qualms about blindfolding the girl and inviting his friend to shaft her teenage pussy. Or, worse still, her bottom. Emerging from the bushes and walking towards Tony's back door, she felt confused and numb. Tony was going to punish her, she knew, as she stepped into his kitchen. Like a lamb to the slaughter.

Climbing the stairs to the sex den, she wondered whether Tony's friend was lurking, hiding somewhere, waiting for the opportunity to ram his cock deep into her rectum. She could hear Tony moving about in his den of iniquity, no doubt preparing the wooden frame, the handcuffs and the bamboo cane. Pushing the door open, she was thankful that he was alone. Although the notion of another man shafting her bum had sent her arousal sky-high, she wasn't prepared to share her body with two males.

'Welcome to my sex den.' Tony chuckled. 'I'd like you to strip naked.'

'What are you going to do?' she asked stupidly.

'You've been a naughty little girl, Belinda. You've tried to cause trouble with Desiree, and I don't like that.'

'I haven't tried to cause trouble.'

'Telling her that a girl stayed here. You lied to her, Belinda.'

'No, I . . .'

'And now you're lying to me. I hope you've shaved for me? I did order you to shave off your stubble. I hope you haven't disobeyed me?'

'No, I . . . I haven't shaved,' she confessed. 'My husband will be home . . .'

'Oh dear.' He sighed.

'No, you don't understand. My husband . . .'

'I understand only too well.'

Belinda knew what Tony expected as he grabbed the handcuffs and leather riding crop. Turning her gaze to the thin bamboo cane lying on the table, she tensed her buttocks. She'd been a naughty girl: she'd defied him, lied to him . . . and had to be punished most severely. She slipped out of her T-shirt and short skirt, removed her bra and panties and stood naked before her master. He ordered her to stand against the wooden frame with her feet wide apart and cuffed her ankles to the posts. Holding her hands up above her head and cuffing her wrists to the top sections of the X-shaped frame, he let out a wicked chuckle.

'I find that it's always best to begin with the riding crop,' he said, lowering the top half of the frame, her naked body bending over until her long black hair cascaded over the floor. He stroked the firm flesh of her naked bottom, and then moved his hand down between her parted thighs and cupped the swell of her pussy lips. 'The crop will warm you up in readiness for the cane.'

The riding crop wasn't too bad, Belinda thought, as the leather loop landed across each twitching buttock in turn. Her naked buttocks warming, turning red, she squeezed her eyes shut and endured the beautiful thrashing as her master chuckled. But she wasn't looking forward to the thin bamboo cane. The swishing

217

sound, the loud cracks ... The cane was a horrendous punishment. But she'd defied him by not shaving her vulval stubble, she reflected. She deserved the cane, she mused, as the leather loop repeatedly lashed her naked buttocks.

Brian would be home soon, she thought fearfully. He'd notice her shaved pussy, her weal-lined bottom and ... Wondering whether to make out that she wasn't well, she pondered on sleeping in the spare room. If she kept coughing, she could suggest that she sleep in the spare room so as not to disturb him. If he was only home for a week, she might get away with it. But, what would happen when he next came home? Trying not to plan too far ahead, she was thankful that there were no telltale signs of anal sex. He'd never discover that she'd had two penises shafting her rectum, pumping spunk deep into her bowels.

'I reckon that you need a double screwing,' Tony said, halting the thrashing. 'One cock shafting your sweet arse and another screwing your hot pussy.'

'Never,' Belinda said, her twitching buttocks stinging. 'There's no way I'm going to have two men –'

'I wasn't giving you a choice,' he cut in. 'I was just thinking that you need a double fucking.'

'Tony, I –'

'With two massive cocks shafting your tight holes, rubbing together through the thin walls of your pussy and your arse ... How about a third cock fucking your pretty mouth? Three cocks, Belinda. Three cocks fucking and spunking your holes.'

To her sheer horror, the notion excited her. But she knew that she'd never commit the debased act. Triple adultery, she mused, as Tony discarded the riding crop and grabbed the cane from the small corner table. Three men, three cocks ... Her naked body jolted as the thin bamboo landed squarely across her glowing buttocks and she let out a shriek. Tony was a monster, she thought anxiously, as the cane again flailed her tensed bottom cheeks. Would he really invite two men to join him in his sexual debauchery?

'No,' she cried as the thin bamboo bit into the crimsoned flesh of her twitching bottom. 'Tony, please . . .'

'Harder?' He chuckled, bringing the cane down across her bum with a deafening crack.

'Please, no more.'

'Do you promise to shave?'

'Yes, I promise.'

'And you want three cocks?'

'No, not three.'

'Two, then?'

'No, Tony. You're not going to share me with other men.'

'You'll agree to three cocks or I'll resume the thrashing,' he stated firmly.

'Only a whore would have three men at once.'

'And you're a whore, so what's the problem?'

'For God's sake, Tony. I'm a woman, a person, not a lump of meat.'

'You're a slut, Belinda, and you know it. I'll be back in a minute.'

As he left the room, Belinda wondered whether he was going to invite two men to join him in using and abusing her tethered body. He wouldn't do it, she mused, desperate to clutch her stinging buttocks. He'd already had another man shaft her rectal duct, she reflected. He wouldn't force her to endure three cocks, would he? Her vaginal muscles tightening, her clitoris swelling between the fleshy lips of her pussy, she tried to push the images of three cocks spunking her naked body from her mind. Her bottom hole, her pussy, her mouth

. . .

'What are you doing?' she asked as Tony returned and brought the frame upright.

'Letting you go,' he said. 'My friends will be round this evening. In the meantime, you can go.'

'Your friends?'

'Three cocks, Belinda.' He chuckled. 'Before you go, I have a little surprise for you.'

'I don't want any surprises,' she snapped. 'Just let me go home and rub some cream into my bum. It hurts like hell. I won't be able to sit down for a week.'

'I bought this especially for you,' he said, fixing a studded leather collar around her neck.

'Tony ... I can't go home wearing this,' she said angrily, tugging on the collar. 'Take it off, for God's sake.'

'There's a small padlock at the back, and only I have the key. Do you reckon that Desiree will like it?'

'Tony, I want you to take it off.'

'It'll remind you that you belong to me.'

'I do not belong to you or anyone else.'

'And this one will remind you that you're my sex slave.' He chortled as he secured a leather belt around her waist.

'Tony ... Look, this has gone too far. Desiree will see the collar. How am I going to explain it?'

'Tell her that it's your new look. By the way, don't bother to try cutting the collar off. Like the belt, it's reinforced with steel wires.'

'Now what ...' she began as he ran a metal chain between her thighs. Securing one end to the front of the leather belt, he pulled it tight and fixed the other end to the back. 'Tony, for Christ's sake ...'

'Nice and snug in your bum crack,' he said with a laugh, releasing the handcuffs. 'And your cunny crack. There, you can go home now.'

'I can't go home like this,' she returned angrily. 'Please, be reasonable.'

'I'm allowing you to go home. That's reasonable enough, isn't it?'

'All right, I'll wear the belt. But at least take the collar off. I can hide the belt, but not the collar.'

Agreeing, he released the collar and watched her dress. Fuming as she pulled her T-shirt down to cover the belt, she was acutely aware of the metal chain running within the valley of her pussy, embedded deep within the ravine between her glowing buttocks. This was crazy, she thought, as she brushed her hair away from her pretty face with her fingers. If her husband saw the belt and the chain ... Tony wouldn't put her through that, she was sure, as he followed her downstairs. He wouldn't be that much of a bastard, would he?

'I'll see you this evening,' he said as she opened the front door.

'I'm not coming here to have three men ...'

'In that case, the belt stays where it is. By the way, the chain is stainless steel. You'll never cut through it.'

'I'm not coming here this evening,' she repeated.

'That's the deal, Belinda. You'll take three cocks or the belt and chain stay.'

Walking to her front door, she knew that he wasn't joking. Her buttocks on fire, the chain tight within her vaginal valley, she thanked God that he'd taken the collar off. At least Desiree was at college, she mused, as she closed the front door behind her. She bounded up the stairs to her bedroom and jumped when the phone rang. She moved to the bedside table and hesitated, her hand hovering over the receiver. It might be Brian, she thought, retracting her hand. She couldn't speak to him wearing the leather belt and the chain.

Lifting her T-shirt as the phone finally stopped ringing, she gazed at her reflection in the dressing-table mirror. The belt was about an inch wide with large metal studs spaced close together. The chain was too tight to allow her to turn the belt to bring the padlock to the front. This was yet another nightmare, she mused angrily, tugging on the belt. Turning and gazing in the mirror at her crimsoned buttocks, she held her hand to her mouth. The weals wouldn't fade for weeks, she was sure. The phone rang again.

'Hello,' she said softly, pressing the receiver to her ear.

'It's me,' Brian announced. 'There's been another change of plan.'

'Oh?' she said, hoping that he wasn't coming home early after all.

'I won't be home next week.'

'Oh, right.' She sighed with relief.

'I'll be home the day after tomorrow.'

'What? I mean –'

'Aren't you pleased?'

'Yes, of course I am. How long will you be home for?'

'At least a week. Are you all right, Belinda?'

'Yes, I'm fine.'

'The first thing we'll do is have a barbecue. Oh, and we'll invite the chap next door.'

'Yes, that'll be nice.'

'Right, I'd better go. This was just a quick call to tell you the good news. I'll see you soon.'

'Yes, that's good news.'

'Bye, love.'

Belinda replaced the receiver, turned and again looked at her reflection in the mirror. The belt had to go, she thought anxiously. And there was no way she was going to shave again. Lowering her T-shirt and pacing the bedroom floor, she tried to calm herself as she felt anger welling in the pit of her stomach. Thinking back to the day Tony had moved in, she shook her head and sighed. He'd taken liberties, used threats and blackmail to have his perverted way, he'd touched Desiree and ... and now he wanted three men to share Belinda's naked body.

Tugging on the metal chain running between her succulent vaginal lips, she recalled the photographs Tony had taken. He could use them as evidence of her

222

debauchery, she reflected. If she didn't do as he asked, when he asked, he could ruin not only her marriage but her relationship with her daughter. Tony obviously had no qualms about using blackmail to get what he wanted. If he threatened to show the photographs to her husband ... The full extent of her predicament hitting her, she jumped as she heard a noise downstairs.

'Is that you, Desiree?' she called, walking onto the landing.

'It's me,' Tony said, standing at the bottom of the stairs and grinning at her.

'How the hell ...'

'The back door was open. I came round to –'

'You can't just walk into my house like this,' she snapped, bounding down the stairs.

'Of course I can. You're my slave, Belinda. You're at my beck and call and –'

'Look, my husband will be home the day after tomorrow. I've got this damned belt and chain, my bottom is glowing a fire red, my pussy is shaved ... Do you want to see me divorced? Because that's what will happen if my husband –'

'There's no need to panic.' He chuckled.

'No need to panic? For Christ's sake, Tony. How the hell am I going to explain all this? I should never have intervened. I should have allowed Desiree to go with you and ... You've done all this. You've caused all this bloody trouble.'

'Calm down,' he said, stroking her cheek. 'The belt is part of your training. You won't be wearing it when your husband gets home, I promise.'

'And my bum? What about the red lines criss-crossing my bum? And what about my shaved pussy? I'm a married woman, Tony. I don't want to be trained as your bloody sex slave. I'm going to talk to Desiree. I'll show her the belt and tell her everything.'

'Is that wise?'

'Maybe not, but I have no choice.'

'What about the photographs? Would you like to show her those, too?'

'What do you intend to do with them?'

'They're my insurance, Belinda.'

'Insurance? What are you talking about? Oh, I see what you mean. You're keeping them to blackmail me. Look, I've agreed to have sex with you and . . .'

'In exchange for leaving Desiree alone.'

'Yes. But, if I end up divorced, you'll lose me. You have to be reasonable, Tony. Can't you see that?'

'I said that I'd take the belt off before your husband gets home.'

'Yes, I know. But I can't shave again. I might be able to get away with saying that I was trimming my pubes and went a little too far. If I keep my bum out of sight, I might be able to –'

'Three cocks, Belinda. That's the deal. No more shaving, no more caning, and the belt goes. But you'll take three cocks.'

Holding her hand to her head as she followed Tony into the kitchen, she knew that she had no choice. But, would he keep his side of the bargain? He'd proved that he couldn't be trusted by touching Desiree. Why should he keep his word now? Three men, she mused uncomfortably. Three men, three cocks . . . The notion firing her arousal, she wondered where Tony would stop. Three men, and then four or five or . . .

'Do we have a deal?' he asked her.

'Do I have a choice?' she returned, taking a bottle of wine from the fridge.

'No, I suppose not. But you're a slut, Belinda. You know how much you'd enjoy three cocks.'

'Why bring other men into this?'

'Because, at heart, that's what you want.'

'Of course it's not,' she hissed, filling a tumbler with wine. 'The next thing you'll be telling me is that you're doing this for my sake.'

'That's a good way to look at it. I'm doing this to give you what you want.'

'You're mad.'

'Come round at seven o'clock. We'll be ready for you.'

'No, Tony.'

'I'll see you later,' he said, leaving by the back door.

'Tony, wait.'

Watching as he walked across the lawn to the bushes, Belinda lowered her head and sighed. Committing adultery with one man was bad enough, she thought dolefully. But three men at once? Her stomach somersaulting as she pictured three solid penises, she wished that she could stop sex from ruling her life. She'd managed to quell her rampant libido successfully during her married life. But now? Why the hell had Tony moved in next door? she mused as she sipped her wine. Why on earth had Desiree fallen for him?

The situation was going from bad to worse, she knew, as she pondered on Brian inviting Tony to a barbecue. Desiree would be there, Tony would be grinning at Belinda – and Brian wouldn't have a clue as to what was going on. Then again, after Desiree's hints, he'd already had his suspicions. He was bound to realise that something was happening. Unless Belinda could compose herself and try to come across as normal. Normal? she mused. Having a barbecue with sperm oozing from the inflamed eye of her anus . . . How the hell could she come across as normal?

Three men, she again mused. Three cocks. Why was Tony so eager to share her naked body? Was he taking money from his male visitors? Why go to all the trouble of creating a sex den? The wooden frame, canes, handcuffs, vibrators . . . There was more to this than met the eye, she decided. Had he built the sex den with Belinda in mind, or his male callers? If he was selling Belinda for sex, then he probably planned to do the same with Desiree. There were too many unanswered questions.

Gulping down her wine and refilling the glass, she wandered out onto the patio and sat down. Suddenly having the notion that Tony was a pimp, she frowned. That would explain everything, she thought. The sex den, the male visitors ... Was he really an IT consultant? she wondered. Or was that a front for his illicit business? More questions, she reflected. The wine going to her head, she let out a giggle as she imagined stealing Tony's customers. Why go to Tony when they could visit Belinda and pay her directly? Cut out the middle man.

'God, what am I thinking?' she said, picturing men queuing at her front door for crude sex. Unable to stop imagining three solid cocks shafting her sex holes and her mouth, pumping her naked body full of spunk, she recalled Tony's words. *Because, at heart, that's what you want.* Was he right? she pondered, her clitoris stirring, her womb contracting. Whether he was selling her body for sex or not, she'd get what she wanted. *That's the deal. No more shaving, no more caning, and the belt goes. But you'll take three cocks.*

Tony expected her at seven o'clock. Desiree would be home. Belinda was going to have to dream up some lie or other, she decided, finishing her wine and wandering into the kitchen. Refilling the glass, she didn't like the idea of lying to her daughter. But, what choice did she have? This was a dangerous game, she knew. But, dangerous or not, the idea of three solid cocks spunking her naked body sent her libido rocketing. Three rock-hard cocks, three swollen knobs ... Seven o'clock.

Thirteen

Desiree joined her mother in the lounge and sighed. 'Tony's still not back,' she said softly. 'It's almost seven o'clock. I wonder where he's got to?'

'He might have been called away on business again,' Belinda suggested.

'He could have left a message or something. The last time he disappeared without a word, he was away for a week.'

'He might have gone out for the evening. Talking of which, I'd better be going.'

'Who is this Chrissy woman you're meeting? An old school friend, did you say?'

'That's right. I bumped into her in the park and we arranged to meet up for a drink. I'll only be an hour or so.'

'I suppose I'll do some studying,' the girl said dolefully. 'Tony's not in, you're going out . . .'

'I'll only be an hour or so, love. I'll be home before you know it.'

'Well, have a good time.'

'I will. I'll see you later.'

Belinda left the house with her stomach somersaulting and her heart racing. She walked past Tony's front gate and stopped a few yards down the road. She could feel the steel chain moving within her vulval crack, rubbing against the eye of her bottom hole. This was crazy, she thought. The belt, the chain . . . Madness. Waiting for a couple of minutes, she turned and retraced her steps slowly, creeping along the path. Tony opened the front door and she slipped into his house and breathed a sigh of relief. If Desiree had been looking out of the window . . . The consequences didn't bear thinking about.

'In here,' Tony said, leading Belinda into the lounge. 'OK, strip naked and we'll get started.'

'Where are your friends?' she asked him, tugging her T-shirt over her head.

'Upstairs. They'll be down in a minute.'

'How much are they paying you? How much are you selling my body for?'

'They're not paying me, Belinda. I'm not selling your body. I'm having fun with your body.'

'Why bring other men into this?'

'Why not? You're a sexy little slut. Why not share you with my friends and bring them some pleasure?'

'I'm not looking forward to this.' She sighed, tugging her skirt down and slipping out of her bra and panties.

'Of course you are.' He chuckled. 'Three cocks, Belinda? This is your dream come true.'

'Hardly,' she said.

She felt like a prostitute as she stood naked before Tony. Stripping out of her clothes, two men waiting upstairs . . . She might as well have been taking money in return for sex, she thought dolefully. It was difficult to comprehend the situation, she mused, hearing movements upstairs. Brian had only been away for a couple of weeks, and Belinda had had more sex during that time than in the last fifteen years of marriage. Massive orgasms, anal sex, oral sex, bondage and whipping . . .

'You really do have a beautiful body,' Tony praised her, slipping a blindfold over her head. 'And the leather belt adorns your waist perfectly. But I'll have to take it off to allow my friends access to your sweet cunt and your tight little arsehole.'

228

'I've never met anyone as crude as you,' she said as he released the belt.

'That will soon change because you're about to meet my friends,' he said with a chuckle. 'Now, get on all fours and I'll call the lads.'

'Why blindfold me?' she asked him. 'Because you're going to take more pornographic photographs?'

'Yes. But there's another reason. I don't want you to see my friends. You might bump into one of them in town and . . . It's best that you don't see them.'

Taking her position on the floor like an obedient dog, Belinda felt her juices of lust creaming her vaginal valley in readiness for a solid cock. She was no better than a common prostitute, she mused, as she peered into the darkness of her blindfold. What was Desiree doing? Would she ring the front doorbell in the hope that Tony would answer? If the girl knew that her mother was about to commit a gross act of indecency, if she knew that three men were about to use and abuse her naked body . . . There was no point in thinking that way, Belinda decided. Desiree would never discover the horrific truth. And neither would Brian.

Hearing the men enter the room, she listened to their crude comments. *Dirty little slut. A nice firm arse. Shaved cunt lips. A fuckable mouth.* A lump of female meat to be used and abused by men to satisfy their lust for crude sex, she reflected. Again wondering how she'd got herself into this situation, she knew that she was about to commit far more than adultery. A secret lover was one thing, she thought, as lewd comments about her naked body resounded around the room. An affair, a fling, a man on the side . . . But this was wanton whoredom.

Belinda bit her lip as a man lay on the floor and slid beneath her naked body. She felt the bulbous knob of his penis slip between the engorged wings of her inner lips. This was it, she thought anxiously, as another man knelt behind her and yanked the firm cheeks of her inflamed buttocks wide apart. Her head pulled up by her hair, a swollen glans pressing against her pursed lips, she opened her mouth and sucked on the unknown man's cock-head. Again thinking about Desiree as she tasted the salt of the man's swollen knob, she knew that she was going to have to keep her two lives apart. The loving wife and mother, and the wanton slut. The wanton prostitute?

Which one was Tony? she pondered as the man beneath her drove the entire length of his solid penis deep into the hot sheath of her contracting vagina. Gobbling on the bulbous knob bloating her mouth, she breathed heavily through her nose as the man behind her managed to force his huge glans past her defeated anal sphincter muscles and sink his solid shaft deep within her tight rectal duct. Her pelvic cavity inflated to capacity, Belinda couldn't believe that she'd taken two massive cocks into the tight holes between her parted thighs. Her naked body rocking with the three-way shafting, she knew that she'd reached the bottom of the murky pit of depravity. She could sink no further, could she?

A thousand thoughts swirled through the wreckage of her tormented mind as the three men found their penile shafting rhythm. Her husband was working abroad to earn money for the family. Desiree was studying in her bedroom, totally oblivious to her mother's debauched behaviour. Family, friends, neighbours ... Everyone believed Belinda to be a good wife and mother. Everyone thought that Belinda was a lovely person. In truth, she was nothing more than a common slut, a wanton whore. Prostitute.

As hands groped the mounds of her firm breasts and fingers tweaked the ripe teats of her sensitive nipples, she felt the bulb of her clitoris stiffen. Her vaginal juices flowing in torrents, streaming down her inner thighs in rivers of milk, she realised that she'd found her niche in life. Crude sex, group sex . . . She couldn't deny that this was her forte. During her teenage years of promiscuity, she'd discovered what it was that boys and men wanted. She'd learned how to please boys, give them what they wanted. Using her hands, her mouth, her vagina, she'd acquired the skills of sucking and riding cocks. Nothing had changed, she reflected as the men began gasping. Once a slut, always a slut. *This is your dream come true*.

Her erect nipples painfully pulled and twisted, Belinda listened to the squishing of her pussy-milk as the three men increased their thrusting rhythms. As the purple glans shafting her mouth battered the back of her throat and her cervix was pummelled by another swollen knob, she felt the third cock-head repeatedly driving into the depths of her hot bowels. This was real sex, she reflected, her naked body quivering as her climax approached. Hard, cold, loveless, crude . . . Why couldn't Brian have been more adventurous in bed?

'God, I'm coming,' the man beneath her announced. Belinda could feel his sperm bathing her ripe cervix, lubricating the tightening sheath of her pistoned vagina as he repeatedly rammed his throbbing knob deep into her abused body. The man behind her grabbed her hips and rammed his cock into her rectum with a vengeance. She felt a deluge of sperm flooding her hot bowels and easing the friction of his cock within her anal cylinder. Her gobbling mouth deluging with creamy spunk, she moved her head back and forth to meet the third man's oral thrusts.

'Dirty little slut,' the man behind her said as she repeatedly swallowed hard. Her clitoris exploding in orgasm against the girl-wet shaft of the cock ramming into her spasming vagina, she moaned through her nose as she continued to drink from the orgasming knob throbbing within her pretty mouth. This was heaven, she mused dreamily, her naked body jolting with the crude three-way fucking. Her sex holes awash with fresh

231

sperm, the squelching sounds of her illicit act reverberating around the room, she rode the crest of her multiple climax to the accompaniment of gasps of male satisfaction.

Her abused body shaking violently as her orgasm peaked, Belinda knew that she was now well and truly hooked on crude sex. After the initial shock of Tony's crude proposal, she'd come to crave sucking his knob and feeling his solid cock shafting her tight vagina. But, now, one cock wasn't enough. The experience of three men using and abusing her, her massive climax gripping her naked body . . . She now knew that she could never deny herself the pleasure of taking three cocks into her sperm-thirsty holes.

Four men? she mused in her sexual frenzy. Four, five, six . . . The idea of charging men for sex loomed in her mind and she wondered how far she'd fallen into the pit of depravity. A bottomless pit? With her husband working abroad and Desiree at college, men could call at the house during the day. She'd charge them for crude sex, commit any and every perverted sexual act in exchange for cash. She could meet men in the park, take them into the bushes and charge them for a quick blow job or . . .

Wondering where her crude thoughts were coming from as the three men withdrew their deflating penises from her sperm-bubbling holes, Belinda tried to think straight. The very notion of becoming a prostitute was ludicrous, she thought anxiously. What sort of woman was she turning into? What sort of woman *had* she turned into? A wanton slut, a whore, a sex-crazed tart . . . Prostitute. Her eyes widened behind her blindfold as she felt a tongue lapping up the sperm oozing from the inflamed iris of her gaping bottom hole – she couldn't believe that Tony would do such a thing.

'You need to be cleaned up,' Tony said with a chuckle. 'You need to have the spunk sucked out of your holes.'

232

'Who . . .' she began, realising that he wasn't kneeling behind her. 'Who's that?'

'She tastes lovely,' a female said, shocking Belinda to the core. 'I'll suck the spunk out of her pussy once I've drained her bottom.'

'Tony . . .' Belinda gasped. 'Tony, I'm not a bloody lesbian.'

'No, but Sandy is,' he returned. 'She's an eighteen-year-old pussy-hungry lesbian.'

The men laughed and came out with lewd comments as the girl locked her full lips to Belinda's bottom hole and sucked out the male cream. Unable to comprehend the bizarre situation, Belinda shuddered as the girl drove her tongue deep into her bottom hole and licked the sperm-slimed walls of her rectum. Her mind aching, she couldn't believe that this was happening. Never in her life had she even dreamed about a lesbian relationship. The idea of another girl licking her bottom hole had never crossed her mind. Could she sink any lower?

As the girl moved down and pushed her tongue deep into Belinda's sperm-bubbling vagina, the men encouraged her with their obscene suggestions. Belinda listened in a state of horror, and again swore to keep Desiree away from Tony if it was the last thing she did. *Suck the spunk out of her tight cunt. Finger-fuck her hot arse. Suck her clitoris and make the slut come in your lesbian mouth.* The sound of the girl's tongue slurping between her vaginal lips, Belinda felt her clitoris swell and pulsate. Desperately trying to deny the pleasure the lesbian was bringing her, she again thought of her daughter.

Tony had lied to Desiree, he'd used her . . . The girl had to be kept away from him, Belinda thought for the umpteenth time. No matter what it took, if they had to move house to keep her away from the sex maniac, then so be it. The man lying beneath her naked body moved down and sucked Belinda's ripe nipple into his mouth as the girl fervently tongued her vaginal sheath. As a finger entered the tight duct of her rectum, Belinda again tried to deny the immense pleasure the young lesbian was bringing her. If Desiree ended up in a bisexual relationship with Tony and the girl . . .

'God, no,' Belinda murmured as the lesbian sucked her solid clitoris into her hot mouth and ran her wet tongue over the sensitive tip. She was going to reach another orgasm, she knew, as her sex-button swelled and pulsated against the girl's sweeping tongue. To come in a female's mouth, to be licked and sucked to orgasm by another girl . . . Her orgasm erupted within the solid nub of her clitoris, a finger massaging deep inside her bottom hole, her nipple being sucked hard . . .

'Suck out my spunk,' a man said, lifting Belinda's head and pressing the bulbous globe of his glans hard against her lips. Opening her mouth and taking his knob inside, Belinda shuddered as waves of pure sexual bliss transmitted deep into her contracting womb as her orgasm again peaked. Three men and a girl, she mused in her sexual frenzy. The man's salty knob waking her taste buds as he mouth-fucked her, she knew that this was depravity beyond belief. But she couldn't deny that it was also immensely gratifying. Never had she experienced an orgasm of such strength and duration. But she wasn't a lesbian, she tried to convince herself, as her clitoris pulsated inside another girl's mouth.

Tony had woken her sleeping desires, her inner cravings, Belinda reflected, as she gobbled on the unknown man's swollen knob. Since he'd first attempted to seduce her, she'd thought about sex, pondered on her virtually asexual marriage. The notion of three men using her to satisfy their debased desires had sent her libido rocketing. And now her clitoris was pulsating in orgasm in another girl's mouth. Where would this all end? she mused dreamily, as her pussy-milk flooded the young lesbian's face. Three men and one girl, and then . . . divorce?

Brian would be home soon, she ruminated. He was coming home to his loyal and loving wife. But, his wife had shaved her pussy for another man; she'd taken another man's cock into her rectum; she had allowed three men to shaft all three holes and a girl to tongue her rectal canal and suck a massive orgasm from her clitoris. It just wouldn't be possible to live two separate lives, she reflected, as her climax began to recede. To live such a massive lie just wouldn't be possible.

Her mouth flooded with creamy sperm and Belinda did her best to swallow the fruits of the gasping man's balls. The white liquid ran down her chin as the finger embedded deep within her rectum massaged her inner flesh and she slurped and sucked and again swallowed hard. Was Tony taking photographs? she wondered, as the finger left the tight sheath of her rectum. More evidence of her debauched behaviour? More material to blackmail her with?

How much more spunk could she take? she wondered, as her mouth overflowed. How much more spunk could the men produce? The deflating cock finally slipped out of her mouth, and she hung her head and hoped that the beautiful debauchery was over. She needed to rest, she knew, as her limbs ached. She needed to rest and recover from the anal abuse, the vaginal thrusting, the mouth-fucking, her massive orgasms . . . What was Desiree doing? she again pondered, imagining the girl watching the clock and wondering when her mother would be home.

'I enjoyed that,' the lesbian said, her mouth finally leaving Belinda's inflamed clitoris.

'I need to rest,' Belinda said, her arms sagging beneath her.

'Lie on you back,' Tony ordered her. 'You deserve a rest before –'

'Before what?' she cut in, rolling to one side and lying on her back. 'I can't take any more.'

'Of course you can,' one of the men said with a chuckle.

'No,' Belinda cried, as the girl placed her knees either side of her head and lowered her gaping sex crack over Belinda's mouth. 'No, I –'

'Give her a good licking out,' Tony said as the men sniggered. 'Give her cunt a good licking out.'

Unable to breathe properly as the girl rocked her hips and ground the wet flesh of her open sex valley hard against her mouth, Belinda again couldn't believe the predicament she was in. Breathing in the scent of the lesbian's vulval valley, she instinctively opened her mouth. The taste of another girl's pussy-milk playing on her tongue, she felt a bulbous knob stabbing at her inflamed vaginal entrance. She'd had more than enough sex for one day, she reflected, as the cock drove deep into her abused sex sheath. Her elongated nipples sucked into hot mouths, her inflamed vagina pistoned by another solid cock, she wondered when she'd be given her freedom.

'Tongue-fuck the lesbian's hot cunt,' Tony instructed her. 'Or I'll give you a damned good arse-caning.' Belinda knew that she had no choice and complied. She couldn't endure the cane, she knew, as she savoured the taste of the girl's lubricious sex-milk. Salty, tangy . . . Committing the lesbian act, she again swore to keep Desiree well away from Tony and his house of debauchery. Desiree was only sixteen, Belinda reflected. But, at any age, she shouldn't be subjected to debauchery like this. Group sex, lesbian sex . . .

'You're good,' the young girl said, peeling the swollen lips of her drenched pussy wide apart. 'I can feel your tongue deep inside me. Give me a nice tongue-fucking and make me come in your pretty mouth.'

'You'll be coming again, then?' Tony quipped.

'I'll be coming in her sweet mouth again.' She giggled. 'God, I'm almost there.'

'Coming,' the man shafting Belinda's tight vagina cried. 'God, you're a dirty little whore.'

His crude words resounding around her racked mind as her naked body rocked with his cock thrusting, Belinda did her best to swallow the lesbian's copious flow of hot pussy-milk. The girl shuddered and gasped, her young body writhing as she ground her open sex valley hard against Belinda's mouth. Riding Belinda's face, flooding her with her creamy juices of lesbian lust, she was fast approaching her climax. The man's sperm flooded Belinda's spasming vagina and she felt teeth sinking gently into the dark discs of her areolae as the lesbian cried out in the grip of her orgasm.

Shaking violently as her own orgasm erupted within the pulsating nub of her clitoris, Belinda sucked out the girl's vaginal juices, drinking from her teenage body as she drifted on clouds of sexual euphoria. In the darkness of her blindfold, unable to see, her senses were acutely heightened. Her clitoris pulsating fiercely as her orgasm peaked, someone lifted her feet high in the air, allowing the man's solid cock deeper access to her contracting vagina. The gasping and squelching sounds of forbidden sex reverberating around the room, she sucked the lesbian's orgasming clitoris into her hot mouth. She was sure that she could sink no deeper into the murky pool of debased sex. There was no sexual act more depraved than this, was there?

The very notion of a girl's clitoris pulsating within her mouth sent tremors of sex through her contracting womb and she knew that she could never remain faithful to her husband. Too much water under the bridge, she mused, drinking from the teenage girl's vaginal duct. Too much sperm in her abused sex sheaths. As the man withdrew his spent cock from her spunk-bubbling vagina, someone lifted her feet higher above her trembling body. Another cock? she wondered. Another fucking? More sperm?

The thin bamboo cane swished through the air and landed squarely across her naked buttocks. Belinda cried out through a mouthful of vaginal flesh. Her quivering body jolting as the cane flailed her tensed buttocks, she knew that there was no escaping Tony and his perverted friends. The lesbian writhed and squirmed as she pumped out her orgasmic milk, flooding Belinda's face as the deafening cracks of the cane resounded around the room. This was the bottom of the pit, she was sure, as the thin bamboo bit into her crimsoned buttocks and the girl pumped out her pussy-cream. She could sink no further, could she?

Again and again, the thin bamboo cane flailed the glowing orbs of her naked bottom until she managed to push the lesbian away and screamed out for mercy. She could take no more. No more orgasms, no more caning . . . The thrashing finally halted and she heard movements, people hurriedly leaving the room. Yanking the blindfold off, she managed to focus her bleary eyes on Tony's grinning face. The others had gone, fled the room. Why? What was going on?

'Did you enjoy yourself?' Tony asked her as she clambered to her feet.

'No, I . . .'

'You loved it, Belinda.' He laughed, running his hand up and down his solid cock. 'And you'll be back for more.'

'Where have they gone? Why did they rush off?'

'The way you were screaming, half the bloody street might have heard you. They've gone upstairs to dress. They'll be back, though. Maybe tomorrow or the next day, they'll be back. And so will you.'

'Never,' she said, grabbing her clothes. 'I must go home. Desiree will be wondering where I am.'

'Was that your first lesbian experience?'

'Yes, it was. And my last.'

'You tongue-fucked another girl, Belinda. I was watching you. You enjoyed it, so there's no point in lying.'

'No, I ... I didn't enjoy it at all.'

'You might fool yourself, but you don't fool me. Three cocks. Did you enjoy three cocks spunking your sex holes?'

'No, I ... Just leave me alone. I need to think.'

'About three knobs spunking you? About drinking from another girl's hot cunt?'

Ignoring him as she dressed, she knew that he was right. She'd loved the lesbian experience, the taste of another girl's pussy-milk. Was she a lesbian at heart? she wondered, veiling her abused sex holes with her tight panties. There was no point in denying the immense pleasure she'd derived from licking a girl's clitoris to orgasm, she decided. Besides, sex was sex. Whether with a male or a female, sex was ... The reality of the illicit act finally hitting her, she recalled her tongue delving into the teenage girl's vagina. The taste, the excitement, the arousal ... No, she decided. She couldn't accept the fact that she'd loved the feel of the girl's clitoris pulsating in orgasm against her tongue. She wasn't a lesbian.

'See you tomorrow,' Tony said as she moved to the door.

'Yes, tomorrow,' she replied, the words tumbling from her lips without her thinking.

'You did enjoy it, didn't you?' he persisted, following her into the hall.

'Tony, I ... Yes, I did. I don't like the idea of going with another girl but ... I did enjoy it.'

'We're two of a kind,' he said, holding her head and kissing her full lips. 'We both enjoy sex to the full. We're going to be very good neighbours. And, very intimate lovers.'

'I have to go,' she said, pulling away and opening the front door. 'I need to think.'

'All right, I'll see you tomorrow.'

Reaching her house, Belinda let herself in and hoped that Desiree was still in her room. If the girl saw the state her mother was in, there'd be no explanation. She could hardly say that she fell over in the park or ... It was pretty obvious that Belinda had enjoyed a session of rampant sex. The odour of sex lingering in her hair, the taste of pussy-milk playing on her tongue, she slipped upstairs to the bathroom and washed away the telltale signs of debauchery.

Wearing her summer dress, she finally went downstairs and made a cup of coffee. Desiree hadn't emerged from her bedroom, but Belinda thought it best not to disturb her. She'd only start asking questions, she was sure, as she gazed through the kitchen window at the garden. The evening sun was sinking, another day was coming to a close. What had happened to her relationship with Desiree? she pondered. Shopping together, doing the garden, cooking, walking in the park ... Things had changed so much, she mused, recalling happy times with her daughter. But there was no turning the clock back.

Walking through the hall as the front doorbell rang, Belinda hoped that Tony hadn't decided to call round to gloat. She'd been through enough, she mused, hesitating as the bell rang again. Was he going to start on about Desiree again? Had he come round to taunt her? Finally opening the door, she stared in disbelief at her husband. Standing on the step with a suitcase in his hand, he grinned at her.

'Surprise, surprise,' he said, dropping the case and flinging his arms around her neck.

'Brian –' she began as he locked his lips to hers in a passionate kiss.

Images of knobs bloating her pretty mouth swirling in her confused mind, she tried to push away. Brian held her tight in his arms, his tongue slipping into her mouth

240

as she recalled drinking sperm from other men's cocks. Could he taste the spunk on her lips? Could he taste pussy-juice on her tongue? Her buttocks were weal-lined from the merciless caning, her pubic hair shaved, sperm oozed from the inflamed entrance to her rectum and the gaping hole of her inflamed vagina . . . Finally managing to push him away, she donned a smile.

'What are you doing home?' she asked, trying to come across as pleased.

'When I rang you, I was at Gatwick airport,' he replied, standing back and admiring her. 'I wanted to surprise you. Where's Desiree?'

'Studying in her room. Brian, I . . .'

'Let's take a look at the garden,' he suggested, closing the front door. 'We'll call Desiree down in a minute.'

Following her husband out into the garden, Belinda wondered whether he'd notice that the fence panel was missing. How would she explain that? she wondered, as he walked across the lawn. Her stomach churned as Tony opened his back door and wandered into his garden. She hoped that he'd not make any lewd comments. If they could behave as friendly neighbours . . . Knowing Tony, she doubted very much that he'd be able to restrain himself from making silly quips. Acutely aware of sperm oozing between her crimsoned buttocks, flowing from her abused pussy-hole, she felt her heart racing, her hands trembling. She should have been pleased to see her husband, she reflected. But . . .

'Tony,' Brian greeted their neighbour, walking across the lawn to the fence. 'I can't believe it's you.'

'Brian?' Tony said, his dark eyes frowning. 'Good grief. How the hell are you?'

'I'm fine. God, I've not seen you for years and . . . and then you go and move in next door to me.'

'Will someone tell me what's going on?' Belinda asked.

'This is Tony, love,' Brian began. 'He used to work with me. He looked after the office computers and . . .

241

When you said that our new neighbour's name was Tony, I didn't think for a minute that it was Tony the computer man.'

'This is amazing.' Tony chuckled, reaching over the fence and shaking Brian's hand. 'It's great to see you.'

'What are you doing now?' Brian asked him. 'What line of work are you in?'

'I'm an IT consultant. Still playing around with computers.'

'Bloody hell,' Brian said with a chuckle. 'Tony the computer man. This is great news. You've met my wife and daughter, of course.'

'Indeed I have. Two lovely ladies. You're a lucky man, Brian.'

'Yes, I am. You'll have to come round for a meal and . . . God, I can't believe this. You'll be able to look after my girls for me while I'm working away.'

'Now, that *is* a good idea,' Tony rejoined, winking at Belinda. 'It will be my pleasure to look after your girls, I can assure you. We've got to know each other quite well, haven't we, Belinda?'

'Yes, yes we have,' she replied, forcing a smile as Tony licked his lips and grinned at her.

'We have a lot of catching up to do,' Brian said. 'So, are you working for yourself or –'

'I'll leave you to it,' Belinda said.

Wandering into the house, Belinda was sure that this was the beginning of another horrendous nightmare. Unable to believe that her husband knew Tony, she shook her head and sighed. What the hell would Brian say when he discovered that Desiree had been seeing Tony? she wondered anxiously. Climbing the stairs, she decided to tell Desiree the bad news. Perhaps this would put an end to the girl's infatuation, she thought, tapping on the girl's bedroom door. With Tony and Brian being old friends, perhaps Tony would back off.

'I heard everything,' Desiree said, moving away from the open window as Belinda walked into the bedroom.

'If your dad finds out that you've been seeing Tony ...' Belinda began. 'It would appear that they're old friends, Desiree. You'll have to forget about Tony now.'

'Why?'

'Because ... because things have become too complicated. Tony is so much older than you, for starters. If Dad thinks that you're having a relationship with him, especially a sexual relationship ...'

'Dad won't know, will he? He won't find out.'

'He'll have to know,' Belinda returned. 'You can't carry on seeing Tony, carry on going round to his place, and keep it secret. I'm not going to lie for you, Desiree. I'd do anything for you, you know that. But I won't lie for you.'

'Would you want me to lie for you?' the girl asked mysteriously, staring hard at her mother.

'Lie for me? What do you mean?'

'Would you want me to lie for you? It's a simple enough question.'

'No, of course not.'

'Earlier, I went round to see whether Tony was back.'

'Yes, I know you did.'

'I went round there after you'd gone out, Mum. After you'd gone to meet your old school friend for a drink.'

'Oh?'

'I looked through the lounge window.'

'I ... I'm not with you,' Belinda said unsteadily.

'You're right, Tony does have other women.'

'Oh, er ... What's happened? Has he left you?'

'No, no. I looked through the window and saw Tony kneeling behind a naked woman who was on her hands and knees. They were both naked.'

'Oh, Desiree.' Belinda sighed. 'I'm so sorry, love. I did try to warn you but ...'

'There was another man beneath the woman and a third man kneeling in front of her.'

'*What*?' Belinda exclaimed, praying that the girl hadn't recognised her. 'Three men and a woman? But ... It must have been really upsetting for you. I only wish that you'd listened to me.'

'I couldn't see who the woman was.'

'Thank God ... I mean ... I can't believe that Tony was with two other men and a woman. I knew that he had no morals, but to carry on like that?'

'The woman had long black hair,' Desiree announced, locking her dark eyes to her mother's. 'I couldn't see her face because the man kneeling in front of her was in the way.'

'So, I take it that you won't be seeing Tony again?'

'Tony has taught me everything I know about sex. You name it, and we've done it.'

'Everything?' Belinda said surprisedly. 'But, I thought that you hadn't ...'

'Everything you can imagine.'

'I ... I had no idea. So, surely you're not willing to share him with other women?'

'The way I look at it is this: I either share him or lose him. I'll be seeing Tony again. I'll be seeing him and ... if I want to keep him, I'll see him and his two male friends.'

'What do you mean? Surely, you're not thinking of allowing three men to ...'

'Share and share alike. Isn't that right?'

'I don't know what you're talking about.'

'I'm talking about sharing Tony. Dad won't find out, will he?'

'Desiree, he's bound to find out. He'll ask me about it and ...'

'And you'll lie for me.'

'No, I won't lie for you.'

'I'll have to lie for you, Mum.'

'No, you won't.'

'Of course I will. Share and share alike. I don't want Dad to discover that I'm a slut. And I'm sure you don't want him discovering that you're a . . . Like mother, like daughter. Isn't that right, Mum?'